THE
BLEEDER

THE BLEEDER

STORIES BY
TAD SIMONS

Published by Pembroke Press

ISBN: 978-0-9961110-0-3

Publisher's Note: This is a work of fiction. The names, characters, and incidents contained herein are products of the author's imagination—because, you know, that's what "fiction" means. Any resemblance to actual people or events is entirely coincidental and beside the point.

Cover Design: DaisyMaeDesign
Interior Design: The Roberts Group

Printed in the United States of America

For My Parents

Contents

THE BLEEDER

Y FIRST CONSCIOUS MEMORY IS OF blood: crimson smears of it on my fingers, red rivulets streaming from my nose, the metallic taste of it on my tongue, pink stains on my teeth, shirts ruined forever—lots of them.

I was a nosebleeder. Still am, sometimes. In fourth grade I'd be sitting in class, listening to Mrs. Anderson tell us about kids with swollen bellies in Africa or how a tadpole turns into a frog, when my nose would start gushing red from both nostrils, as if a tiny plumber in my sinus cavity had turned on the spigot. Once, the little girl who sat next to me—Suzy something—screamed so loud when she saw the blood on my face that I sprayed her with scarlet snot, so startled was I by her ear-splitting squeal. Often I wasn't aware that I was bleeding, and such unsettling scenes were how the matter came to my attention.

Whenever the nosebleeds happened, I had to excuse myself and go to the bathroom, where I'd sit in a stall, stuff my nose with toilet paper, lean my head back and wait. Sometimes it only took a few minutes for the bleeding to stop, but other times it might keep pouring for half an hour or more. On those not in-frequent occasions, Mrs. Anderson inevitably hunted me down and sent me to the nurse's office. There, I would be greeted warmly and taken care of by Miss Simms, the first woman with whom I ever truly fell in love.

Of course, I was only nine years old, so many people say

that the ache I felt for Miss Simms wasn't *love* love. They say it was some sort of childish infatuation, a harmless crush, because nine-year-olds aren't capable of feeling true, romantic love. This is nonsense, of course. If you ask me, a fourth-grader can feel love just as deeply—maybe even deeper—than an adult. At any rate, when a nine-year-old feels love, it's not all cluttered up with the misgivings and apprehensions that plague adults; it's pure and true and simple—and no one can tell me it's not real.

The events I am about to relate happened a long time ago. Working up the courage to put them down in writing has taken a while, and, even though I've been told a thousand times that what happened wasn't entirely my fault, the guilt weighs on my heart like a rock even as I write this. Parts of the story were in all the papers, of course, but not the parts that matter. Newspapers are fairly good at giving you the who, what, and where, but they stink when it comes to the why. The truth is far too complicated for the likes of them.

It all started after Christmas break, during a troublesome period when I was experiencing at least one nosebleed a day. What caused my nose to start erupting so frequently, I don't know. It could have been the dry winter air, or the result of subtle shifts in barometric pressure, or—as my state-sanctioned psychiatrist has always suspected—the manifestation of darker, deeper dimensions in my young psyche that had no other avenue for expression. Whatever the reason, it usually happened after lunch, in the middle of phonics or math, when the threshold of boredom had moved from stifling to painful. As if on cue, my sinuses would burst and I would scamper up the aisle between the desks in the middle of the room, snatching a Kleenex from Mrs. Anderson's outstretched hand on my way out the door. Sure, the other kids laughed at me and teased me, but as soon as that door closed I didn't care. All I could think about was Miss Simms: her soft cool hand on my forehead, her skin as smooth as fleece, the acrid bite of rubbing alcohol in her office—these were the sensations I had begun to crave.

The nurse's office was a tiny room adjacent to a much larger office occupied by the school principal, Mr. Lufton. A small cot, just long enough for me to stretch out on, was pushed against the wall. On the other side of the wall was Mr. Lufton's office. Often, as I lay on the cot waiting for my nosebleed to abate, I could hear Mr. Lufton's muffled voice as he talked on the phone. Just knowing Mr. Lufton was there made me nervous. This was back in the days when it was still admissible for a principal to pull your pants down and whack you on the ass if you got out of line, and Mr. Lufton did not hesitate to exercise this privilege. A long wooden paddle used just for this purpose hung on the wall of his office, and though I never personally got paddled, I heard the ritual through the wall often enough that the mere sound of Mr. Lufton's voice made my stomach clench.

Fear of Mr. Lufton—and what he might do if he ever found out how much I looked forward to my daily nosebleed—was the price I paid for being able to see Miss Simms, though. And as long as I was in Miss Simms' care—that is, as long as my problem was medical—there was nothing he could do to me.

Or so I thought.

Miss Simms reacted to my nosebleeds in precisely the opposite way of most adults. Instead of getting impatient or disgusted with me, she treated each successive nosebleed with ever deepening layers of compassion. Each time I entered her office, she clicked her tongue and said, "Oh, my goodness," then swiftly exchanged the bloody Kleenex I held clamped to my nose with a fresh, clean tissue (one that always smelled better and felt softer than Mrs. Anderson's Kleenex) and insisted that I lie down. "There, there," she always said, "just relax and you'll be fine." She never got mad, never scolded me, never even asked if I might be picking my nose too much or shoving a No. 2 pencil up my nostrils to make them bleed. No, she was always gentle and caring, and each day as she opened up a new dimension of her heart to me, I felt the sweet pain of love grow stronger in my own tiny heart.

After a while, Miss Simms and I had established a comfortable routine. I would show up at her office sometime in the early afternoon, whereupon she would tend to me and insist that I lie down on the cot in her office "for however long it takes, honey," she always said. Miss Simms' voice had the slightest hint of a Southern accent, like a sprig of mint in a glass of iced tea. Every time she said the word "honey," her tongue lingered on the first syllable, "hun," half a beat longer than you'd expect, holding onto the "n" like a child clutching a balloon, then letting the "y" free to fly on its own, turning the whole word into a smooth, delightful sort of mouth music. I literally felt my heart melt the first time she said it, and every time thereafter.

After I took my position on the cot, we often did not exchange a word. I would lie with my eyes open, studying the perforation patterns in the ceiling tiles, while she sat at her desk, leafing through binders and reports, or reading from an assortment of fat textbooks. I got the impression she was taking some classes somewhere, studying to be something other than what she was—a school nurse—but I could not think of her in any other way. I could not imagine her wearing anything other than her white nurse's smock, or envision what sort of life she might have had beyond the walls of her ten-by-ten office, though she undoubtedly had one. Often the only verbal communication we shared was when she would ask, every so often, "How're we doing?," to which I would answer with a simple nod of my head or a perfunctory "okay." In those brief exchanges, her eyes said much more than her mouth ever did. Her eyes—green and clear, like a lily pad or a field of fresh-cut grass—could reach inside me, all the way to the core of my tender being, and squeeze my heart with an exquisite tenderness. Whenever I said I was feeling better, the corners of her mouth would curl upward ever so slightly and a sensation of warmth would flow throughout my entire body, as if she had wrapped me in a blanket. In those moments, I would look at her out of the corner of my eye and see the sparkling sheen of her clean, blond hair, the wet glint of purple on her fingernails, the gentle taper of her calf as it went into her shoes, and be certain that there was no greater bliss in the world.

One day I came to Miss Simms' office and she wasn't there. I waited around, and then, after some time, she emerged from Mr. Lufton's office. She seemed upset. Her face was pink and blotchy, as if she had been crying, and she barely acknowledged me when she saw me in her office. She simply pulled a new Kleenex out of the box and handed it to me without saying a word, then took one for herself and blew her nose.

As I've said, I had never been in love before, so the emotions that overcame me when I saw her like that—so sad and empty-looking—were powerful and strange. I didn't know what to say or do, yet my chest felt like it was going to explode, so I knew I had to do something. But what? Then I remembered that it was also Valentine's Day, and that I had made Miss Simms a card. I reached into my back pocket and took out a crumpled envelope, into which I had stuffed a small heart-shaped card, cut out of red construction paper, with the simple message, "Happy Valentine's Day" written inside. The important part was that I had signed it, "Love, Joey,"—and I meant it. I had never used the word "love" in a piece of correspondence before, and I remember how the significance of each letter—"L" "O" "V" "E"—seemed to multiply as I wrote it. By the time I put the comma in and signed my name, the entirety of my nine-year-old soul was sealed in that envelope.

To this day I think Miss Simms sensed that the depth of my feelings for her were more profound than a simple schoolboy crush. When she read the card, she broke out in tears, and, to my surprise, so did I. Then she did something that I will never forget for as long as I live. She motioned for me to come closer to her, then put her hands on my shoulders and pressed her lips against my forehead. What happened to me at that moment is beyond my powers of explanation, for it felt as if she had injected the world's most irresistible and addictive drug directly into my frontal cortex, causing my legs to go all rubbery and my mind to go utterly blank. An intoxicating combination of terror and ecstasy coursed through my veins. A tingling sensation traveled from my head to my feet, and my face got all red and hot. Her lips seemed to linger on my forehead for an eternity. Then, ever so slowly, she pulled her lips away and whispered, "Thank you, you're such a sweetheart."

An instant later, the capillaries in my nose swelled and burst, and a trickle of blood dribbled down my lip. Overcome with shame, I held my hand under my nose so that I wouldn't drip blood on Miss Simms' clean tile floor. She handed me a Kleenex and smiled.

"Lie down, honey," she said. "It'll be all right in a minute."

Shortly after that kiss to my forehead—I don't remember exactly when—I discovered that I no longer needed to wait for my nose to bleed: I could *will* it to happen. That is to say, at some point my nosebleeds—some of them, anyway—stopped being accidents. All I had to do to make one happen was think about it for a few minutes—to imagine the blood vessels in my sinus cavity swelling and bursting—and a warm dribble would suddenly ooze out my nose and down to my lips. For the purposes of feeding my delicious infatuation with Ms. Simms, this proved to be an extremely valuable skill.

By the end of February, my spontaneous nosebleeds had tapered down to one or two a week, but I still tried to visit Miss Simms every day. Which meant, of course, that I was becoming an expert at controlling my nosebleeds, willing them to happen whenever I felt like getting out of class, a habit I began to indulge on a more or less daily basis.

It was mid-morning, I remember, and the sky outside was gray, with clouds that looked like brains. I usually didn't visit Miss Simms until after lunch, but Mrs. Anderson had just begun telling us about the Lewis & Clark expedition, which meant that she was doing her usual trick of transforming fascinating episodes of history into stupefying stretches of boredom.

Rather than listen to her prattle on about courage and sacrifice and frostbite, I focused all my attention on my nasal capillaries and was subsequently excused from class. I had long since stopped going the bathroom; it was a waste of time. Instead, I headed directly to Miss Simms' office, while the blood was still fresh and my immediate need of her assistance obvious.

When I arrived, Miss Simms was not in her office. I poked my head around the corner and checked the cafeteria, but didn't see her. The only person there was the school janitor—a fat, humorless fellow named George—and he was busy eating a sandwich. I didn't want to be caught roaming the halls without a pass, though, so I returned to her office and lay down in my customary position on the cot against the wall.

I was content to wait, for merely being in Miss Simms' office gave me a great deal of comfort. I felt safe there. No one bothered me when I was lying down in her office, because they assumed I had either puked in class or was coming down with some infectious disease they didn't want to catch.

After a few minutes I got tired of staring at the ceiling tiles and closed my eyes. The school was very quiet when all the students were in class; even the least little bit of sound—the hiss of a student drinking from a water fountain, the thud of a teacher kicking a doorstop loose and shutting the door—echoed through the concrete-and-tile corridors like small explosions.

As I lay there that day, I heard some sounds coming from Mr. Lufton's office. His door was closed, as it usually was when he was making phone calls or in a conference—or, most ominously of all, when he was giving a student the paddle. In Texas, when I was growing up, a few firm whacks on the ass was thought to be the most effective corrective for poor behavior, and the threat of it always loomed large and terrifying. I knew the drill, and I had overheard it enough times to know that I never wanted to be on the receiving end of Mr. Lufton's wrath.

It usually didn't last long. The student would show up with the teacher. The teacher would explain what the student had done to deserve their march to the principal's office. Mr. Lufton would thank the teacher for bringing the matter to his attention and dismiss them. Then he would close the door and give the student one of several versions of the same speech on the need for respect and discipline in an educational setting, not to mention the world at large. I only heard the actual words to the last part of the speech, though, because he liked to start low and build to a fiery, evangelical crescendo, which I could hear fine. His final words were always something along the lines of, "Discipline is a function of pain. Pain is a function of suffering, but also of power. Though it pains me to do so, I am about to show you who has the power around here."

After that, a period of ominous silence would follow—the moment when, I supposed, he took the paddle off the wall. The next sound was three or four sharp smacks—the distinctive slap of a hard board against exposed flesh—delivered in a slow, agonizing rhythm, as if he wound the paddle up like a baseball bat and smashed it against the student's bottom as hard as he possibly could. Immediately afterwards, Mr. Lufton would open his door and send the student on his or her way. He preferred that the students arrive back at class still crying, I think, because it helped spread the fearful legend of The Paddle.

On this particular morning, however, he did not seem to be delivering the usual speech. I could hear the mumble of his voice, but the cadence of the words was all wrong; they came in short bursts, two or three at a time, followed by a weird laugh that, through the wall, sounded like the snort of an animal, a pig or a dog maybe. There was another voice too, softer and more feminine, but too low for a girl. Mr. Lufton was in his office with a woman, I realized, and the moment I realized this, I also understood that the woman in there with him was Miss Simms.

I cupped my ear to the wall in order to hear them better, but the only noises I could make out were the unintelligible murmurings of Mr. Lufton and Miss Simms and the occasional scrape of a chair moving on the tile floor. It didn't occur to me to wonder what they might be talking about for so long. As far as I could tell, all adults had a seemingly infinite capacity for meaningless chit-chat. It was not until I heard the first distinctive "swack" of the paddle that I began to wonder what sort of conversation they were having.

A second smack of the paddle was followed by a high-pitched but very short squeal, as if Miss Simms were clenching her teeth, holding back a much longer, more painful scream. Then there was a third smack, and a fourth. My ear was crushed against the wall; I could hear heavy breathing and a stifled scream after each whack of the paddle. When, somewhere around the fifth or sixth whack, I heard Mr. Lufton's scratchy, lizard-like laugh, I could take no more. I knew that Mr. Lufton was allowed to paddle students if he deemed it necessary, but it didn't seem right for him to extend this form of discipline to teachers and nurses, most especially Miss Simms—who, as far as I could tell, endured enough of Mr. Lufton as it was.

When it became clear to me—judging from the screams and moans I heard—that Mr. Lufton was hurting Miss Simms, and that Miss Simms had no one to protect her, I knew I had to do something. An incandescent anger I had never felt before began to dictate my actions. I was no longer thinking, just acting on impulse. I sprang to my feet and raced to the closed door of Mr. Lufton's office. I quickly turned the knob, opened the door inward and poked my head inside.

"Excuse me, Mr. Lufton, I'm looking for Miss . . ."

But I never completed my sentence, for as soon as she heard my voice, Miss Simms screamed louder than I've ever heard anyone scream in my life. She had been bent over Mr. Lufton's desk, with her skirt hiked up, exposing her bottom, which, in the brief flash I saw, was pink and dimpled with the symmetrical pattern of holes in Mr. Lufton's notorious paddle. She quickly stood up and smoothed the front of her skirt. The look in her eyes was one of pure terror and panic. She looked at me, then at Mr. Lufton, then back at me—and I, in turn, looked at Mr. Lufton, then at her, then back at Mr. Lufton, who was resting the paddle on his shoulders as if he were standing in the on-deck circle at Wrigley Field, waiting for his turn at bat.

I was of course too young to understand what was actually going on in that room, but what I *imagined* was going on was horrible enough.

At that moment, something—someone—pushed me from behind and I practically fell into the middle of the room. George the janitor had heard Ms. Simms scream and had come running, but hadn't bothered to stop when he came to me or the door.

"Is everything okay?" George asked.

"It was nothing," Mr. Lufton quickly replied. "Miss Simms here saw a mouse, that's all. See that you set a trap or two in my office tonight, will you, George?"

George looked a bit confused, but took Mr. Lufton at his word.

"I'll do that," he said as he backed out of the room. "Sorry for interrupting, sir."

"Not at all," said Mr. Lufton, congenially.

When I saw that George had believed Mr. Lufton, and was going to close the door behind him, leaving me alone in there to face the paddle-wielding principal and the flustered Miss Simms, I did something I probably shouldn't have—but at the time, there seemed to be no other choice. I concentrated as hard as I could on the blood vessels in my nose, commanding them to burst. When I saw the gush of blood on my shirt, I turned to face George the janitor and screamed, "He's lying! That's not what happened! What happened was . . . HE HIT ME!" I lied, pointing directly at Mr. Lufton. "WITH HIS FIST!"

There is a type of person who can identify another's weaknesses and knows instinctively how to exploit those vulnerabilities for their own personal benefit. Mr. Lufton was one of those people. By the time George closed the door, Mr. Lufton had already figured out how he could punish me and use me at the same time. To him, I was just a walking sack of insecurities waiting to be manipulated, a nine-year-old runt who had no choice but to do as he said or face the consequences.

Before I had a chance to open my mouth again, Mr. Lufton had already determined that I had violated any number of school ordinances, among them being caught out of class without a hall pass (Mrs. Anderson only had one, and she had stopped giving it to me), failing to knock, attempting to see the principal without a scheduled appointment, and feigning personal injury to get out of class. By far my biggest crime, however, was violating the school's "honor code" by lying about being hit by Mr. Lufton, a lie which, much to my dismay, Miss Simms confirmed.

I thought I would be expelled for the stunt I pulled, but that didn't happen. Instead, Mr. Lufton decided to make me pay for my insubordination in a way that was—to me, anyway—infinitely more painful and humiliating than getting smacked with his infamous paddle or expelled from school for a week.

Among the weaknesses Mr. Lufton saw fit to exploit was my affection for Miss Simms. There were plenty of others, of course—my status as a lowly fourth-grader; my dread of having the school call my parents; my fear of Mr. Lufton's paddle and the pain it could inflict; my desire to avoid the shame of detention, suspension or expulsion—but my main concern was whether I would be able to continue visiting Miss Simms. Mr. Lufton seemed to sense that this was my greatest vulnerability, and he devised an ingenious way of leveraging my fear to get what he wanted.

At first, I could not believe my good fortune. Since I was in the nurse's office almost every day anyway, Mr. Lufton proposed that a trip to Miss Simms' office be made a regular part of my schedule. In much the same way that other kids got excused from home-room for advanced math or science, I would be excused for an hour each day to assist Miss Simms. A "first-aid mentorship" was what Mr. Lufton called it. I could learn about first aid and human biology, take a CPR class, help organize Health Week, become the student expert on infectious agents and airborne illnesses. It was a "win, win" for everyone, said Mr. Lufton. I didn't quite understand what he was winning, but it didn't take long to figure it out.

My new schedule put me in Miss Simms' office on Mondays, Wednesdays and Fridays, from 1:30 P.M. to 2:30 P.M. On my first official day as Miss Simms' "first-aid assistant," Mr. Lufton greeted me with a smile and a pat on the shoulder, but the look in his eyes made me uncomfortable. It was the kind of look a tiger at the zoo gives you just to let you know that, given the opportunity, he could devour you in a second. Miss Simms sat in the chair of her tiny desk, while I sat down on the edge of the cot and Mr. Lufton remained standing, with his arms folded and his feet spread a little too wide.

"Joey, you're taking on a big responsibility—you know that, don't you?" he said. I nodded and Miss Simms nodded with me, as if she too were receiving the same lecture.

"Every student in this school is counting on you, so you can't let them down," he continued. "That means you need to remain alert and aware of your duties at all times. Do I make myself clear?"

"Yes, sir," I said.

"Good. Now, Miss Simms will go over the duties she wants you to perform. But first, she and I have some important business to discuss. Your first responsibility is to make sure that no one disturbs us, do you understand?"

Again, I nodded.

"If anyone comes around asking to see myself or Miss Simms, tell them to come back in an hour. Do you think you can handle that?" Mr. Lufton asked, tucking his chin into his chest and boring through my skull with his animal eyes.

"Because if you can't, I'll find someone else who can."

"No, I can do it," I managed to mumble.

"I know you can, Joey. Let's shake on it, man to man," he said, extending his long, bony hand toward me. I put my little palm in his and he wrapped his fingers around my hand like a snake ensnaring its prey.

"Don't disappoint me," he added, tightening his grip on my hand until the moment it started to hurt. He then released his grip and nodded at Miss Simms, signaling for her to follow him into his office. Miss Simms gave me a strangely maternal smile—a smile that said, "everything's going to be all right" and "thank you for being here," all at the same time—and disappeared behind Mr. Lufton's door.

As it turned out, Mr. Lufton and Miss Simms had a lot of important business to discuss. In the weeks that followed, Miss Simms spent the first fifteen or twenty minutes of each hour-long shift I had as her first-aid assistant in Mr. Lufton's office. What business the principal and the school nurse had to meet about so frequently was beyond my comprehension at the time, but I took my duty seriously in the belief that this is what Miss Simms wanted from me as well.

I tried to listen in, of course. When the coast was clear, I would press my ear to the wall and strain with every fiber of my being to hear what they were talking about. I could make out a word here or there, but most of the time their voices were too soft to penetrate the wall, and often I could only hear a rustle of papers or the scrape of a drawer closing shut. Sometimes, I didn't hear anything at all.

On some level, I believe I knew what was going on in there—that Mr. Lufton and Miss Simms were engaging in that most mysteriously adult of activities—but my feelings for Miss Simms wouldn't allow me to believe that she was using me in any way, only that she needed me. She seemed grateful for the lookout service I provided, and this made me feel special. She even kept a bowl of candy in the medicine cabinet—mostly little Snickers bars and Tootsie Pops—and made a point of offering me one each time she emerged from Mr. Lufton's office.

"Go on, take one—a little sugar is good medicine," she would always say. And I believed her, because I always felt better by the time I finished my candy and Mr. Lufton and Miss Simms had completed their "business." It meant that the rest of the hour was ours, alone, unless some sick or injured kid showed up, which hardly ever happened.

The first couple of weeks I just accepted the time Miss Simms spent in Mr. Lufton's office as another stretch of boredom that had to be endured before I had Miss Simms to myself. But gradually I began to resent the fact that she was giving so much attention to Mr. Lufton, and not to me. I was her assistant, after all, and there was no one to assist if she wasn't there. I wasn't consciously aware of what was going on in Mr. Lufton's office, but that didn't protect me from being overwhelmed by waves of weird emotions every time she emerged from his office. I got a peculiar charge from watching her smooth her skirt and check her face in the mirror, a mildly intoxicating rush of pre-adolescent elation—but mixed with that feeling was a sick swirl in my stomach, a nauseating knot of tension and heat, as if I'd eaten a spicy burrito then jumped on the Zipper ride at the state fair. Reconciling these feelings was more than my young constitution could bear, so by the time I left her office I was often a confused, conflicted wreck. Nevertheless, I did my best to protect their privacy and took a great deal of pride in my job. And as long as Miss Simms was happy, so was I. It was when Miss Simms started being unhappy that everything began to unravel.

My first clue that something was wrong was when Miss Simms started coming out of Mr. Lufton's office with a blank, hollow look on her face and kept forgetting to offer me candy. (I had to keep reminding her.) Then I started to get the feeling that she was forgetting I was even there—or worse, that she wished I wasn't. On those days, she would make me do stupid things like inventory the Q-Tips or draw a picture of a germ, then just bury her head in one of her textbooks and not turn the page or say a word for the rest of the hour. Other times she would emerge from Mr. Lufton's office with that splotchy look on her face, as if she had been crying, and the droopy shadows under her eyes would make her look tired and sad.

It didn't take long for me to realize that when Miss Simms was unhappy, I too was unhappy. When she was sad, my young heart ached to help her, but I didn't know what to do. I felt helpless. I was only nine years old, after all, and it wasn't like she was running to me for solace or protection. Still, I felt bad for her, and was frustrated when I couldn't cheer her up or at least get her to smile a little. On days when she didn't feel like talking, the minutes would creep by at an agonizingly slow pace, more painful even than Mrs. Anderson's history lectures—more painful than anything I had ever known.

One Wednesday (I remember it was Wednesday, because we always had fish sticks in the cafeteria on Wednesdays), I was lying on my cot, waiting for Miss Simms to come out of Mr. Lufton's office, when I heard Mr. Lufton raise his voice.

"The hell you will!" he yelled, as if each word were a rock he was throwing.

"You can't stop me," I heard Miss Simms say.

"The hell I can't!"

"It's my decision."

"The hell it is."

There was a loud thud, as if Mr. Lufton had slammed his hand down on his desk. Then Miss Simms came out of his office and sat down at her desk. She cried for a long time. She tried to keep me from hearing her deep, heaving sobs, but they were impossible to ignore. At one point, the school receptionist—a plump woman who looked like she had been sixty all her life—poked her head in and said, "Is everything all right in here? Are you okay, dear?"

Miss Simms stopped crying just long enough to say, "I'll be fine, Mrs. Flynn. I just got some bad news, that's all. Family stuff." But as soon as Mrs. Flynn left, another wave of tears came, then another, one right after the other, for the rest of the hour, until I had to leave.

Something inside me let go that day, some internal harness or restraint; whatever it is inside that prevents us (most of the time) from doing what we are thinking. Whatever that preventive mechanism in our brains is, it stopped working the moment I decided what do about Mr. Lufton—or rather, *for* Miss Simms. From that moment on, my thoughts and actions had a strangely crystalline clarity to them, as if my whole life had been pre-ordained, leading me to that precise moment in time. I had no doubts. No fear. No second thoughts. I knew what I had to do, and from that moment forward I was swept along like a leaf in a raging river, unable to alter my course in any way.

The gun wasn't hard to find. My stepfather kept it in a gray metal box on the upper shelf of his closet. The box had one of those number locks that you spin with your thumb, and I had long since discovered the combination by simply spinning the numbers until the box opened.

Until then, I had never actually touched the gun; I had simply opened the box a few times to look at it. It was a .32 caliber service revolver that my stepfather had gotten when he was in the Army Reserve. As far as I know he never used it, but—like many people—he kept it handy, just in case. He didn't bother to hide the bullets in a separate place, either; they were right there in their own little box, lined up in neat rows like little soldiers ready for battle.

The barrel and chamber were black, but the grip had plates of nubbly brown plastic on either side, and the hammer itself was scuffed, as if it had been banged against something or used so often that the paint wore off. It was heavier than I expected, and the chamber spun around with the smooth glide of something engineered for a higher purpose than mere play. I had plenty of toy guns, of course, but none of them felt as substantial as the real thing. There was something mesmerizing about the weight and feel of it in my hand, and I'll admit that the thing held a certain fascination for me—but I was not a gun-crazy kid, nor was I obsessed with violence or bloodshed. I had plenty of other interests—yo-yos, comic books, model cars, magic tricks, basketball, Legos, etc.—and if Mr. Lufton hadn't been . . . well, *Mr. Lufton* . . . I'm fairly certain none of the events I am sharing with you would have transpired.

It's also worth pointing out that, in retrospect, I didn't realize what a bullet does when it comes into contact with human flesh and bone. It didn't register as "real" that when one shoots a gun, a piece of flaming hot metal spits out of the barrel toward its target at three thousand feet per second. To me, at the time, a gun was just something you pointed at something else to make it go away—a kind of magic wand for making bad things disappear.

Mr. Lufton was the bad thing I wanted to disappear. I had seen the effect he had on Miss Simms, and through the wall I had heard him punish my friends without remorse or regret. As far as I could tell, the man had no redeeming qualities whatsoever, and he ruled his little fiefdom like a cruel dictator, wielding fear and intimidation like a club and meting out corporal punishment with his precious paddle, the closest thing to an actual club the law would allow. Getting rid of him would be doing everyone a favor, I thought. I think I even convinced myself that if I could make Mr. Lufton disappear, I would be celebrated as a hero in the eyes of my classmates, and certainly in the tear-soaked eyes of Miss Simms.

Another thing to consider when judging my actions (and judge them you must) is that I'm not sure I understood what death was at the time, either. A few pets of mine had died, sure, but I never felt bad about it because my mother had explained to me that they had gone to a "happier place," and I figured if there was a place where hamsters could be happier than they were in my room, tucked in a ball under a pile of cedar shavings, where was the harm in dying? At times, in fact, my mother made death seem like a fairly decent alternative to the torture of grade school. Not that I wanted to kill myself, mind you—just that at the time, death was not high on my list of things that ought to be avoided. Girls, homework, vegetables, chores, baths, church, thank-you notes, haircuts, poop-scooping—all of these struck me as considerably less desirable than eternal sleep. Heck, I figured, I might even be doing Mr. Lufton a favor, for he seemed like the kind of person who could use a little extra happiness.

I chose to shoot him on a Friday, in the absurd belief that the weekend would give everyone time to forget what was going to happen. When I arrived at Miss Simms' office on that fateful day, she wasn't there. This was not unusual, for she sometimes got called away to examine a student in class or retrieve a sick child from the bathroom. She was never gone long, though, so I didn't have much time. Considering the magnitude of the crime I was about to commit, I felt strangely calm. My movements were deliberate and purposeful, and my attention was focused so sharply that, had it been a school assignment, I would have passed with stars and smiley faces.

The gun was in my backpack. As quickly as I could, I set my pack on the cot and put my ear against the wall. At first I heard nothing. Then I heard Mr. Lufton's muffled voice—a few words at a time, then silence, a few more words, a chuckle, then silence again. It sounded like he was on the phone, which meant that when I entered his office, he would be sitting behind his desk, a big cherry-wood monstrosity that stretched half way across the back of the room. I decided that I would aim for his heart, because that seemed to be the most diseased part of him, but in truth I had no idea how to aim a gun other than the notion of pointing it in the general direction of what you wanted to shoot. Once I got inside the door, I would only be ten or fifteen feet away, so I figured he would be hard to miss.

I unzipped my backpack and took the gun out. It felt lighter in my hand than it did at home, but it still had the solid heft of a device built for business, not pleasure. Quickly, I checked the cylinders to make sure none of the bullets had fallen out, then I went to work.

The coast was clear down the hall, and the receptionist was around the corner, so she couldn't see me. I slipped out of the nurse's office and made my way to Mr. Lufton's door. I held the gun in front of me, so that if anyone came up behind me they wouldn't see it. Mr. Lufton's voice was less distinct through the door, but I could still hear him. I tried to picture in my mind where he would be sitting when I opened the door—middle of the desk, phone to his ear, leaning back in his black leather chair—and when the image was clear in my mind, I reached for the doorknob.

They say that when you're about to get into a car accident, time seems to slow down as your mind tries desperately to make sense of the horror that is about to happen. I don't know if that's true, but I do know that the next two seconds of my life have lasted a lifetime, and I expect them to stretch into eternity.

I turned the knob and pushed the door open. There, behind his desk, sat Mr. Lufton, just as I had imagined him, leaning back in his chair, mumbling something, with an odd sort of smile on his face. He didn't have a phone in his hand, but I didn't notice it at the time, nor did I care. Silently, I leveled the gun at him and sighted down the barrel at his chest. He must have seen me in his peripheral vision, because his eyes suddenly got big and wide, and he put both of his hands in the air, as if I were a mugger or a bank robber.

"Joey, what the? . . ." he managed to spit out before (or perhaps while) I pulled the trigger. Then, it happened: The instant the muscles in my hand contracted around the trigger, Miss Simms' head suddenly appeared where Mr. Lufton's chest had been. She looked at me, and I at her, and there was frozen millisecond in which both of us were aware of the unstoppable velocity of the moment—a flash of mutual recognition that what was happening was nothing but a senseless, unnecessary tragedy. The most terrible thing of all was that in that transcendent moment when time stood still and her eyes locked on mine, those green eyes of hers were not filled with anger, confusion or dismay, they were filled with the very thing you would least expect at a moment like that: forgiveness.

Then the gun exploded in my hand and she was gone.

I was of course blamed for the whole thing. Troubled kid. Compulsive liar. Bad seed. Mr. Lufton wasted no time informing the press that I was a delinquent child whom he had tried to help but had clearly failed. He even claimed to take "responsibility" for the accident, by which he meant I would be immediately placed in a juvenile correctional facility, where I would no longer be a threat to the public. Safety at the school would be restored, he said, and preventive measures taken to ensure that such a calamity never happened again. I believe he even got an award for his bravery in a situation involving "deadly intent," as well as a commendation from the police chief for the new security protocols he established after I was whisked away and subsequently imprisoned, for the rest of my life, in that horrible moment.

The pills they give me in these little institutional cups are supposed to prevent it from happening, but I still live that moment over and over again in my dreams, which are never sweet. On the nights when the dream cannot be stopped, the gun goes off and I instantly wake up. Without even looking I already know that my face and chest are covered with blood. I walk down the hall to the bathroom and stuff a wad of Kleenex in each nostril, then I sit down in one of the toilet stalls and lean my head back against the cool tile.

Once seated, I know from bitter experience that there is nothing left to do but be patient and wait for the bleeding to stop.

. . . .

EXIT 43

A scorched pumpkin sky was fading into a cool, moonless night as Jude Mathers eased his blue, six-cylinder Acura, freshly washed and vacuumed, onto Eden's expressway, southbound toward downtown Chicago. Traffic was flowing freely and that was a relief. Fifteen minutes to the off-ramp, five or ten to park the car—less if he used the valet—and a couple minutes give or take to reach the door. The timing was tighter than he would have liked, but if traffic kept moving and the parking gods smiled favorably on him, he stood a reasonably good chance of getting to the door of the Tambe d' Oro before the maître d' scratched his name off the list as a no-show. Just such a calamity had recently occurred to his roommate Glen, who had shown up a mere fifteen minutes late, and Jude did not want to share that fellow's unfortunate fate. The restaurant's ruthless punctuality was part of its allure. Slackers, procrastinators, and johnny-come-latelies were not tolerated. This was a dining establishment for people who valued their time. People who didn't—people who lollygagged and dawdled and allowed the rest of the world to disrupt their schedules—got turned away, whether or not their name was on the list.

Jude knew the risks involved.

He'd made the reservation three weeks ago, and things had progressed far enough with Kim since then that Jude felt certain he would get laid tonight. All the preliminary indicators were pointing in that direction: for the occasion she had worn a burgundy dress, not quite red but close enough. An opal necklace hung between her pillowy breasts, drawing attention to a portion of her body that was normally shielded by thick, hand-made sweaters and a layer or two of assorted undergarments. Her toenails were painted to match her lipstick, and Jude could tell by the sheen of Kim's legs that they were freshly shaved. Kim had greeted him at the door with a warm, playful kiss and was now sitting beside him, legs crossed, tiny purse clutched in her left hand, head swaying ever so slightly to the song on the radio, a Jack Johnson tune he recognized but could not name.

The restaurant to which they were headed was one of the trendiest places in the city, and he was prepared to drop up to $200 for the privilege of dining there. He had worn his nicest suit-and-slacks combo, and had purchased a new necktie that very afternoon, yellow with blue accents, like Kim's hair and eyes, though he wasn't aware of the connection. The saleswoman at the store had even persuaded him to buy a vial of men's cologne, the selling point of which was that it had a laboratory-tested pheremonal effect on a woman's libido, especially if she happened to be ovulating. He wondered about that lab and what sort of credentials one needed to work there. Per the saleswoman's instructions he had dabbed a little on each side of his neck, just beneath his jaw line, where Kim could "discover" the scent in an intimate embrace. All of those ingredients put together made for an almost certain nightcap of carnal exploration, Jude felt; it was as close to a sure thing as he could imagine.

"Are you wearing cologne?" Kim asked as Jude slipped into the traffic stream and over to the middle lane. It occurred to him that, since she could smell it four feet away, he may have applied more pheremonal sex juice than was technically necessary.

"Me? Certainly not. You must be picking up my natural scent, the wild and unpredictable essence of me," he joked. "Do you like it?"

"I don't know. I might have to get closer to find out," she

purred. She put her hand on his leg, then leaned over and sniffed the air near his ear like a dog.

"Mmmmmm. Essence of mountain yak, I'm guessing."

"African wildebeest, actually—from the Serengeti plains," he said, and they both laughed.

Though they hadn't spoken of it, both Jude and Kim felt an extra tingle of anticipation in the air that evening. They were young still—he twenty-seven and she twenty-six—but for the first time in either of their lives they both felt like adults, fully grown people who had escaped the uncertain chaos of childhood and were now embracing the vast, unlimited promise of their dreams. Jude had a good job in a brokerage firm, one with plenty of "upside potential," as his boss liked to say—and Kim was a freelance designer on the verge of getting a permanent position in an agency she had worked for on several occasions, one that did pro bono work for such humanitarian causes as the American Breast Cancer Society and PETA, the animal rights group. Working there, she didn't feel as if she would have to compromise her values by designing packages for cigarettes, say, or creating logos for companies that used sweatshop labor in third-world countries. Compromising her values was something she promised herself she would never do in the working world, and she was proud of herself for making it through four years of professional life without selling out. Jude, too, was proud of her. Kim was easily the sanest, most stable of his girlfriends to date. She had her artsy side, but he felt he could count on her to keep bringing in an income after they were married—*if* they ever got married. She wasn't the smartest girl he had ever dated, or even the most fun, but she was a solid, practical person with a truly decent heart, and he liked her for that. He might even come to love her, he thought.

Kim, like Jude, had endured her share of dissatisfying relationships. She felt like Goldilocks: some of her boyfriends were too hot, some too cold. Jude was just right—spontaneous without being irresponsible; funny but not too glib; aware of what was going on in the world but not consumed by it; spiritual but not self-righteous; romantic without being emotionally needy. To her, Jude represented a genuinely happy medium. She wasn't crazy about him, and she was grateful for that. At this point in her life she wasn't looking for explosive emotional fireworks. She didn't want volatility and speed, she wanted comfort and reliability, a man she could count on for the long haul. Indeed, she had thought for years that she would end up marrying someone at least ten years older than herself—a man who already knew who he was and would appreciate her all the more because her body was a decade behind his in the wrinkle and sag of matrimony.

Jude was still a bit boyish, and she was sometimes surprised that this didn't irritate her more, but she figured he would eventually grow up and assume the yoke of fatherhood without too much fuss. She might have to give him a poker night with his buddies every now and then, and occasionally host a Super Bowl party, but that was a small price to pay for a man's cooperation. If he asked her to marry him at some point, she was inclined—though not compelled—to say yes, and this gave her an odd feeling of power. She could take or leave him, really, and if he ever cheated on her, she reasoned, the divorce would be that much less painful.

A car whizzed past them on the left then darted into the fast lane and disappeared.

"Jerk," said Kim.

"I hope he gets nailed."

"Me, too."

"I hate people like that."

"I know. What makes them so special that they can just go out and put everyone else's life in danger?"

Jude checked his rear-view mirror. "Hold on, here comes another one," he said.

A silver Toyota Camry blew by them in the next lane over but did not veer into the fast lane, as the other car had. Instead, it darted into the sixty-foot gap between Jude and the car in front of him, a late-model pickup truck with a missing taillight.

"Omigod, he's going to hit that truck!" Kim shrieked.

Jude saw it too, but didn't say anything; his arms were tensed at the wheel, his eyes locked on the road in front of him. Unaware that he was doing it, Jude lifted his foot off the accelerator and began applying pressure to the brakes. A car in the right-hand lane prevented the Camry from shooting the gap and going around the pickup. The Camry jerked to the left as the driver realized he could not go around the right side of the truck. At about the same time, the driver must have realized he was traveling too fast to avoid slamming into the back of the pickup, for there was a moment of hesitation, then the Camry's brakes locked up and the car swerved to the left, its tires screeching in a sickening wail of concrete and rubber. The Camry began skidding sideways. Briefly the car gained some traction, then fish-tailed violently across two lanes of traffic, almost colliding with an E-class Mercedes on Jude's left. The rear of the car slammed into the cement divider in the middle of the freeway. A shower of sparks sprayed into the air. Then, as if it were a spectacularly doomed vehicle in a video game, the car began to flip and roll, side over side, five or six times, in a strange gymnastic of rubber and steel. On its final flip, the car did a half-pirouette on its front bumper and landed with a heaving crunch upside down, in the middle of the freeway, about fifty feet in front of Jude.

To Jude, the whole episode seemed to unfold in slow-motion silence, just the way they say it does when death looks you straight in the eye but decides to pass you by. There was also something about watching it through a pane of glass, insulated from smell and sound, that made it seem unreal, as if he were watching the whole thing on TV. The rest of the traffic around and behind them had slowed to a crawl. Miraculously, no other cars were involved in the accident. The cars ahead of the crash kept moving, opening up an acre of empty concrete beyond the crumpled vehicle that now lay in the middle of the road, upside down, its wheels spinning in lazy circles like a child's toy hurled across the room.

"Oh my god, did that just happen!?" Kim gasped.

In order to maneuver around the obstacle now in front of him, Jude nudged his way into the left lane. Shiny pebbles of shattered glass surrounded the car as if someone had spilled a sack full of diamonds. A liquid of some sort was crawling along the bottom chassis and dripping from the front bumper, creating an oily puddle on the road. There was no sign of movement; the force of the crash had completely crushed the top of the car so that the hood was level with the road. Both of the vehicle's airbags had deployed and inflated portions were now sticking out of the windows like bloated limbs. On the driver's side, where there should have been a person, there was nothing but a gray balloon of polypropylene protruding like a head out onto the road.

It was hard to imagine anyone surviving such a crash. There was no sign of the driver; the space where he would have been had disappeared, having been crushed by two tons of steel hurled to the ground in a violent display of pitiless physics. Whoever was driving that vehicle was still inside, probably dead but perhaps not—perhaps only paralyzed and bleeding, perhaps in shock and now suffocating, his face smashed into the plastic airbag intended to save him—and the worst part was, there was nothing Jude felt he could do about it. Slowly, he navigated around the perimeter of the vehicle and eyeballed the damage. Total destruction was his assessment: the car would have to be scrapped, the driver buried, and the road cleaned of debris. Traffic would be backed up for hours. The news crews would be on the scene shortly. It was going to be a madhouse. There was still time to get to the restaurant, he thought, and there were hardly any cars on the road ahead of him. If he stepped on it, they could still make it in time, he reasoned.

As soon as Jude cleared the debris of the crash he punched the gas and breathed a sigh of relief.

"What are you doing?" Kim asked.

"I'm getting us out of here," said Jude. "If we hurry, we can still make it to the restaurant."

"What are you talking about?" she said. "How can you think about eating at a time like this? We have to stop."

"Stop?"

"Of course."

"Why?"

"To see if anyone needs help."

Jude glanced over to see if Kim was serious.

She was.

"The car is upside down. The cab was completely crushed. The driver is probably dead. What could we possibly do?"

"I don't know," Kim said. "That's why we have to stop—to see what we *can* do."

"We're not doctors. We'd just be in the way."

"You don't know that!"

"Yes, I pretty much do," Jude replied. "If I thought I could help, I would—but I'm fairly certain I'd be useless in that situation. I haven't even taken our company's CPR training."

"I know CPR. I used to be a lifeguard," said Kim.

"Well, my guess is that guy is going to need more than a little junior-lifeguard CPR."

"That's a guess based on what? We can't really know unless we stop."

"I don't need to know! I saw the accident, and I think any reasonable person would agree that whoever was driving that car is extremely messed up and probably already dead."

Kim shot him an icy glare. "Oh, so suddenly I'm not a reasonable person?"

"I didn't mean it that way," said Jude. "I just meant that the guy, the driver, is probably beyond help at this point."

"What if everyone thought that way?" Kim snapped. "What

if nobody ever stopped to help?! What if that was you under there, clinging to your life, wondering when help was going to come?"

Jude sighed in a way that communicated a bit too clearly how little he thought of Kim's opinion, and how much he resented her turning the episode into something *personal*.

"Someone will stop," Jude assured her. "In fact, my guess is that too many people will stop, traffic will get backed up, and it'll just take longer for the ambulance to arrive. I think the most helpful thing we can do for that guy is keep moving and get out of the way so the police and medics can do their job."

"But we are *witnesses*," cried Kim. "We saw the whole thing happen. The police will want to talk to us, for their report."

"There were plenty of witnesses," Jude said. "Besides, the police can reconstruct what happened from the skid marks and crash pattern. They don't need us."

"They might," said Kim. "There's no way to know for sure unless we stop."

"If we stop, we run the risk of getting killed by some other jackass in a hurry," Jude argued. "It happens all the time. Remember that story on the news a couple of weeks ago? Old lady stranded on the side of the road with a flat tire, guy stops to help and *bam*, he gets clipped by some numb-nut in a Ford F-150 driving on the shoulder. Forget it."

"I'm calling 911," said Kim, pulling a cellphone from her purse. Jude shrugged, as if to say "whatever." Kim dialed and put the receiver to her ear.

"It's busy," she said. "How can 911 be busy?"

"Lines are probably overloaded from the four hundred people behind us calling 911," said Jude. "Really, Kim, there's nothing more we can do."

Jude accelerated and the crash scene receded in the rear-view mirror. Traffic had come to a standstill and, one by one, cars maneuvered around the upside-down car, lying on its back like a dead insect in the middle of the road. Jude and Kim rode in silence for a minute, each afraid to say anything for fear of sparking a larger argument. In that minute, each of them reviewed the main points of their disagreement and came to the same definitive conclusion: the other person was wrong. Without realizing it, the substance of their discord had congealed and hardened into a dark, solid mass that separated them as surely as a wall of bricks.

"We should have heard sirens by now," said Kim.

"I'm sure Chicago's finest are on their way."

"Evidently not," said Kim. "What if they're at the scene of some other accident? What if they're caught in traffic? What if they can't come right away?"

"They'll get there as soon as they can," Jude said.

"What if they don't even know about it yet? What if no one could get through because everyone was dialing at the same time?"

"Someone must have gotten through," Jude said, trying his best to reassure her.

"But if someone had gotten through, we would have heard sirens by now. An ambulance would be on its way already."

"Maybe it's coming from a different part of the city, so we can't hear it," Jude offered.

"Maybe it isn't coming at all."

On the side of the road Kim saw a small rectangular sign with a bed on it that read: "Hospital."

"Get off at the next exit," Kim ordered.

"Why?" he asked.

"Please, just do it."

"Do you have to use the restroom?"

"No."

"Because if you do, we're like five, ten minutes away from the restaurant, max."

"I don't have to go to the bathroom."

"Okay. Can it wait, then?

"No," Kim said. "Please."

"But we'll miss our dinner reservation."

"Screw the dinner reservation!" Kim screamed. "Just get off at the next exit and take me to the hospital!"

Jude arched his eyebrows in disbelief. "Is something wrong?" he asked.

"Yes. Someone is back there either dying or dead and no one is doing anything to help them!"

Jude started to say something, but Kim cut him off. ". . . so just shut up and take me to the goddamn hospital."

Jude pulled off at exit 43 and followed the signs to the hospital. At Kim's request, he pulled up to a white brick building with the word "emergency" above the doors lit up in big block letters, red as blood. Jude let Kim out of the car. She rushed inside and Jude pulled into the nearest parking lot, still wondering if it might be possible to make their dinner reservation, given that there was nothing wrong with Kim and, other than her obstinance, they had no reason to be at the hospital in the first place.

Jude walked through the double doors at the entrance of the emergency room and saw Kim at the registration counter talking to the receptionist. She seemed agitated. Her head was bobbing up and down and she was gesturing emphatically with her hands. The receptionist looked bored and vaguely suspicious, as if she were trying to determine what sort of medication Kim was or wasn't taking.

As he walked up beside Kim, Jude heard the receptionist say, "I'll look into it, ma'am."

Kim looked exasperated.

"She says they haven't heard anything about a crash on the freeway."

"They probably won't hear about it until the paramedics call it in," Jude offered.

"Which means an ambulance hasn't gotten there yet."

"Maybe not. It's only been about five minutes since it happened."

"That's what I've been trying to tell this person," she whispered, "but she won't listen."

Jude rested his elbows on the counter and leaned toward the receptionist. "Excuse me, but we just witnessed a terrible accident on the Eden's just north of here. I'm certain there was at least one badly injured person and maybe more, so an ambulance needs to get there right away."

The receptionist rolled here eyes up toward Jude without moving her head. "Are you a doctor?" she asked.

"No, but . . ."

"Then, as I've already explained to the young lady here, all I can do is report what you've told me to the proper authorities," said the receptionist.

"Who are?" Jude intoned.

"The police dispatcher and my supervisor."

"Could we talk to your supervisor?"

"She's not in the building at the moment."

"When will she be in the building?" Jude asked.

The receptionist rolled her big, brown, heavily made-up eyes at Jude and said, "Look, son, don't pull any of that 'I need to talk to your boss' crap with me. Believe it or not, we have systems in place to deal with these things, and trust me, it will be dealt with as expeditiously as possible. It may not happen as fast as you might like, but then again, what does? Am I right? So why don't you and your lady friend have a seat and a nurse will be right with you."

"There's nothing wrong with us," Kim said. "We just wanted to report an accident."

"Okay. So you've reported it," said the receptionist. "Are you waiting around for someone to give you a medal?"

Kim stomped her foot and emitted a child-like squeal of indignation. "No, I just . . . look, if there was an accident on the Eden's expressway just north of exit 43, which there was, wouldn't they bring any injured people here?"

"Maybe. Maybe not," said the receptionist nonchalantly. "Depends."

"On what?"

"Nature and extent of the victim's injuries. Flow of traffic. Current rotation of medical personnel. Availability of beds and equipment. Driver's knowledge of the roads. Other incidents in the vicinity. That kind of thing."

Kim bit her lip in frustration. "Can you at least tell us how long it usually takes for someone to get here after an accident?"

The receptionist looked up at Kim through her eyebrows. "Depends."

"On?"

"Traffic to the accident site. Number of people and vehicles involved. Nature and extent of their injuries. How easily they can be pulled from their vehicles. Whether or not they need traction. Competence of the medics on the scene. Time of day. The weather. Traffic between the accident and the hospital."

"Okay, we get the idea," said Jude. He put his hand on Kim's shoulder in a way he hoped was comforting. "Look, I don't think there is anything more we can do here. Why don't we just let these people do their jobs and try to put this whole thing behind us. It doesn't have to ruin our evening. If we hurry, I'm sure we can still make it for dinner. Then we can get a drink and salvage some enjoyment out of the evening. What do you say?"

Jude thought he sounded conciliatory and reasonable, or at least hoped he did—but Kim was not in the mood to be placated.

"No."

"No?"

"I'm going to wait here to see if they bring him in," said Kim.

Now it was Jude's turn to be exasperated. "Oh come on, Kim. Only one of two things can happen here: Either they bring him in or they don't. Either way, there's nothing you can do about it. And besides, it's really none of your business. Why don't you just let it go?"

Kim looked at Jude with steel in her eyes. Suddenly she couldn't believe that mere minutes before she had been toying with the idea of someday marrying the man who stood before here now, a man so indifferent to injury and death that he ranks it below "dinner reservations" on his list of personal priorities; a man so callous and cruel that he would refuse to come to the aid of a dying man for fear of getting held up in traffic. Could such a man ever be trusted to do the right thing? What if he were faced with a choice between taking his own sick child to the doctor and missing a tee time at the country club? Could he stop thinking about himself long enough to make the right decision? Faced with a thousand and one such decisions during the course of family life, could such a man be counted upon to put the family's needs above his own? The notion instantly struck Kim as absurd. The clear, unavoidable answer was—no.

And just like that, though he didn't yet know it, Kim struck Jude from her list of potential husbands and possible soul mates.

"You do what you want," Kim said. "I'm going to stay here."

"For how long?!" cried Jude.

"As long as it takes."

An hour passed, during which Kim and Jude barely spoke a word. He slouched in a chair in the waiting room flipping through six-month-old copies of Sports Illustrated; she leafed through the pages of Redbook and, every fifteen minutes or so, wandered up to the front desk to see if any news had arrived on the crash or the whereabouts of the injured driver. The answer was always the same: no. No, the hospital dispatcher had not received any word on the crash, and no, no one involved in an automobile accident had been admitted to the emergency room.

It was close to 9:00 P.M. when Jude announced that he was starving and could not put off eating any longer. He informed

Kim that he was going to find the hospital cafeteria and asked if she wanted anything.

"Do what you like," Kim replied. "I'm not hungry."

The story was the same at 10:00 P.M. By then Jude had eaten and had taken a short, though hardly restful, nap. He had flipped through every issue of every magazine on the rack and had learned from half-a-dozen issues of *People* more than he ever wanted to know about the tragic breakup of Brad Pitt and Jennifer Aniston.

"Kim, can we go now?" Jude asked plaintively.

She looked at him with angry, empty eyes. "I want to go home," she said.

"Then let's go."

On the expressway, driving in the opposite direction, they passed the spot on the road where the accident had happened. The car had been towed away, the road cleaned up, and traffic was flowing briskly, as if the accident a few hours before had never happened. When they arrived at Kim's apartment building in Rogers Park, Jude walked her to the door. She thanked him for the ride, and, without so much as a perfunctory peck on the cheek, opened the door and slipped inside. The bolt of the security lock clicked into place behind her and she disappeared up the stairs into the dark interior of the building, out of sight. He stood on the stoop for a minute or two in the hope that she might change her mind and invite him up. When it became evident that this wasn't going to happen, that she had said goodbye to him for good, Jude climbed into his car and drove the back way home, along Sheridan Road to Evanston, where he and his college roommate, Glen, had lived for the past year and a half since getting their MBA's from Kellogg.

Glen wasn't home when Jude arrived. He tossed his car keys onto the kitchen table and noticed the blinking red light on the answering machine, indicating that there was a message. Thinking that Kim might have called and left an apologetic word or two for him to make up for the evening she had ruined, he rewound the tape and pushed the play button. The message was from a nurse at Cook County Hospital. Something about Glen being there and the need to contact a family member. Jude called the number and waited for the nurse, Doreen something, to be paged.

"Hello. This is Doreen O'Connell."

"This is Jude Mathers. You called about my roommate, Glen Doyle. Is he okay? What happened?"

"We need to contact a family member," said the nurse. "Do you know how we can get in touch with the nearest relative?"

"His parents are divorced," said Jude. "His mom lives in France, and I think his dad lives somewhere in Atlanta."

"Does he have any brothers or sisters in town?"

"No."

"Do you have a phone number for the father?"

"Well, I might be able to find one," said Jude. "Why don't you ask Glen? I'm sure he knows it by heart."

There was an awkward silence.

"I'm afraid Mr. Doyle has been involved in a serious accident," said the nurse.

"Is he going to be okay?" Jude said with a twinge of panic in his voice. "I mean, how serious is it?"

"If there are no immediate family members available, we're going to need you to come down to the hospital as soon as possible," said the nurse coolly.

"Will you at least tell me what's going on?" Jude said, his voice rising in both pitch and volume as the words came out of his mouth. "Is he alive or dead?!"

"The best thing you can do for your friend right now is come down the hospital," said the nurse. "Will you do that?"

"He's dead, isn't he?" Jude blurted. "You won't—can't—answer my question because he's dead. Isn't that right?"

"We can give you details at the hospital," said the nurse.

"Why won't you at least tell me if he's alive or dead?!" Jude cried.

"Again, Mr. Mathers, all I can say right now is that you're needed at the hospital," said the nurse. "Please, try to get here as soon as you can."

Jude hesitated for a moment to collect his thoughts, which were rapidly spinning out of control.

"Sure, I'll be right there," he said quietly. "Anything I can do to help."

• • • • • •

THE VISION

For the 750 workers at Ace Manufacturing Corp., the unveiling of the company's new vision statement was an occasion of great ceremony and speculation. Two years in the making, the statement was forged by a twenty-five-person committee representing people from all levels of the organization, from line workers on the shop floor all the way up to the president himself. Charged with the responsibility of articulating a corporate philosophy that would guide the company through the challenges and complexities of the twenty-first-century marketplace, the committee had embraced its task with uncommon gusto, sometimes working for weeks on end to hammer out the elusive language for what had come to be known simply as The Vision. Those whose jobs went undone during this period of creative ferment were excused from their usual duties by the CEO, who had declared that the committee's all-important work was the company's top priority. And, since members of the committee had been forbidden to discuss anything that went on in their vision-statement meetings, an air of potent mystery surrounded the unveiling.

Rumors about what the statement might say had been circulating for months. Some thought it would be a modern formulation of the original three P's—People, Performance, Profit—espoused by the company's founder, R.F. LeBlanc, who died the previous year of a heart attack, at home, while trying to prove to his six-year-old great grandson that he could still do twenty push-ups. (He couldn't.)

Many hoped the statement would solidify the company's dedication to its employees by ensuring a harmonious balance between work and home, job and family. Others thought a far-reaching, grandly ambitious vision was what the company needed, one that inspired all of Ace's employees to perform at their peak each and every minute of every day. Their CEO went further than that even, announcing at the project's inception that the company's vision statement would "solidify everything that is good and great about our company in one bold, declarative sentence—a sentence so wise and so compelling that its truth will be self-evident, its power irrefutable, its genius unsurpassed."

Not many sentences get this kind of buildup, so, naturally, everyone wanted to know what these magic words might be. If the statement was anywhere near as magnificent as the ceremony itself, success was a foregone conclusion.

A banquet hall at the nearby Hilton had been rented for the occasion (it was the biggest room they had), and the decorating committee had outdone themselves by festooning the room in blue and gold, the company's official colors. Blue and gold balloons dangled from an enormous chandelier, which hung from the ceiling like a giant crystal wedding cake, and the walls were adorned with blue-and-gold bunting that encircled the entire room, twice—"one for good measure, and one for good luck," as Marjorie Lemke, head of the decorating committee, was fond of explaining. There was plenty of food and coffee, too. Baskets were piled high with muffins, croissants, bagels, pastries, and scores of other treats, including miniature pecan pies and a generous selection of melon slices and berries. Hot, strong coffee poured from gleaming brass urns, and real cream flowed from miniature pitchers that were dutifully re-filled by an attentive and courteous waitstaff.

Clearly, something big was about to happen.

Brad Horn was especially interested in the new vision statement because, as one of the company's senior analysts, he was painfully aware that the old vision—one that had served the company well for fifty years—was failing. Revenue was down 12 percent from the previous year, profits had taken an 8 percent hit, and just about every business cost imaginable—market research, product development, raw materials, health insurance, office-space rental, technical infrastructure, gasoline (for the truck fleet), office supplies, etc.—was rising at an alarming rate. The company had passed on as many of these costs to customers as it could, but now even customers were starting to revolt, many of them defecting to competitors who operated with lower overhead costs and, of course, lower standards of service and quality. Ace Manufacturing was still the top company in its field, but that status, Brad knew, was perilously close to evaporating.

What Brad Horn wanted from the new vision statement was perhaps more than a mere sentence could deliver, however. What he wanted was a sense of security, the assurance that his job—indeed, his company—would exist for the next twenty years or so, at least long enough for him to put his three kids through college and buy his wife, Carol, the Lexus she had always wanted. He wanted a statement that relieved him of worry; that promised him a brighter, more prosperous future; that inspired him and made him believe that his dreams and aspirations were possible to achieve. Though he dared not hope for it, and certainly didn't expect it, he wanted all of that from the new vision statement—all of that, and more.

After draining a cup of coffee and quickly refilling it, Brad took a seat near the back of the room, next to Rob Vernon, one of the many white-toothed, starch-collared denizens of the marketing department. Brad and Rob played an occasional racquetball game together, but otherwise they knew almost nothing about each other.

"Not a bad turnout," Brad observed as he sat down.

"For a mandatory meeting," Rob retorted.

"Any inside intelligence on what the committee has come up with?" Brad probed.

Rob emitted a sound somewhere between a snort and a snicker. "Intelligence? Out of this bunch?"

"I just hope it's not one of those gargantuan, Dickensian mission statements that takes up a whole page and has forty semi-colons."

"Dickensian?" Rob smirked.

"Yes, Charles Dickensian. Didn't they teach you anything at Cornell?" Brad ribbed.

"Dead white dude? Bestseller list a couple of centuries ago? Wrote books that make lousy movies, and even worse video games?"

"Glad to see your education hasn't been wasted."

"I'm looking for something a bit more Hemingwayesque myself," said Rob. "Something I can grunt while I'm on the toilet."

"Tsk, tsk, your cynicism is showing again," Brad said. "Better cover it up before someone from upper management sees."

"Not much chance of that," Rob said. "Those guys are blind to everything except profit."

"Those *people*," Brad corrected. "Remember, Anne Hutchinson's on the board."

"You're right, she's got bigger balls than I do," Rob said. "Not to mention hairier legs."

"And smaller boobs."

The CEO of Ace Manufacturing, Leonard B. Hastings, who had bigger boobs and hairier legs than both of them combined, stepped up to the podium and cleared his throat.

"Greetings one and all. Before we begin, I'd like to thank everyone on the decorating committee for their hard work in putting this event together. The room looks marvelous." The observation drew a round of polite applause while Marjorie Lemke stood and bowed. "I'd also like to thank everyone in this room for their patience and input during the past year. Our vision-statement committee could not have done its important work without your cooperation and support. I'd also like to thank everyone on the vision-statement committee for the energy and insight each of you has brought to this process. I am confident the end result will speak for itself. And it better," he said, leaning into the microphone, "because I don't want to be up here all day!"

A burst of laughter filled the room then died as quickly as it had come.

"Which brings us to the moment at hand. Every great company needs a vision, an idea of where it's going. Great companies can't afford to rely on the past as a guide. No, great companies always look ahead. That's why, two years ago today, I asked our vision committee to distill the essence of this company into a single sentence—one bold statement that would encapsulate everything this company is and is going to be. As it turns out, they did me one better. This stellar committee not only captured this company's vital mission in a single sentence, they slashed it down to four powerful words that I'm sure you'll agree articulate everything we're about here at Ace Manufacturing.

"Big deal, you might say. I could do that in five minutes, you might think—just hand me a pen. If you actually tried to do it, however, I am certain you would come to a different conclusion. As any poet can tell you, reducing eternal truths to the fewest possible words is no easy task, and the fewer words one seeks to employ, the harder the task gets. So you see, what I am going to share with you today is not just four simple words— but four *perfect* words. Four words of pure business poetry."

Brad leaned over to Rob and whispered, "Said words to be preceded by the longest, most tortuous preamble in history."

"I'm pretty sure he said 'turds,'" Rob whispered back.

"Turds, curds, what's the difference? I just wish he'd get on with it," Brad replied. "I've got work to do."

Someone shooshed the two of them to be quiet, and Hastings continued: "But before I do, allow me to say what a privilege it is to work with such a fine, dedicated group of people. I can say without a doubt that we have the best people in the business, so take a moment to give yourselves a well-earned round of applause." Hastings then began slamming his meaty hands together in front of the microphone, sending a thunderous boom throughout the room every time the ample flesh on his palms collided. An enthusiastic burst of applause issued from the front of the room and rippled back to Brad and Rob, who were half-heartedly clapping while simultaneously surveying the room to see who was making the bulk of the noise. It was, as always, the gang from sales, who, in Brad's opinion, spent so much time slapping themselves on the back that their children were going to be born with an extra set of arms.

After the applause withered and died, Hastings cleared his throat and began applying his words with an extra layer of sincerity. "And now, I'd like to draw your attention to the screen behind me," he said.

A veil of black curtains parted and a projection screen fifteen-feet wide and ten-feet high was revealed. On it was projected an iridescent blue background with the Ace Manufacturing logo—the letters "A" and "M" intertwined like a pretzel—tucked neatly into the lower right-hand corner.

"As you all know, our vision committee has been working toward this moment for two years. Last year, you all participated in a company-wide self-assessment survey. The results from that survey were collated along with an analysis of best practices from other companies, as well as feedback solicited from our vendors, clients, and shareholders. A number of benchmarking tools were also employed, and after all the data was aggregated, a common theme emerged—a theme that unites us all in the everlasting pursuit of excellence. So, without further ado, allow me to share with you Ace Manufacturing's official Statement of Vision for the twenty-first century!"

The CEO gestured toward the screen with a dramatic sweep of his hand. Four gold-colored words dissolved into view one by one on the iridescent blue canvas of the PowerPoint slide. The words were:

"Do"

"More"

"With"

"Less."

An uncomfortable silence hung over the auditorium as the employees of Ace Manufacturing sorted out the meaning of these words. "Do more with less," was not a motto anyone in the auditorium expected, but no one had known quite what to expect, either. Bigger words, maybe. A more powerful verb, perhaps. Whatever it was, no one could put it into words themselves, so the longer these particular words remained on the screen, immovable and immutable, the more authority they accumulated. A few tentative claps punctured the silence, followed by a few more, but the cumulative response from the employees of Ace Manufacturing never quite reached the level of applause. Only one person kept clapping, as loudly and conspicuously as he could: CEO Leonard B. Hastings himself.

Hastings kept clapping long after everyone else in the room had stopped, his hands coming together again and again in an aggressive, defiant thump as he stared appreciatively at the screen. After what he deemed was an appropriate amount of time to let the words on the screen to sink in, he turned again toward his audience and sidled up to the microphone.

"I'm not going to bore you by standing up here and taking a bunch of questions," Hastings said. "I think you'll all agree that this statement speaks for itself, and I'm confident that if we all embrace it and apply it to each and every aspect of our work, a brighter, more prosperous future awaits us all. Thank you."

A small army of women began passing out t-shirts, visors, and rubber wristbands with the new vision statement imprinted on them. In the back of the room, Brad Horn and Rob Vernon stood up and stretched.

"That's it?" Brad wondered out loud. "Two years of arguing and deliberation and thought, and all they come up with is four lousy words?"

"Like the man said, think of it as poetry," Rob offered. "Mercifully short and entirely beside the point."

"Funny. But tell me, oh wise one, how are we supposed to do any more with any less? We've already cuts costs to the bone. We've already layed off as many people as we can. Everyone here is already doing the work of two or three people. Where does it end?"

Rob Vernon gave a philosophical shrug. "It never ends," he said.

At first, the changes were barely noticeable. Instead of cleaning the offices every day, for example, the janitorial service began coming every other day. In the coffee machine, a cheaper brand of brew was substituted, which meant that the sludge it produced was only marginally less drinkable than the previous swill. When 100-watt light bulbs burned out, they were replaced with cheaper 75-watt bulbs, except in places where it was determined that no extra light was necessary, in which case the dead bulbs weren't replaced at all. The cost of snacks went from ninety-five cents to a dollar, because a time-and-motion study had determined that employees wasted an average of twenty-seven seconds every time they rummaged around in their pockets for spare change before putting a dollar in the machine anyway. On the assembly line, new gloves were not issued to workers until they had worn holes through to the skin in the old ones, and safety glasses had to be cracked, not just scratched, before they could be replaced. Buyers for raw materials—aluminum, stainless steel, plastic, glass, oil, glue, paper, various kinds of fabric—were simply required to purchase a grade level down, a move that was applauded by the shareholders for yielding an immediate 4-percent return.

In these and other subtle ways, life at Ace Manufacturing began to change. Brad Horn noticed it first in the chatter, or lack thereof. On Brad's floor, the sixth, the collective clucking of administration hens had dwindled to a disconcerting murmur. Twenty of their sisters had been layed off in the month since The Vision was unveiled (due mostly to the company's acquisition of a new software program that did their jobs more efficiently), which left only nine of them to chirp and gossip the day away. In the past, these daily exchanges were often punctuated by loud, riotous laughter of the sort one only hears in places choked by tedium. Lately, however, the hens had taken to whispering to each other conspiratorially, as if they were prisoners planning a jailbreak. Brad didn't realize how accustomed to the previous level of office chatter he had become until it was gone; now, without it, he found it difficult to concentrate on his work, like someone who can't sleep without the hum of a fan to keep the encroaching silence at bay.

The whispering also took its toll on morale, since everyone assumed that the information exchanged via whispering was more sensitive and confidential than the information exchanged out loud, in the open. It wasn't, but when the hens were huddled in the break area and talking to each other like attendees at a librarian convention, one couldn't help speculating that they might have heard something about another round of layoffs or another initiative implemented in the name of cost-effectiveness and efficiency. After all, when their ranks were full the hens did sometimes become aware of classified information before Brad did, which aggravated him. Furthermore, their communication network was far more sophisticated and diverse than Brad's, since his job didn't require him to converse with many people at all.

Plus, Brad was a man, and a numbers man at that. He did not possess the gene for idle chit-chat, and his DNA was not equipped to deal with, or play, the sort of office politics that might be necessary to save his job from the combined forces of free-market economics and corporate Darwinism. He was doubly handicapped in that he didn't trust his instincts, either. His instincts had failed him on numerous occasions, after all, most recently when he had tried to say something funny to Ms. Driscoll, the office manager, and had received only a vacant stare in return.

One morning, an announcement came over the loudspeaker: "Will all employees please sit down at their desks to hear an important announcement from the president."

A wave of murmurs rippled through the office as everyone did what they were told. It was 11:00 A.M. on Friday, May 14, a day that was destined to become known as Black Friday to those who remained with the company, and Independence Day to those who were released.

Leonard B. Hastings wasted no time in getting to the point. As soon as his image flickered to life on everyone's computer screen, he began: "Good morning, fellow colleagues. As you all know, we are competing in an ever more challenging marketplace, and our competitors are growing stronger every day. In order to survive, we need to make the best possible use of our resources, and in the past few months we have taken up initiatives to do exactly that. I believe we can do better, however—which is why I am addressing you today. In the interest of creating a more focused, efficient company—one better able to hold its own in today's challenge-rich business environment— we are, starting today, consolidating a number of business units to leverage certain departmental synergies and eliminate work- force redundancies. For many of you, this means that today will be your last day at Ace Manufacturing. I want to thank you all for your contributions and unwavering dedication to the com- pany, and I wish you the best of luck in your future endeavors. No one likes to let people go, but it is sometimes necessary, and this is one of those times. For those of you who are remaining, I want to assure you that Ace Manufacturing will continue to be Number One in our industry and that quality and excellence will not suffer because of these changes. Indeed, we are taking these steps to *improve* the company's overall performance and generate even higher levels quality and excellence. Thank you."

Throughout the rest of the day, a dark, foreboding cloud of doom hung over the offices of Ace Manufacturing. For most, the end was quick and tidy—a tap on the shoulder, the closing of an office door, a few minutes to convey the inevitable, a handshake and goodbye. For some, though, the news of their dismissal was difficult to accept. Larry Edwards had been with the company for fourteen years and had recently registered his best sales quarter ever. "It's not fair," he protested, and everyone in the room nodded in agreement. No, it wasn't fair. "What am I going to do?" Edwards pleaded. "Where am I going to go?" No one could answer these questions, but Larry Edwards was reassured that he was a valued (if expendable) member of the team, as well as a talented salesperson. He would land on his feet, they assured him, because good people always do.

Ellen Hofstedter couldn't control her tears. The moment she felt the hand on her shoulder she burst out crying, as if the hand had turned on an especially noisy spigot, one that could not easily be shut off once it got going. She snuffled and sputtered as it was explained to her that she would receive a week's pension for every year she had worked at Ace, or sixteen weeks—almost four months!—of paid time off to find another job, which was better than most. Unfortunately, the prospect of so much unstructured time combined with the pressure of finding a new job felt to Ellen as if she had just been pushed out of an airplane. She couldn't enjoy the fall because she wasn't sure she had a parachute. Certain death awaited her at the bottom, she suspected, so the only reasonable thing to do was to panic. Which she did, requiring three paramedics to come to her rescue, because her superiors feared, for insurance reasons, that she might be having a heart attack.

Brad Horn was not among those released that day, but his marketing cohort, Rob Vernon, was. Before he left, Rob poked his head into Brad's office and said, "See ya 'round." There wasn't much else to say. Both men agreed that they should get together sometime to play racquetball, but it never happened. In fact, Brad Horn and Rob Vernon would never see each other again as long as they both lived, their brief friendship dissolved and forgotten, lost to the indifference of time and, not incidentally, their indifference toward each other.

The following Monday, Ace's remaining employees arrived at work to find that several keys on their computer keyboards had been removed. A statistical analysis of typographical keystrokes had evidently determined that there were keys on the company's computers—namely the ~ suene, the ^ carat, F2, F9, and NumLk/ScrLk keys—that went almost entirely unused. In a memo distributed later that day, it was explained that these unused keys had been removed from everyone's computers so that the plastic could be recycled.

Other inefficiencies were identified and addressed as well. For example, a study of office traffic patterns determined that, left to their own devices, people in the office got up to use the bathroom an average of seven times a day, which was four times more than the government deems necessary for a healthy adult. Each trip to the bathroom took an average of six minutes. If everyone in the company went to the bathroom four times more than they needed, it meant that they were wasting twenty-four minutes a day. Multiplied by the number of remaining employees, 400, that was 9,600 minutes, 160 hours, or 6.6 days of wasted worker time *every day*—just in superfluous bathroom breaks. Calculated on a per annum basis, that meant that each year, the company literally pissed away more than six years of potentially productive work time. If the children at Oak Hills Elementary school could limit themselves to three bathroom breaks a day, management reasoned, so could the employees of Ace Manufacturing. Potty breaks were thus restricted to one in the morning, one at lunch, and one in the afternoon. Exceptions had to be approved by an employee's supervisor.

The use of office supplies was subjected to the same exacting scrutiny. Paper clips were rationed on a need-to-clip basis in order to prevent people from taking a whole box and letting it spill at the bottom of their desk drawer. Paper and staples were issued in lots of fifty, and usage by each individual employee was meticulously tracked. Ball-point pens were distributed at a rate of one every two weeks, and employees received one packet of post-it notes a month, no more.

Once it was discovered that inefficiency and waste ran rampant in even the most mundane operations of the company, the admonition to "do more, with less" went from an aspiration to a compulsion. In the shipping department, FedEx-ing anything overnight was forbidden. Instead, employees were urged to "think ahead" in order to avoid having to overnight anything. The water cooler was no longer stocked with paper cups; employees were urged to bring their own cups and reuse them. (This measure only lasted a week, until someone realized that the water cooler itself was an unnecessary luxury, because perfectly good water ran from the tap for free.) Printing any document just because an employee wanted to became impossible. Instead, employees were required to fill out an RFP (request for printing) any time they needed to print something, after which the printing approval committee might or might not deem the item print-worthy. Since this process could take days, it had the unintended benefit of working even better than expected, since by the time the committee got around to approving a print request, the person who submitted the RFP in the first place had usually forgotten about it.

In these and many other ways, Ace Manufacturing began transforming the way it did business. There were grumblings and complaints along the way, of course, but that was to be expected. Change was always hard, Hastings knew. Besides, this wasn't just change for change's sake, it was a true "paradigm shift," a necessary restructuring of operations to "align the company and its goals with the new business realities of the twenty-first century," just as the consultant he hired had explained numerous times. Hastings had always liked the sound of this. It was just the sort of pro-active, forward-thinking strategy advocated by the authors—geniuses all—of the mountain of business/management books stacked on his credenza, all of which he fully intended to read someday.

As the weeks went by, and changes were made to do much more with quite a bit less, Hastings felt he had stumbled upon on an undiscovered business principle that he himself ought to write a book about one day. Hastings had noticed that if he had a team of ten people doing a predetermined amount of work and one of the people was fired or quit, the amount of work the team accomplished did not go down 10 percent, as one might expect. Instead, the remaining workers, in order to maintain the team's overall productivity, would figure out how to absorb and distribute the lost worker's job responsibilities amongst themselves. In short order this new nine-member team would end up doing just as much work as the old ten-member team did.

To the company, this phenomenon represented a 10 percent *increase* in productivity, because the company was now paying only nine people to do the work of ten. It also confirmed for the entire executive team that the company's new vision statement, "do more, with less," wasn't just an empty slogan, it was the concise articulation of a brilliant business philosophy, one that ensured healthy numbers on the bottom line by disciplining the company to make the best possible use of its resources. What's more, the benefits did not stop there. Once the new nine-member team got used to doing the work of ten people, yet another person could be eliminated from the team and the same phenomenon would assert itself. There would be some initial protests from the remaining team members, but these would quickly subside and the team would once again figure out how to redistribute the departed worker's tasks amongst themselves. Soon there would be *eight* people doing what was previously the work of ten. Then seven. Then six. The secret was redistributing the work gradually, rather than all at once, so that employees didn't notice how much more productive they were being.

The success of this program confirmed for Ace's executive team what they had suspected all along—that most employees of the company were not working up to their full potential. One could look around the offices on any given day and see that people weren't working as hard as they could every moment of the day. Time was constantly being wasted on idle chit-chat, unnecessary trips to the bathroom or snack machine, personal phone calls, illicit Web surfing, obsessive e-mailing, poor organization, agenda-less meetings, extended lunches and any number of other activities that did nothing to further the company's goals. Only by rooting out these inefficiencies one by one in a disciplined, organized fashion, could the company hope to achieve its full potential.

Against his will, Brad Horn became the architect of his own department's reorganization. One by one, over the course of many weeks, Brad had to break the news to members of his staff that they were no longer needed. First was Greg Morrison, then Barbara Felt, then Angie Baxter, then Paul Littleton. Soon, Brad had eliminated more than half his department.

Brad had expected each firing to be more painful than the last one, but to his surprise he found that the opposite was true: the more people he let go, the easier it got. It was just business, he told himself, and there was nothing he could do to prevent it, so why sweat it? Certainly he felt bad for those who had to go look for another job, but part of him was also slightly envious of them as well—they, at least, had the prospect of finding something more enjoyable to do. He, on the other hand, had no choice but to persevere, if only because his wife, children, bank, and creditors expected him to.

To compensate for the people he had fired, Brad, without fully realizing it, had taken on a considerable amount of their workload himself. Whereas he had been putting in a relatively comfortable thirty-five-hour workweek, now he was regularly working fifty-five to sixty hours a week; ten hours a day and whatever time he could squeeze in over the weekend.

Intuitively, he knew that he could not keep taking on more responsibility and doing more work forever; there had to be a breaking point. He barely had time to think about where that point might be, however, because his days were fuller and busier than ever. Only when the numbers began to fall did he begin to worry for real. When he ran the reports, Brad saw that overall production was off 26 percent since the new vision statement had gone into effect. Productivity per individual employee was more than it used to be, but only because each employee had been saddled with more work than they could possibly handle. Everything else had gone down: revenue, profits, margins, shipments, you name it.

At some point, Brad stopped worrying about the security of his job and replaced that worry with an even larger, more ominous concern about the viability of the entire company. Week after week went by and the numbers continued to plunge, yet upper management didn't seem to notice or care.

One morning he got a memo in his e-mail with a subject line that said, simply, "Way to go." The attached message said: "Management just wants you to know how much they appreciate your hard work. Way to go."

The following week he got another memo with the subject line, "Thumbs up," and the attached message: "What direction is Ace manufacturing headed? Up—two thumbs up!

A few days later, Brad got another memo with the subject line, "Smiles are contagious," and the enclosed message: "Studies have shown that smiling is good for you—and for our customers. Going forward, employees will be required to smile at least once every five minutes."

Another company-wide memo bore the subject line, "Expect the expected," with the message: "As expected, for the second straight quarter Ace Manufacturing has exceeded its customers' expectations."

For a while, Brad dismissed these periodic messages from above as the flotsam of management—harmless happy talk to keep the troops motivated. But the more bizarre the messages got, the more confused Brad became about their purpose and management's intent. Soon, the messages even stopped having messages—all they contained were words in the subject line: "Be the best." "Perform with purpose." "No is yes in disguise." "Stand or get stepped on." "Don't react, act." "Embrace excellence."

These were supposed to be inspirational messages, Brad guessed, but without any context, and blurted out at random as they were, they made almost no sense whatsoever. Meanwhile, the payroll continued to dwindle by a few dozen people a week, key indicators of the company's financial health were still deteriorating, and morale among the few remaining employees was growing toxic.

One Monday morning, Brad's assistant, Jennifer, called in sick, saying that her doctor had diagnosed her as having a rare auto-immune disease caused by relentless stress (it was most common in soldiers returning from the front lines of intense, protracted battle) and that she didn't know when, or if, she was ever going to return to work. Without Jennifer's help, Brad had no hope whatsoever of getting through the pile of reports on his desk before the next round of reports were due. In one jagged moment, his job had gone from almost impossible to completely absurd. No one person could do what he was being asked to do. He needed help, and he needed it now.

Fed up, Brad decided it was time to confront management—to raise the red flag, shoot off a flare, blow the whistle, whatever it took to get the suits upstairs to recognize the dire situation unfolding in the aisles and cubicles of their company. Someone had to tell them, he reasoned. Someone had to inform them that things had reached a crisis point, that people were suffering—indeed, that *action* needed to be taken. How they did not know this already, he could not fathom. But it was clear to him that they must *not* know, or else they would have done something already.

Frank Toynbee was the man to talk to first, Brad felt. Toynbee was the company's Chief Financial Officer, and if anyone could appreciate the tragedy of the balance sheets Brad was processing, it was Frank. Technically speaking, Brad was going over his boss's head in seeking out Toynbee, since his boss reported to the man. But Brad's boss had quit the month before and had never been replaced, so Frank Toynbee was his de facto boss for the time being, though this reporting relationship had never been formalized, or even acknowledged, by anyone. After all, there was only one person left in the HR department, and she had her hands full processing the paperwork of people who were being layed off.

Toynbee's office was on the eighth floor, two floors up from Brad's. It had a big glass window and a polished cherry-wood door, but the window shades were drawn and the door was closed when Brad approached. He couldn't tell if anyone was inside or not, so he gave the door three quick raps and waited to see if anything would happen. Inside the room he heard a low, gravelly voice say, "Come in," so he took a deep breath, turned the doorknob and leaned into the room.

Frank Toynbee was a slender stalk of a man with a thin coating of grey fuzz on his aging head and an Adam's apple so large it looked like he had swallowed a golf ball. As Brad entered his office, Toynbee looked up over the rims of his reading glasses. He seemed not to recognize Brad, and gave no visible indication that Brad's intrusion was either welcome or unwelcome.

"Brad Horn from the sixth floor, sir."

"Horn," repeated Toynbee. "Have a seat."

Brad eased himself into one of the two chairs facing Toynbee's desk and took a moment to look around. On the shelf behind Toynbee was a framed eight-by-ten photo of a much younger Frank Toynbee standing in a boat holding up a fish about three feet long, a tiger muskie by the looks of it. In the picture, Toynbee had a dark tan and was smiling. Except for the unmistakable Adam's apple, the man in the photo looked nothing at all like the pale, gaunt man behind the desk.

"What can I do for you?" Toynbee asked, but his tone made it perfectly clear that he had no interest in doing anything.

Brad cleared his throat and said, "Well, sir, it's about the current, uh . . . *situation*."

"What situation?"

Brad thought for a moment about how to phrase his assessment of the company's current predicament, but his thoughts refused to come to his lips fully formed. "The work situation," he said, finally. "It just seems that in the past few months we have cut so many corners and let so many people go that the work is starting to pile up. I'm putting seventy to eighty hours a week now and only getting to about a third of the work on my desk. It's too much."

Frank Toynbee peered over the rim of his glasses and pointed his cold, grey eyes at Brad.

"So, what you're saying is, you're not up to the challenge?"

Brad gulped. "No, what I'm saying is, there is too much work to do and not enough people to do it."

"Damn straight," Toynbee blurted.

"Pardon?"

"Nature of the beast," Toynbee barked.

"Beast, sir? What beast?"

"*Business*, boy!"

Brad blinked and searched his brain for a coherent response. "I'm afraid I don't get your meaning," he said, at last.

Toynbee peered wearily over his glasses. "Better to have too much work than not enough, eh?"

"Yes, I suppose, but . . ."

"No buts about it," Toynbee interjected.

"What I meant was . . ."

"You're not a socialist, are you, Horn?"

"No, not at all . . ."

"Then you understand the need to run a business as efficiently as possible."

"Yes, but . . ."

"And the need to embrace change."

"Sure, but . . ."

"And you understand that business goes in cycles."

"I guess, but . . ."

"And that we're in a down cycle."

"I suppose . . ."

"Do you know why they call it a down cycle, Horn?"

"Uh, because profits go down?" Brad ventured.

"Exactly! Profits go right down the goddamn toilet! And what happens when a toilet gets full?"

Brad didn't understand what Toynbee was trying to say, and it showed in the increasingly perplexed expression on his face.

Toynbee pounded his fist on his desk and leaned toward Brad as if he were about to spit on him. "You have to *flush* it!" Toynbee shouted. "And that's exactly what we've been doing—a little flushing."

Toynbee sat back down in his chair and tapped on the spacebar of his computer a few times. It was clear to Brad that Toynbee felt nothing more needed to be said, and that the matter had been concluded to his satisfaction. Brad sat in uncomfortable silence for more than a minute, waiting in vain for Toynbee to say something else, but the man just sat there, mute and still, as if he were made of wax.

Unable to find the necessary words to express his own confusion and dismay, it then occurred to Brad that perhaps he was talking to the wrong person—that maybe the right person to be talking to was none other than the man at the top, Leonard B. Hastings himself. It was possible, Brad thought, that Hastings was suffering from a lack of reliable information on exactly what was happening among the rank and file, and that he wasn't aware of the deteriorating mood and morale of the people he employed. Perhaps he would be doing Hastings a favor by telling him, Brad thought. After all, he had read that people were afraid to tell CEOs anything they didn't want to hear, which led to the rather common problem of people in power being surrounded by yes men and sycophants, people whose plan to get ahead was simply to please the boss. To achieve their goal, these professional parasites would tell whatever lies were necessary to maintain the illusion of their leader's courage and genius. As long as the illusion held, they reasoned, their jobs were safe. It was a survival strategy, nothing more—a defensive posture to protect themselves from an economy where nothing was certain; where competitive pressures put companies out of business every day; where job security was largely a matter of uncontrollable burps and gurgles in the stock market; where a company's loyalty to an employee only extended as far as the last paycheck; where personal survival depended solely upon one's ability to stay one step ahead of decision-makers themselves. It was a self-defeating strategy, though, because ultimately it was bad for business, bad for everyone.

Someone had to speak up, Brad told himself. Someone had to tell Hastings what was going on, even if the man at the top didn't want to hear it. And that someone, Brad decided, would be him.

"Thank you for your help," Brad said to Frank Toynbee, whose attention had gone back to his computer screen.

"Not at all," said Toynbee, without looking up.

Brad walked around the corner and down to the end of the hall, where the office of Leonard B. Hastings was located. Hastings' door was closed, and Brad could see through the blinds that the light in his office was off. This did not necessarily mean Hastings wasn't inside, however, as he was known to take long naps in the middle of the day. It was only ten o'clock in the morning, though, so Brad didn't know quite what to think.

He'd also heard that Hastings often left the lights in his office off throughout the day because he didn't like the glare—a result, it was said, of the blood pressure medication he was taking, which made his eyes sensitive to light.

Brad tried to peek through the blinds to see if Hastings was at his desk, but he couldn't tell. He tried three timid knocks on the door, then three more raps, harder and faster. Nothing. He glanced to his right and left to see if anyone was looking. Satisfied that no eyes were on him, he slowly turned the knob to Hastings' office and opened the door a couple of inches. No one was sitting in the chair behind the desk, so he opened the door a few inches more and scanned the room. Not only was Hastings' chair empty, everything else in the office was gone as well. All the books and knick-knacks on the shelves had been removed. No plaques or awards hung on the wall, and the various photos of Hastings shaking hands with important people—Ronald Reagan, Henry Kissinger, Rudy Guiliani, Bob Dole, Newt Gingrich—had disappeared as well. In fact, there were no personal artifacts whatsoever in the room anymore. Except for the computer monitor on the desk, the room was entirely empty.

Brad crept out and closed the door quietly behind him. The air in the hall was so still that Brad could hear himself breathing. The lady who watered the plants was making her rounds, ambling down the hall toward the bathroom, where she could refill her watering can. In her hands she held a clump of dead leaves, pruned from plants suffering from the strain of photosynthesizing nothing but fluorescent light. She saw Brad standing in front of Hastings' door and nodded.

"Looking for the boss?" she said as she walked past him.

"That's right," Brad said.

"He resigned is what I heard," she said. "Got a twenty-million-dollar settlement package and headed off to one of those little islands in the Caribbean."

Brad looked at her and blinked a few times, but said nothing.

"Twenty-million—imagine that," she muttered as she rolled past him.

"Uh, any idea who is running things now?" Brad blurted just as she was about to enter the women's bathroom. The plant woman paused, her watering can dangling by her side in her gloved left hand, the dead brown leaves clutched in her right.

"Ain't hardly anyone left," she answered. "Maybe *you* are." She then leaned her shoulder into the restroom door and disappeared inside, leaving a faint whiff of pine-scented disinfectant in the air. On the floor lay a dead leaf that she had dropped. Brad looked at it for a few seconds. He could have picked it up, but decided not to. That wasn't his job.

Yet.

* * * * * *

MOTHER'S DAY

OD, I HATE MOTHER'S DAY. THE one day in the whole stinking year my work is supposed to get acknowledged—the only day people (namely George and the kids) are supposed to at least *pretend* what I do matters—and I get a day like this, imported directly from the seventh circle of Hell.

Is a little gratitude too much to ask? Is it too big a burden for my family to take one little moment out of their year (I don't really need an entire day) to throw a "thank you" my way for all I do around here? They don't even have to mean it; I'd just like to hear it, once in a while, out loud, without any coercion or manipulation on my part. It wouldn't hurt for George to hear our wedding vows again, either, because I don't think he remembers a goddamn word. Come to think of it, I don't remember him saying a thing at our wedding ceremony; he *mumbled* so much that everyone just *assumed* he was saying what he was supposed to. I'm beginning to wonder if he didn't secretly make up some idiotic, self-serving bullshit on the spot, just to get off the hook with the big guy upstairs when he started treating his gorgeous and devoted wife (that would be me) to huge, heaping helpings of *cream-of-asshole* soup!

Oh well, what do I expect? Mother's Day is a crock no matter how you look at it. Everyone feels (or should feel) obligated to be nice to you because it's *that day*, but in reality everyone starts to resent you for having this *special* day—for being forced by the Hallmark card company to acknowledge your contribution to the harmony and balance of life on this planet—and then they all start getting pissy and mean and the whole day swirls straight down the toilet. I'll tell you what: They'd sure as hell have to acknowledge me if I stopped doing the laundry for a month. But then I'd be left staring at a month-high pile of dirty underwear, which would just get me back to where I started, so I guess it wouldn't be much of a protest. There is really no way to win.

Unfortunately, it seems there are plenty of ways to lose, and I keep finding them. Want examples? Here are several, arranged in chronological order, so that when I murder George, there is no mistake about who killed him or why. Some people leave suicide notes; I want to leave a murder note. All you have to do is imagine the following words pinned with a ten-inch Wustof chef's knife to George's scrawny, hairless, pitiful excuse for a chest:

(*A side note*: I don't really want to kill George. I just feel like killing him sometimes, and when that feeling comes over me, I find it therapeutic to *imagine* him in various stages of bodily dismemberment and/or primordial pain. You understand.)

The day started this way: We had company over on Saturday night, the evening before Mother's Day. Rob and Erin from down the street; the ones with the yippy little Yorkshire terrier. They're nice enough people, but he's an engineer (yawn) and she's a florist, so, except for the fact that they have a seven-year-old girl (Mandy), who is as obsessed with the American Girl doll cult as our own daughter, Beth, we have next to nothing to talk about. Which means it's up to me, and me alone, to keep the conversational ball rolling, because god forbid if George ever had to open his mouth and *converse* with anyone. His defense: "I hate small talk." Then why not try medium talk?, I say. Or big talk? If everyone is so damned boring, why not share with the rest of us some of the genius that is supposedly swimming around in that balding little head of yours? Elevate the conversation a little, why don'tchya? Here's a cosmic mystery you might try explaining: Why is watching a bunch of grown men on steroids tackle each other such a satisfying way to spend an afternoon? (Honest to god, if a football game is on in our house, I could strut naked into the living room, sit spread-eagle on the couch and pour canola oil all over my body, and George wouldn't lift an eyebrow or anything else. I might have more luck if I poured cold beer all over my body, but I doubt it. He'd just think it was a waste of good beer.)

Sometime during the evening I evidently said something that irritated him, because he clammed up even more (if it's possible for a closed clam to seal itself any tighter) and went to bed right after Rob and Erin left, sticking me, of course, with the cleanup duties. Around 12:30 A.M. I looked at the clock and said to myself, "Gee, look, it's Mother's Day. I could use a cocktail." So I made myself a gin and tonic, and then another one. Pretty soon I had a decent buzz going and was feeling like I needed to do something to keep from feeling so damned empty inside. So, despite everything, I decided that I would trudge upstairs and go through the motions of making up with him. I disrobed, spritzed on a little Chanel, and slid under the covers. George was asleep, snoring like a chainsaw, as usual, and I started tickling him with my fingernails, which he always likes. Well, almost always. This time he woke up just long enough to tell me to leave him alone. When I didn't obey His Majesty's orders—when I crawled over and tried to fulfill what I thought was pretty much every man's fantasy—he didn't respond. Not at all. After a while he just farted and said, "Sorry, ain't gonna happen," and went back to sleep.

The next day, My Day, was also Beth's first communion. Big day, big deal, lots to do, not enough time to do it. You get the picture: one of those days when Mommy could use a little help. The schedule called for church at 11:00 A.M., lunch at the Mall of America's Rainforest Cafe (Beth's choice), followed by an afternoon at Camp Snoopy and dinner with George's mother (who is a passive-aggressive psychotic) and father (whom I adore, but only in small, non-lethal doses) in the evening. Arguably more than one family should have to endure in a day, I'll grant you, but certainly not unprecedented and, under normal circumstances, not at all beyond the entertainment threshold of yours truly, who is regularly called upon to perform such miracles yet gets barely any news coverage at all, much less acknowledgement that the maternal magic required to accomplish all of this *and make everyone happy at the same time*, is remarkable in the extreme.

First things first, of course—if we're going to have guests for dinner and be gone most of the day, we have to tidy up and get everything ready in the morning, right? So, after George has had his coffee and has perused the sports section ad nauseum, I ask him to go down to the basement to get a six-pack of Diet Pepsi. Guess how long it takes him? AN HOUR?! It's not like he had to *find* the stuff, either—a case of it was right out in the open, next to the cooler, which I also asked him to bring up. He did rinse the inside of the cooler (at my request, because it's not something he would do on his own), so you can factor in the extra time needed for that—but still, an HOUR! During that same hour, I managed to clean and vacuum the first floor, dust under the radiators, Windex the dining-room windows, Swiffer the kitchen floor, iron Beth's communion dress, and get a load of laundry going.

I offer this comparison because I am beginning to believe that men and women (or at least George and I) travel through time at different speeds. While I am traveling eighty miles per hour on the freeway with my cellphone in one hand and a cup of Kenya AA in the other, George seems to be taking his sweet time through life, as if he's stuck in some sort of existential pedestrian zone that goes around in big, lazy circles, like the track around a football field. That may be it exactly, in fact. It's like he never left high school, except now he's too tired to run around the track anymore, so he just walks, checking out the cheerleaders along the way and grabbing a beer whenever he can. Mind you, I wouldn't trade—couldn't trade, even if I wanted to, because people who walk in circles don't *get* any- where—but I sometimes envy him. It must be nice to go into the basement for an hour to fetch a few cans of soda and know, without a doubt, that *your wife is upstairs doing everything else!*

After cleaning, I of course had to dress Beth and get her ready, which included doing her hair. Beth, being a very par- ticular and idiosyncratic type of girl, wanted her hair done in an elaborate braid that wasn't so much French as Gordian—which is to say, it was an extraordinarily complex architecture of swirls and curlicues that took nearly an hour to manufacture, and all I had to go by was a single picture from a recent issue of Vogue (yes, I am a subscriber) that Beth had retrieved from the recy- cling pile—so, as you can plainly see, I had my hands full.

While I was performing this amazing feat of cosmetic im- provisation, George had one task, and one task only, to accom- plish: dress Alex, Beth's older brother by two years, in some acceptable clothes for church. Now, I don't need to tell you how much easier boys are to dress than girls, because a) they don't care what they look like, b) most of their clothes are *not* fit for church, and c) the process of elimination does most of the hard decision-making for you. Since Alex only has *one* decent pair of corduroys and *one* nice shirt with a collar and buttons down the front, it shouldn't be *too* difficult to figure out what he should wear to church. But no—we're already running ten minutes late when what do I see piling into the minivan? Alex, wearing jeans, a Spiderman t-shirt and dirty tennis shoes—and George, wearing nothing but a black t-shirt under his sport jacket, looking like some kind of hipster/bachelor/gangster heading off to a casino! Imagine: wearing black to your daugh- ter's first communion? What kind of message does *that* send? When I asked him what the hell he was thinking, he said he gets too hot in his sport jacket, so he was trying a new "look." This is a man who has had the same haircut since he was four years old, and suddenly he's concerned about how he looks? On Mother's Day, no less?

The implications were alarming, certainly, but I didn't have time to deconstruct them all because we were already twenty minutes late and, in circumstances like these, Reverend Palmer does everything he can to make sure you pay for each tardy minute at the collection plate. This on top of the fact that on communion day, parents of the communicant are expected to be extra generous when the plate comes around, or else the nuns will bad-mouth you for the rest of the year. I only had three dollars in my purse, though, so we had to go by a cash machine on the way. Four blocks away is a bank with a twenty-four-hour drive-through machine. We stopped, I stuck my card in and asked for $100. A little message pops up on the screen that says, "We're sorry, but this account has insufficient funds to fulfill your request." Impossible!, I think, because I just deposited a $200 check my mother sent to buy Beth a communion present. Then I ratchet down my request—$80, $60, $40, $20— and each time the same message pops up on the screen, but there's nothing we can do about it because the bank is closed. Fine, I reason, we'll just have to write a check—but obviously I don't want to write a check until I figure out what's up with our bank account. Because the only thing worse than not giving any money at all to Our Lady of the Sacred Heart Catholic Church on communion day is giving a check that bounces. If that ever got out, the gossip would never stop; we'd have to change parishes for sure.

On the way out of the bank, I noticed that George was being strangely quiet and looking a little sheepish, like a little kid who has done something wrong and is trying to hide it, but secretly wants you to find out. What is it, I ask? Do you have a clue as to why there is no money in our account? He's not sure, he says, but it may have something to do with the fact that he bought me a present (the obligatory Mother's Day gift) and hadn't cleared the financial side with me. (I do all the bills, and he is under strict instructions not to purchase anything until he consults me first.) Said he wanted to surprise me.

The confession was supposed to melt my heart, I suppose, because our little off-ramp to accounting hell was paved with good intentions. But, as usual, George found a way to take a potentially happy scenario (me getting a gift I did not anticipate) and magically transform it into a situation that ended up pissing me off more than if he had done nothing at all. Needless to say my heart did not melt; it began to simmer instead, and though I didn't know it at the time, was headed for a full, rolling boil.

Ned and Patricia, George's parents, met us at the church. As we entered the chapel and took our seats, Patricia made sure she sat next to me, even though she knows I can't stand being within twenty feet of her when she's freshly "powdered." Patricia is one of those perfume people—you know, the kind of women who baste themselves in drug-store perfume to cover up the smell of being old. And I am one of those anti-perfume people, the type whose sinuses swell up at the first whiff of a *cloud de cologne*, whose eyes begin to water, whose temples begin to pound, and whose mood quickly deteriorates—but who is also too polite to say anything and therefore doomed to suffer in silence.

Patricia, on the other hand, doesn't do anything in silence. The second a thought pops into her head it comes out her mouth, damn the consequences and to hell with anyone who thinks otherwise. We hadn't been sitting down for more than twenty seconds when she leaned toward me and whispered, "My, the dresses some of these girls are wearing are very fancy, aren't they?" Meaning of course that, comparatively speaking, Beth's dress was rather plain and that I am too much of a cheapskate to spring for the expensive dress with the elbow-length gloves and the taffeta hemline. Then she threw in the kicker (there's always a kicker): "It appears that some of these families take this occasion *very seriously*." Meaning, of course, that I do not—that my efforts on behalf of her grandchild are and always will be short of the mark; the mark having been set by her, the mother of George, the man who, at that exact moment (one moment among many that he could be using to support and defend me against the passive-aggressive attacks of his lunatic mother) was otherwise engaged in a heated thumb-wrestling match with Alex, and, judging from the hoots and finger-poking, apparently winning.

Meanwhile, Ned, my father-in-law, was hunched over and fiddling with something in his lap. I thought maybe he was putting film in his camera or dog-earing the pages of a hymnal, but upon closer inspection I saw that he was doing neither of these things. Instead, he was playing blackjack on one of those pocket gambling toys from Walgreens. And, judging from the muttering and cursing under his breath, *he* appeared to be losing.

So, this is the snapshot *I* remember: me listening to my mother-in-law spray her sanctimonious nonsense as thickly as she applies her toxic perfume, while the jewel of her parental efforts, George, is busy being the oldest ten-year-old boy in the congregation, and her own husband is sitting in the Lord's house trying to figure out how to improve his odds of beating lady luck the next time he's in Las Vegas!

At moments like these I have to wonder: Can the end of civilization be far behind?

In any event, the communion ceremony was lovely, with all the girls in their little white dresses and gloves, and all the boys in their smart little jackets and ties, like tiny businessmen. The ceremony went on a bit too long for my tastes, but it's a solemn, important Catholic tradition, so naturally they have to draw it out. Beth was near the back of the pack when it came time to eat the wafer (excuse me, "accept the body of Christ"), and I got a good photo of Reverend Palmer laying the wafer on her tongue. Which is a good thing, because that photo may some-day be the only hard evidence that she ever took communion.

Why do I say that? Because when Beth returned to her

seat—and while Reverend Palmer was leading the final prayer—I looked over and saw Beth fiddling with the hem of her dress. Then I saw her stick part of the dress in her mouth. Even more disgusting, I then witnessed her rubbing her tongue with it!

I instantly realized that she had not eaten the communion wafer; she had somehow kept from swallowing it, and was now using her communion dress as a napkin, into which she was spitting the remains of the wafer, as if it were a piece of bone or gristle.

As soon as the ceremony ended I marched over to her pew and demanded to know what she thought she was doing? Didn't she realize, I explained, that not only had she rejected the body of Christ and therefore nullified virtually all of the communion ceremony's symbolic power, possibly damning her to a life of unrepentable sin and infinite purgatory—she had also defiled a perfectly good dress, which would now have to be dry-cleaned? Why on Earth would she do such a thing, I wondered? Had I, as her mother, failed to communicate that using one's dress as a napkin is unacceptable in polite society? Did I overlook some essential lesson in manners that led to this grotesque lack of awareness on the part of my darling daughter? Please, I begged her, tell me where I went wrong?!

Her reply?

"Daddy said I didn't have to eat the cracker if I didn't want to."

In the car, on the way to the Mall of America—where we had promised Beth lunch at the Rainforest Café and an afternoon riding the rides at Camp Snoopy, the indoor theme park situated smack dab in the middle of the mall—it was all I could do to keep my attention focused on the road (George doesn't like to drive). I'm sure George's you-don't-have-to-eat-the-wafer advice to Beth was offered innocently enough, without any awareness of the possible repercussions or consequences, perhaps even with the intention of easing Beth's misgivings about eating something that is supposed to represent a chunk of flesh and washing it down with something that is supposed to signify blood. We'll never know, though, because when I confronted him with the fact of Beth's stained dress and her damning testimony against him, he claimed not to know anything about it. He might have said something to that effect, he said, but then again maybe he didn't—he couldn't be sure one way or the other. How the hell would he know, he added—he doesn't keep taped transcripts of everything he says. And besides, he said, what's the big deal? The whole thing is kind of creepy when you think about it. I mean, it's like some sort of ecclesiastical episode of Fear Factor, he said, except they don't have a bucket up there for people to puke in.

He didn't know it, but I was the one at that moment who needed a bucket. I didn't respond to the comment, though, because for once Patricia piped up and said something useful.

"Shame on you for talking like that, Georgie," she scolded.

Ned then had to immediately negate it, of course. "George is right," grumbled Ned without looking up from his blackjack game. (I could see him in the rear-view mirror.) "The whole thing is a freak show."

"Ned!" Patricia bleated.

Then (and I do not understand this at all), all three of them burst into laughter—howling, slap-your-knee, bend-over-and-gasp-for-air guffaws—as if they had just heard the funniest joke in the world. Soon the kids chimed in, even though they had no idea what was so funny, and pretty soon everyone in the car (except me) was hooting and hollering and trying to catch their breath, declaring how incredibly hilarious whatever they were laughing at was. I might add that this happens on a fairly regular basis, and usually catches me by surprise because, although I think I have a healthy sense of humor, I am inevitably mystified when it comes to understanding what George and his parents find so damned funny all the time, and even more so when they try to explain it. This is quite an alienating experience, as you can well imagine, because no matter what the object of their idiotic mirth is, I can never shake the feeling that they're secretly laughing at me.

This time I was too mad to care, however; I just kept quiet and drove, round and round the Mall of America's astronomically huge north parking ramp, until I found a spot, on the roof, in the upper atmosphere, not too close to the sun, a mere mile-and-a-half away from our destination, the Rainforest Café.

If you've never been to a Rainforest Café, consider yourself fortunate. One doesn't eat lunch at the Rainforest, one has a lunchtime "experience." The experience begins at the reservation desk, where a plastic alligator in a small pond snaps its jaws at you, requiring you to fish all the spare change out of your purse and give it to the kids, who gleefully toss it into the alligator's mouth. This is an apt metaphor for the rest of the Rainforest experience, which is designed not so much to entertain and delight people as it is to separate parents from their money in the most efficient, superficial way possible. The only thing missing is a row of slot machines.

Once you've received your safari "passport" (i.e., your reservation number), your Amazonian ordeal starts with a realistically tortuous forty-five-minute wait, which requires you to browse through the gift shop, where a seemingly infinite array of jungle-themed t-shirts, stuffed animals, and toys are available for purchase, and if your kid is anything like Beth, she wants them all, now. And if your kid's siblings are anything like Alex, he requires you to buy items of equal or greater value for him, too. Otherwise he—terrorist that he is—will throw an embarrassing temper tantrum and ruin everyone's day, just for the fun of it.

To placate Beth and Alex I bought them each a Beanie baby (the cheapest viable way to avoid a nuclear sibling meltdown). Beth chose a dolphin and Alex chose a walrus. It didn't seem to matter to them that neither of these creatures has anything to do with rainforests, and I can assure you that the rest of the adventure was just as educational. The restaurant itself is decorated like some sort of Dr. Seussian drug dream, with giant toadstools for chairs, Jack-in-the-beanstalk vines snaking all over the ceiling and a band of monkeys that periodically jump out and sing, just like real monkeys, only not. The highlight for the kids is the thunderstorm, which happens every fifteen minutes or so. You know the storm is coming when the lights dim, the thunder starts to rumble and the strobe-lightning flashes. You know the storm has arrived when a fine spray of mist descends from the ceiling, capturing all of the airborne germ molecules on its way down and depositing them directly onto your food. The food itself is expensive and large (the better to catch bacteria with), making up in volume what it lacks in quality. But at least it's authentic rainforest food: Amazonian-sized cheeseburgers with french-fry mountains, for example; hot dogs as long as an anaconda; and Oreo-cookie milkshakes that look like mud, or river sludge, depending on which part of Brazil you are traveling. Bottom line: I hated it (always do), George, Patricia, Ned and the kids loved it—and I, for reasons as complicated as they are dysfunctional, ended up paying the bill.

George and his dad did not want to shepherd the kids through Camp Snoopy, so they made up some lame story about needing to check out a sale at Sears—a sale on what, they wouldn't say, but I had my suspicions. One of those new high-definition televisions was at the top of George's wish list, I knew, but he already knows that it will be a very frosty day in Hell when I agree to buy a $2,000 television set. I simply won't raise my children in a home where the primary forms of entertainment are TV and video games, and he knows it. Whether he likes it or not, books and music and homework are going to be the priorities in our house for the next ten years at least; if he can find a 50-inch plasma television for $100 then, we might be able to talk.

The other item George has wanted for some time, and which I think is absolutely ridiculous, is a gas-powered leaf-blower. George thinks these things are brilliant because all you have to do is walk around and blow the leaves off the sidewalk; you don't have to rake. I say no, you idiot, you still have to rake because all you're doing is rearranging the leaves, not removing them. How would it be if, say, I ran the vacuum cleaner backwards and just blew the dust bunnies into different corners every day? He says no, it's not the same thing, because the leaves are *outside*, where, evidently, the laws of filth and grime are different. In a way he's right, I suppose. *Outside*, you can blow your leaves onto your neighbor's lawn, unless of course your neighbor has a leaf-blower too, in which case you just cancel each other out.

Anyway, because I was suspicious of their motives, I let George and Ned go with strict instructions that under no circumstances was George to *buy* anything. While he was there he could check out the prices on something we *really* need, like a new dishwasher, but that was all. No juvenile impulse purchases; not today. The last thing we need is to fill the garage with another ping-pong table or miter saw no one will never use. This was to be an information-gathering expedition *only*, I said, and any potential future purchases were to be cleared through me. I do not think I was unclear in communicating any of this.

After George and Ned wandered off, Patricia and I herded the kids toward Camp Snoopy. For the uninitiated, Camp Snoopy is the largest indoor theme park in the world—the "theme" evidently being insanity. It's located in the middle of the Mall of America, which is essentially a giant box covered by a vast roof of Plexiglas. Exactly who came up with the idea of putting a theme park in the middle of a shopping mall I don't know, but I am reasonably certain they weren't adults. Because, while Camp Snoopy may be fun for kids under the age of twelve, it's a torture chamber for anyone old enough to remember who Charles Schulz was.

Alex wanted to ride the Ripsaw rollercoaster, of course, because it, the log ride and Paul Bunyan's axe are all rides Beth is too short for. She can't even reach the line on the height chart when she stands on her tippy toes, so it's the carousel and the Magic School Bus ride for her. Luckily, Alex is old enough now that he doesn't have to be supervised every second, so I let him ride to the rollercoaster alone while Beth rode the carousel, which is located adjacent the rollercoaster. In between the two rides is a calliope with a dancing monkey that pops out every ten minutes and bangs a pair of cymbals to the tune of "Yankee Doodle Dandy." We agreed to meet by the dancing monkey in half an hour, which, if Alex was lucky, might give him time for two rides.

Now, the only reason I let Alex ride the rollercoaster alone was because he had done it before without incident, and because I had to watch Beth. As rollercoasters go, the Ripsaw isn't all that adventurous—it just winds around a lot and doesn't go very fast—and I figured I could at least keep an eye out for Alex while I watched Beth on the carousel. Patricia wasn't so sure, and she let me know about it.

"Do you think it's a good idea to let Alex ride that thing alone? What if something happens? What if someone kidnaps him out of the line? Beautiful boy like that, I wouldn't be surprised. There's nothing stopping anyone who had a mind to do it, as far as I can tell. And what if he stands up? Or falls out? Or hits his head on something? It happens, you know. I read about a kid at Disneyland who stood up and bam, it was over before he knew it. Such a shame. Are you sure it's safe? It doesn't look safe to me. It wobbles. Yes, I can definitely see it wobbling. Are you sure they've never had an accident here, because I can definitely see how an accident could happen. Just because they're strapped in with a seat belt doesn't mean they can't get out. Someone Alex's size, all he has to do is wriggle one way or the other and he's loose. That's why I would never let my Georgie ride one of those things. Children are just too precious to take risks like that. Parents these days don't realize what a gift they have. There's no discipline. They just give their kids everything they want, and then they wonder why their little brats are so spoiled. It's no wonder. Doesn't it make you nervous that you can't see Alex? It makes me nervous. I just love that boy so much. If anything bad ever happened to him, I don't know how I would cope. And Ned, he'd simply be *devastated*. Ned thinks the world of that boy. I know he doesn't show it all the time, but he does. He lives for these visits. If it were up to him we'd visit more often, but I keep telling him no, they don't want us old fogies hanging around all the time. We won't be around forever, though, so we have to make the most of the time we *do* have . . ."

Jesus, what a bitch. Not that I haven't heard all this before; she's been talking this way to me since before George and I were married. It doesn't matter what the subject is—my cooking, my housecleaning, my clothes, my weight, my hair, my upbringing, my education, my politics, my taste in movies, my choice of diet soda—she'll find something nasty to say about it, and she'll do it in a way that makes her look like a saint and me look like a witch.

It doesn't really matter, though, because I tune most of her prattle out. In between the corny carousel music, "Yankee Doodle Dandy" and the deafening din of children screaming on the rollercoaster, I could barely hear her. I was busy watching Beth, who had insisted on riding the carousel alone because she is a "big girl" now. Not so big, unfortunately, that going around in circles while riding up and down on a winged horse doesn't make her nauseous. From where I was standing, I could see her face going pale and her eyes droop as she clutched the brass pole. Then up it came—the entire rainforest, burger, shake and all—just as the carousel came to a stop.

Most of it went on the horse, but the bottom half of her dress caught its fair share.

I whisked Beth off to the bathroom to clean her up, and told Patricia to wait for Alex by the dancing monkey.

It is impossible to get streaks of Oreo vomit out of a white communion dress with a paper towel, but I did my best. By the time I was done, Beth said she felt fine and that she wanted to go on another ride. Kids and dogs are like that, I guess—they puke, then go right back to doing or eating whatever it was that made them hurl in the first place. It's sick. I told her there was no way she was going on another ride, and you would have thought I poured boiling water on her head. She screamed for ten minutes, then said she was hungry.

Alex was just coming off his second turn on the rollercoaster when we got back to the dancing monkey, but Patricia was nowhere in sight.

"She spewed, didn't she?" Alex said as we approached. Beth stuck her tongue out at Alex and he jumped back as if he were afraid she was going to throw up on him, too.

"Where's your grandmother?" I asked him.

"Beats me," Alex replied with a shrug.

Twenty minutes later we found her, in a store called "The Butterfly Shop," which, true to its name, contains nothing but refrigerator magnets and other useless knick-knacks in the shape of a butterfly. The moment she saw us, her eyes opened wide and she started beating the air with her hand, motioning for us to come toward her.

"You have to see this, dear," she said to me, pointing her bony finger at a gold brooch that looked to me more like a molting moth than a butterfly. "Isn't it beautiful?!" she exclaimed. "If anyone is looking for something to give me for Christmas, I wouldn't mind seeing *this* under the tree," she said in her sing-songy voice, the voice she uses when she wants something but doesn't want to pay for it herself. No apology for abandoning her post. No sense of shame or guilt for walking off without telling anyone. Not even the faintest glimmer of awareness that she could have *endangered Alex's life*, the very crime she had been accusing me of. This is how I know that practically everything she says is nonsense. Alex only matters to her insofar as he can be used to make me look and feel like a lousy mother. It's sad, its sick, and it's what I have to live with, alone in my in-law prison, because George never sees this side of his mother. Not that she doesn't say or do these kinds of thing right in front of him; he is simply incapable of seeing his own mother as a duplicitous, back-stabbing, bad-mouthing bitch. I can only hope that Alex has the same blind spot for me when he grows up.

We were due to meet George and Ned at Legoland, which meant we had to hoof it three-quarters of a mile around the perimeter of the mall. George and Ned weren't there yet when we arrived, so the kids sat down at a Lego table and began building something. Beth wanted to build a dinosaur the size of the ones on exhibit in the Lego store. These are creatures about six feet tall that probably took six engineers a week to assemble using four million pieces of Lego. When Alex informed her that there weren't enough Legos at their table to do it, she began to cry. I didn't know why she was crying until *after* I snapped at Alex—"Dammit, what did you do to your sister?!"—which of course provided Patricia with more proof that I am indeed a bad mother.

George and Ned finally showed up eating ice cream cones. The kids immediately wanted one too, even though it had only been an hour since lunch. Ned offered to treat, and my will to fight was weak, so I relented, figuring that if anyone else puked, it'd be their own damn fault. No one did, but on about Beth's third lick, she made the classic mistake of pushing her scoop of strawberry cheesecake ice cream off the cone and plop, onto the floor—or onto the carpet, rather. When I explained to the pimply kid behind the counter what had happened and asked if she could have another scoop, he said yes, but I would have to *pay for it*. I pointed out that this wasn't a very customer-friendly response (at Baskin-Robbins, for instance, replacing a dropped cone is automatic and free) and he said there was nothing he could do because the cone had landed on the carpet, not on the store's tile floor. If the ice cream had landed on the store's tile, he could have replaced the cone, he said—but, since the carpet was considered part of the mall proper, store policy prohibited him from providing a free replacement scoop. It didn't matter that the ice cream had landed only *three inches* from the store's tile, he had to charge me, he said—it was the store's *policy*. I pointed out that the ice cream never would have fallen if he had scooped and secured it properly, but he wouldn't budge. He just looked at me like I was an idiot.

This struck me as a prime example of how things have gone completely haywire in this country, so I asked to see the manager. The kid said the manager wasn't there, and I said surely he has a cell-phone, and surely you have the number in case something goes wrong on your shift? Because I am here to tell you that something has gone *tragically, horribly* wrong, and I want to report it. At this point George stepped in and said, "Honey, why don't we just pay for another damned cone?" The way he stressed the word "damned" indicated quite clearly to me that he thought my argument was frivolous—that I was making a big deal over nothing. But it wasn't *nothing* to me; it was the principle of the thing. I just hate to think that we now live in a society where a little girl who accidentally dumps her ice cream on the floor can't get it replaced for free, with an understanding smile, just because some jackass lawyer has written a *policy* that prohibits it.

The kid continued to claim that he had no way to contact his manager, so I said fine, have it your way. Then I bent down, picked the fallen ice-cream scoop up off the carpet and flung it onto the store's floor, right in front of the cash register. "There, now it's on your precious tile," I said. Then I wiped my hand with a napkin and grabbed Beth's arm. She cried all the way out to the car and half-way home. Everyone else—George, Alex, Patricia, and Ned—just sat in silence, afraid of what I, the crazy bitch, might do if any one of them opened their mouth.

Dinner, as you might expect, was a complete disaster. I won't go into *all* the sordid details, but the highlights should give you the overall flavor of the evening.

It is the custom, in George's family, to eat red meat on

Sundays. Don't ask me why, because even they don't know. It's just something they do, and have been doing ever since anyone can remember; probably some leftover habit from the Depression. Anyway, for whatever reason read meat is "special" in their book, so it gets the Sunday slot.

Personally, I couldn't care less if I never eat another bite of red meat in my life. I'm not against it, but I'm not a big fan, either—I'll take pasta or chicken over red meat any day of the week. But, in deference to their family custom, I bought a rib roast for dinner—a big, fat chunk of juicy red beef, identified by the butcher himself as the best cut of meat for the money he had. I was shaking some salt and pepper on it, getting it ready for the oven, when Patricia came into the kitchen and let out a little gasp.

"Oh my, you're not serving that for dinner, are you?" she said.

"No, Patricia, this is breakfast," I replied. "What do you think?"

"It's just that, well—what about that mad cow disease?"

"What about it?"

"They found it in a cow in Michigan," she said. "It's in all the papers."

"So what?" I said as I slid the roast into the oven.

"How do you know that meat isn't infected?" she said, crunching her eyebrows in a worried grimace.

"I don't. But I'm willing to take my chances," I said, wearily.

"Well, just the same, I don't think Ned and I can eat it, knowing what we know. You understand," she said, then strutted out of the kitchen.

"Yeah, I understand perfectly," I muttered under my breath. "*You* are a mad cow."

She heard me, unfortunately, and went running off like a five-year-old to tell George what I'd said. George, being the dutiful and utterly subservient son that he is, came into the kitchen to talk to me about the "incident." I, however, had just picked up the aforementioned ten-inch Wustof chef's knife to cut up some vegetables. I must have looked intimidating, because he seemed to be choosing his words very carefully, as if he knew deep down that I would stab him in the chest if he didn't proceed with exactly the right tone and choose precisely the right words.

"Look, honey, it's been a rough day, I know," he began. "And I haven't forgotten that it's Mother's Day, so I apologize if things haven't gone the way you might have liked."

It was clumsy and garbled, and he could have expanded on the theme of "my ruined day and what he was going to do about it," but his intentions were good and he was headed in the right direction. I had to give him credit for that. Then he nuzzled up behind me and kissed me on the neck. Another positive move.

"Come into the living room," he whispered into my ear. "I've got something I want to give you."

Now we were getting somewhere.

"Trust me, it's something you deserve," he said, nibbling on my earlobe.

He told me to close my eyes and led me by the hand into the living room. He made me stand there for a few seconds to draw out the suspense, then said, "Okay, you can open them now."

I opened them, and there in front of me, with a big fat red bow on it and two "Happy Mother's Day" balloons tied to the handle, was a brand new Toro SuperShot 3000 leaf-blower.

George saw the disappointment in my eyes, followed by the lightning flash of anger. He tried to tell me that he hadn't bought the thing that afternoon—that he had bought it a week and a half earlier and had been planning to give it to me all along. Then he told me what a great deal he'd gotten on it, and tried to show me all the marvelous features it had—12-amp motor, 250 mile-per-hour blowing capability, push-button starting, "not just a leaf-blower, but a complete *debris management system*," he said, but his words rushed over and around me like water around a rock. I was too mad to even cry.

I didn't say anything. I just went upstairs into our bedroom and shut the door. I've been up here for the past five hours, and, once again, it's approaching midnight. I know what they've been saying about me down there—that I'm too high-strung, I take things too seriously, I'm ungrateful, I'm mean, I'm unreasonable, I'm not enough of this, I'm too much of that. Worst of all, of course: I'm not like *them*.

Around 8:00 o'clock, I smelled the roast burning and heard the smoke alarm in the kitchen go off. I trust one of them had the sense to take the thing out of the oven. The kids came in for a kiss goodnight at 9:00 P.M., and I apologized for yelling at them. George knocked on the door around ten, but I told him to go sleep on the couch and I haven't heard from him since. I'm sure he did just that. If I wanted to kill him, now would be a good time.

I'm not going to kill him, though—instead, I'm going to let him make it up to me. Meanwhile, I'm going to call my own mother, whom I almost forgot in the chaos and fury of the day. She lives in Los Angeles. It's two hours earlier there, so I should still be able to catch her before she goes to bed. In fact, I'm dialing the number right now. It's ringing. I can hear her pick it up.

"Hello?" she is saying in a worn, nicotine-hoarsened version of the voice I have heard all my life.

"Hi, Mom. Happy Mother's Day."

* * * * * * *

SOME KIND OF ANIMAL

Anold Simkin sat at his desk, deep in thought. Unfortunately, Arnold was not paid to think; he was paid to enter various words and acronyms into a central database that would eventually be used as a search index for more than three million documents being scrutinized by lawyers on the nineteenth floor, for a case involving . . . well, Arnold didn't quite know, exactly.

He had learned, though, that if he stared at his computer screen and typed the same sequence of letters over and over—A-S-D-F-:-J-K-L–Delete—he could put his body on auto-pilot and escape the office cubicle in which he was imprisoned through the back door of his imagination. His physical body could then serve as a decoy while his mind, unchained from the painful tedium of his job, was free to roam the wilderness of his dreams. During these mental work breaks, Arnold made occasional forays into the dark and tangled jungle of his aspirations, and dwelled at times on the smorgasbord of fears and anxieties that plagued him almost constantly. But the truth is, he spent most of his daylight dream-time wallowing waist deep in the fetid swamp of his desire for Ellen Reese, who sat three cubes away and smelled like lilacs.

Arnold and Ellen worked with nineteen other under-employed misfits, most of them ex-liberal-arts majors in various stages of self-destruction. The legal case they were working on had something to do with two biotechnology firms fighting over the intellectual property rights to some sort of AIDS-related drug research. But the details of the case did not concern Arnold. In fact, he preferred not to know the details. Because if he understood the case—if he could see the big picture—he felt certain it would violate any number of ethical principles that he claimed to stand either for or against. If he were aware of these ethical breaches, he would feel even more hypocritical and conflicted than he already did. So he was content to toil away in his purgatory of ignorance, tapping mindlessly on his computer keys, waiting for a random draft of the office's air-circulation system to bring a whiff of Ellen's loveliness into his cube. One breath of her sweet and earthy scent was good for at least fifteen minutes of auto-erotic daydreaming; more if she happened to be wearing her green chenille sweater. He cherished those moments of the day when he could transport his weary spirit out of his body and travel to a secluded Caribbean beach with her by his side, or to one of those little Italian villages with pastel-colored houses fused to the side of a mountain overlooking the Mediterranean. Or humping each other in a . . .

Arnold was a romantic at heart, or so he believed. Which is why he felt guilty whenever the travel-magazine patina of his daydreams dissolved and, next thing he knew, he and Ellen were desperately screwing to cartoon jazz in a Las Vegas motel room.

Sometimes the daydreams were so vivid he convinced himself that while Ellen pecked away at her keyboard, she must be thinking the same thoughts as he. This would go a long way toward explaining the intensity of those imaginary couplings, he figured. If two consciousnesses were thinking the same thing at the same time, it stood to reason—or to Arnold's reasoning, anyway—that there would be twice as much psychic energy invested in that thought, and that the thought itself would be amplified for both parties. When people said they were "on the same wavelength," perhaps they weren't speaking metaphorically after all, Arnold speculated. Perhaps their brainwaves were aligned in such a way that transmission between them *was* possible, and that two such harmonically tuned people could indeed share psychic as well as physical energy.

For these reasons and many others, Arnold was willing to do just about anything to be near Ellen Reese. Anything except talk to her, that is. At this point in their relationship, talking would be too much, he thought. Talking would spoil the illusion of perfection, and he wanted to hold on to that illusion for as long as humanly possible. There would be plenty of time for talk when their destinies finally converged, which was inevitable, he felt. The day their psychic, spiritual, and physical worlds intersected, they would compare notes on their mutual out-of-body experiences at the office and discover that they were bound by threads both cosmic and profound, ties that reached across space and time connecting her yin to his yang, harnessing their love in an endless meadow of soft green clover fed by an underground spring of infinite bliss. Theirs would be a love that transcended the mundane realities of the material world, that transported them to places only they could imagine, where they would do things to and for each other that only they dare share. They would find that Las Vegas motel room and . . .

Arnold couldn't help himself. That he continually tainted the purity of his love for Ellen with scenes from "True Clit," an X-rated video he had rented one long and lonely Valentine's Day a few months back, was a source of deep shame for him. So, as a mental exercise, whenever the scene of his mental meanderings began to devolve into the grunting, slurping, heaving biology of his lust, he started training himself to desist by thinking about the least lustful thing he could imagine—which was, conveniently, his job.

His job.

Arnold was what the legal profession calls a "coder." Which means that he spent his days sifting through documents too boring or insignificant for an actual lawyer to examine, looking for key words, acronyms, or names—BMG, HTC, Edison, mucus, benzene, phenicol, Darvon, AZT, etc.—posted in a master list on the wall. Every day, new words were added to the list—BHT, renal failure, zygote, enzyme—but no context for the words was ever provided, and their significance to the case as a whole was never explained. They were just arrangements of letters, and his job was to hunt for them, like a chicken picking through piles of its own droppings in hopes of finding an occasional seed.

Once in a while he would come across a document that looked as though it might be important—a check for an unusually large amount of money, say, or a memo with two or three coherent sentences in it alluding to some murky bit of research. In these instances his heart would start to pound and a rush of adrenaline would dampen his upper lip. Energized by the prospect of stumbling upon something that might actually be significant to the case, he would, as instructed, bring the document in question to the attention of his supervisor. Each time, the supervisor—a plump, bespectacled woman in her mid-forties whom Arnold detested—would glance at the document and assure him it was nothing.

That Arnold was the first line of defense in the war against legal irrelevance gave him no solace. A more boring or thankless job he could not imagine. Yet he had been doing it—putting up with the tedium, enduring the drudgery, suffering the bad coffee—for almost a year now. His first day had been so bad he almost didn't come back. After the first week, he told himself he would stay for a month, tops. But, like the proverbial frog in a pot of water heated ever so slowly, he had not jumped out. He had allowed himself to grow accustomed to the mind-numbing routine; indeed, he had taught himself how to tolerate the intolerable. Now, both his mind and soul were in danger of being par-boiled, but he no longer cared. As long as the simmering soup that was destroying him contained a pinch of Ellen Reese, he would gladly stew in his cube until what remained of his soul was little more than a thin cloud of vapor and mist.

\. . . . . . .

Arnold's largish nose was the first part of him to notice Ellen's absence. His brain and penis, which were connected even more closely than the average women's magazine would have you believe, were not far behind. It was not uncommon for Ellen to miss a day or two here or there. She was a woman, after all, and in Arnold's experience women were prone to all sorts of mysterious ailments that prevented them from doing things—usually things like going on a date with him. But Ellen had never been gone for an entire week before. And never in the time they had worked "together" did Arnold have the feeling she wasn't coming back. Until now.

On a bathroom break, Arnold snuck a peek into her cubicle and the awful truth slapped him hard in the face: Ellen Reese had quit. Gone was the little black Nerf puppy perched on top of her computer monitor, the Power Puff Girls blow-up doll, the Arizona Highways sunset calendar. Gone was the cup full of colorful pens she kept on her desk, the ones arranged so carefully they looked like an exotic flower. Gone was the little lumbar cushion on her chair that she used for lower-back support.

Missing most conspicuously of all was her fragrance. In the mornings, when her perfume was fresh, its effect on Arnold was intoxicating. The sweet, silent cloud of her essence would tumble over the wall of his cubicle and into his nostrils, where it would activate a number of neural pathways that Arnold was fairly certain led to a level of ecstasy the likes of which he had never experienced before. He didn't know what kind of perfume she wore, but he imagined it was a potion with a name like "Destiny" or "Obsession," or "Impulse"—a name that suggested unappeased appetites and uncontrollable desires. Acting like a machete to the jungle of his sexual ambivalence, Ellen Reese's scent made him want to do things primal and beastly. It made him want to turn into a goat-man and prance through primeval forests in search of milk-skinned nymphs; to roam the open prairie like a wild stallion; to reduce his responsibilities in life down, like a stud bull, to the brute dissemination of sperm; to live without the complications of consciousness or the complexities of conversation, in a simple state of nature, perpetually aroused and ready to thwart the forces of sterility and death at any time. Or at least have a good go at it.

Arnold was fortunate that Ellen Reese's mesmerizing scent tended to fade throughout the day as it mingled with the odors of rancid coffee and microwave popcorn. Otherwise he would get no work done whatsoever. The day Arnold learned of Ellen Reese's departure, however, he also discovered that he was incapable of doing his job without her presence nearby.

That afternoon was the longest of his life. Each document he examined turned before his eyes into an unintelligible jumble of numbers and letters he could not muster the will to decipher. Each minute seemed to crawl by like a caterpillar on Valium. Every time he tried to escape through the back door of his imagination—to daydream a few excruciating minutes away—he found the door locked.

Ellen was, evidently, the key. But whatever flights of fancy Ellen's presence had made possible before were now nullified by the crushing reality of her absence. Before, it was as if Ellen Reese were a magnet that pulled fantasies out of him spontaneously. He didn't have to think about it; it just happened, with no effort on his part. All he had to do was sit back and let his eyes lose focus, the way they did when he was standing in front of a urinal or watching a Ken Burns documentary on PBS. In no time a fuzzy dreamscape would appear, his groin would swell, he would feel himself leave his body and poof, twenty minutes would disappear. Now, trapped in his chair, unable to think or act, he had no choice but to listen to the relentless hum of his computer while it waited, with eternal patience, for him to do something.

Brad Delaney, a fraternity type who lifted weights during his lunch hour and sat in the cube next to Ellen's, got out of his seat and sauntered stiff-legged into the snack room. Arnold had never talked to Brad before, but he had seen Brad and Ellen chat a number of times. Arnold was intensely jealous of these exchanges, and despised Brad because of them. But that did not prevent him from recognizing that Brad might have some useful information concerning Ellen's whereabouts.

Arnold decided he had a sudden craving for a Twix bar, and followed Brad into the snack room, where he stood in front of the snack machine, arms folded, with a perturbed look on his face.

"No Snickers," Brad said as Arnold walked in. "Can you believe it?"

Arnold nodded. "Three Musketeers are good," he said. "Less fat."

"All air," said Brad. "No peanuts."

"Almond Joy?" Arnold offered.

"Can't do almonds," said Brad. "or coconut." He paused, then pushed B-5. "Oreos it is, then." The vending machine's corkscrew dispenser swirled and a six-pack of Oreos fell with a thud into the bin below. As Brad reached for it, Arnold said, "Uh, say, I couldn't help noticing that Ellen has cleaned out her cube. Did she quit or something?"

"Nah, she got a *real* job," Brad said.

"Where?"

"The zoo."

"The zoo?" Arnold repeated.

"Yeah, not much else you can do with a biology degree, I guess," Brad said, and headed back to his cube.

Arnold poured himself a Dixie cup full of water and gulped it down like a shot of tequila. The reality of Ellen's departure was still sinking in, but at least now he could conjure a mental picture of her. That she had a biology degree surprised him. He had guessed something a little less organic, like political science or business administration. That she was working at the zoo surprised him even more. Arnold didn't normally think of zoos as the sort of places where people had paying jobs. Now that he thought about it, though, he supposed *someone* had to feed the animals and clean up after them. He could not stretch his imagination far enough to understand why anyone would aspire to that sort of work, however, least of all Ellen. Then again, Arnold couldn't understand why anyone would ever choose Cheerios over Cap'n Crunch either, since the latter was so clearly a superior cereal. Such distinctions were beyond him.

The next few days were torture for Arnold. Each morning he came into the office, sat down, and felt the weight of the world pressing on him. He felt heavy and slow, like the first blob in a new bottle of ketchup. Time oozed along almost imperceptibly, and the boredom that came with it was as painful as a toothache. It started as a spasm in the back of his neck, then seemed to move through the marrow of his bones until his entire body was in a kind of mute agony, unnoticeable on the outside but relentless and inescapable nonetheless. The line between a job and self-inflicted torture had become a blur.

When he became aware of the Micro/Macro it was even worse. He got glimpses of it every now and then, when the .01 percent of his brain he needed to do his job was occupied and the other 99.9 percent of his gray matter was free to amuse itself. In this mental state, random images and thoughts floated through his brain while he was working—images that he classified into two main categories: Micro and Macro. In micro mode, he was keenly aware of every minute detail: the concave curl of the computer keys, the insistent blink of the cursor on his computer screen, the slightly loose jiggle of the space bar every time he hit it, the spring action of the keys under his fingertips. In Micro mode, he sometimes felt as if he had reached a sort of Zen-like state of consciousness in which all things great and small were of equal value.

These moments didn't last long, because they were inevitably shoved aside by the Macro, which was a humiliatingly keen awareness of his place in the cosmic food chain. In Macro mode, he often saw himself as a small maggot feeding off the waste of human activity—or the activity of lawyers at any rate. On one end of the food chain were scientific researchers guided by such lofty and righteous goals as saving the world from the scourge of AIDS or relieving the suffering of people with renal kidney failure. Below that were the companies that paid the scientists and packaged and marketed their products. Below that was the universe of doctors and patients and healthcare professionals who relied on the researchers for their livelihoods and lives. Below that were the insurance companies, which tried to prevent doctors, patients and healthcare professionals from getting paid—and below that were the lawyers, who were equal-opportunity parasites feeding off of everyone's dissatisfaction with the chain itself. Well below that, near the invisible bottom, was Arnold, who helped masticate and digest the enormous volumes of waste created by everyone above him. He felt like a worm or a beetle, one of the teeming masses of vermin that live off the excrement of others. Except that he felt lower than that, because at least maggots and weevils and bacteria had a useful purpose, at least they served the greater good by decomposing all the icky organic substances in this world that need to be decomposed, such as feces, rotten food, and the flesh of dead, decaying bodies. But as far as Arnold could tell, his work served no useful purpose whatsoever, which put him on roughly the same level as politicians and professional golfers.

On Wednesday, Ellen's cube was taken over by a large man in his mid-forties whose feet were so wide he had trouble keeping his shoes tied. And just like that, any evidence that Ellen Reese had ever existed was gone.

Each day thereafter seemed longer than the day before. Stacks of documents several feet high arrived in fat square boxes twice a week, but there was no way to get through one shipment of documents before the next shipment arrived. Thus it was impossible for Arnold to feel as if he were making any forward progress, because the pile of work to be done was always growing faster than the pile of work he had finished. Arnold had calculated that if an average of five boxes went un-coded every week, and he worked there for fifty more years, there would be roughly 6,200 boxes of documents left to code when he died. That's why, in the middle of the afternoon, when the drudgery was most intense, Arnold sometimes felt as if he were actually living backwards in time, getting farther away from who he was and who he wanted to be, not closer. At times, the whole idea of goals, ambition, and achievement seemed preposterous, because it was clear to him that, in his life anyway, the true flow of space and time rendered such ideas meaningless.

Something curious was happening to Arnold's memory of Ellen as well. It had not faded or diminished, as he had expected—it had intensified. With each passing day his feelings for Ellen grew stronger and the ache in his heart grew more painful. As he toiled away at his desk, love clichés raced through his mind at a furious pace. "Absence makes the heart grow fonder." "You don't know what you got 'til it's gone." "One is the loneliest number." He had heard them all a thousand times before, but now these banal axioms pulsed with fresh profundity. Every inane song on the radio suddenly seemed to be speaking to him, to be shouting, "Hey, we've been there too! Love stinks! Love hurts! Sure, these lyrics might sound insipid to some, but *they're the truth!*"

To be in love, to be tortured by love—it was the oldest story in the book, Arnold knew. But if there was any comfort to be found in feeling connected to the rest of the human race, if only by a single thread of despair, Arnold couldn't locate it. He felt more estranged from the people around him than ever; more alienated from humanity than any bug-eyed creature from space; emptier inside than he ever thought possible.

It was 2:30 P.M. on a Tuesday afternoon. No matter how much coffee he drank or how many Snickers bars he consumed, Arnold could not keep his eyes open. The boredom of his job had reached the threshold of pain, and his body was shutting down in self-defense. When Arnold had taken the job he knew going in that it wouldn't be particularly rewarding; what he couldn't predict was the toll all that daily tedium would take on his psyche. The machinery of the Industrial Revolution, he knew, had reduced human labor down to the level of a cog or piston in the great engine of the economy. The pure exchange of money for labor had reduced work for most people down to a kind of prostitution, and the relentless need to make money in order to buy goods and services had, at the lower end of the economy, where Arnold dwelled, resulted in a kind of slavery wherein one was forced to do humiliating, de-humanizing work in order to survive. Sure, he was "free" to leave the job anytime he wanted, but the need to pay rent and buy food would force him to accept another, possibly worse, job somewhere else. He was trapped, like a wild animal, in a cage that allowed him to see beyond the bars of his prison but not to escape. There was something so sick and twisted and wrong about it all. As Arnold's eyes fluttered shut, he began wondering where Western civilization had gone wrong. In agrarian societies, at least people were in contact with the land and connected to the cycles of Nature; at least they knew where their food came from and what went into it. On the job/boredom scale, pulling beets out of the ground all day probably got old after a while too, Arnold figured—but at least you were outside, working with your hands, able to smell something besides microwave popcorn and your own surreptitious farts.

Such were the thoughts careening around in Arnold's head when his eyelids closed completely and his mind began to drift. Up through the inky emptiness inside him he went, through the electrostatic fireworks behind his eyelids to a chamber in his psyche where everything was dark and quiet, like a cave, and all he could hear was the beating of his own heart. It is here that he had The Dream, which he would later think of as a capital "V" Vision, a mystical beckoning from beyond which he could not resist—the sort of life-defining moment of alternate reality that shamans, holy men, Carlos Castaneda, and Oprah talk about but hardly anyone ever actually experiences themselves. How he achieved this state of heightened consciousness in the spiritual purgatory that was his cube, on a diet of peanut butter and jelly sandwiches, was not his concern. All he knew was that the Vision felt real, and everything that happened after it was pure, inescapable fate.

The Dream, like so many other dreams, started in a field of flowers. Blue lupins, to be precise—acres of them spreading to the horizon, coloring the landscape as if Van Gogh had woken up one day and found nothing but crushed flower petals on his palette. The sun was high and warm, and the sound of rushing water nearby seemed to beckon him. He started walking toward it, noticing as he went that his feet were bare and he was wearing nothing but a leather pouch around his privates, held in place by thin strips of leather tied around his waist.

There was a footpath through the flowers, and though the ground was somewhat rocky, he felt no pain in his feet. He walked along the path toward the burbling hiss of water crashing on rocks. The path wound around a large boulder, and as he rounded it the water's playful music was accompanied by a pounding, thunderous bass he could feel deep his chest. A delicate mist cooled the air as he got closer to the rumble of the rushing water. Suddenly he was standing in a clearing surrounded by gigantic redwood trees—trees that hadn't been there before, but now thrust their enormous trunks toward the sky, blocking most of the sunlight that was trying in vain to get through the forest canopy. He walked about thirty yards farther and came to the edge of a large pool of water. To his right was a majestic waterfall cascading down from the ledge of a rocky plateau about a hundred feet above him. As the water crashed onto the rocks below, it sent plumes of mist into the air, which caught a few beams of sunlight and created a rainbow. Arnold's eyes followed the arc of the rainbow downward and saw a figure sitting across the pool from him, on the rocks near the bottom of the waterfall. It was a woman. Since this was a dream vision taking place in Arnold Simkin's mind, the woman was of course Ellen Reese—and, naturally, she was naked.

From across the pool, Arnold watched as Ellen twirled her long wet hair into a rope and squeezed the water out onto the rocks at her feet. As she did this, she looked up and saw Arnold staring at her. She did not cry out or look afraid. Instead, she smiled warmly and waved to Arnold, signaling for him to join her. The terrain around the pool was too rugged to climb, so the only way to get to the other side of the pool was to swim. Arnold stuck his toe in the water at the edge of the pool. It wasn't nearly as cold as he expected, so he waded in up to his waist and eased himself in. The warm blue water enveloped his body like a hug.

He started swimming toward Ellen (using the breast stroke, of course) but as soon as his feet lost contact with the bottom of the pool he heard a loud blast of noise that sounded like a trumpet. He saw some movement in the trees near Ellen. As he swam, keeping his head above water, Arnold swore he could feel the ground around the pool shake. Next he heard an explosion of snapping branches and another trumpet blast. Ellen did not seem particularly concerned by the noise; she just sat on the wet rocks, smiling at Arnold as he made his way across the pool, her eyes as blue and deep as the water in which he swam. Ellen's nonchalance puzzled Arnold, because what had emerged from the forest and was now standing not thirty feet away from her was a giant elephant, with gleaming tusks almost ten feet long and ears the size of a patio umbrella.

Wait a minute, thought Arnold—how did an elephant get into this dream? He was under the distinct impression that in dreams involving naked women and idyllic waterfall scenes, the only creature allowed to appear was a unicorn. But this, evidently, was not the case.

The elephant took a few steps toward Ellen, swinging its massive trunk from side to side. It then raised its prodigious snout into the air and released another trumpet blast. Alarmed, Arnold began swimming faster, but no matter how hard he swam he didn't seem to get any closer to shore, or to Ellen. Ellen herself did not look frightened. Far from it. Instead of trying to get away from the enormous creature, she stood and walked toward it, holding her hand out as if the beast were a puppy or a baby goat at a petting zoo. Arnold watched in horror as the elephant sniffed Ellen's hand and appeared to fondle Ellen's hair with its nimble proboscis.

Fearing for Ellen's life, Arnold churned the water in a furious attempt to reach the shore. Exactly what he was going to do when he got there he wasn't sure. It didn't matter, though, because despite his most heroic efforts to reach Ellen, he was now getting farther away from her—or, rather, the pool itself was growing larger, so the relative distance from Arnold to the shore was increasing. Arnold's arms were beginning to feel like two wet logs, and his breath was now coming in short, desperate gasps. He stopped swimming and began treading water to catch his breath.

The elephant had not killed Ellen yet, but Arnold felt it was only a matter of time before the beast turned homicidal. Arnold had barely enough energy left to keep his own head above water, much less save a damsel in distress. Helpless, Arnold watched as Ellen stroked the elephant's trunk. In response, the elephant laid the bottom third of his mighty snout on the ground. Ellen then stepped onto it, one foot then the other, and, to Arnold's dismay, the elephant lifted her into the air. She stood for a moment like a bird on a tree branch, then sat down on the elephant's left tusk.

Arnold was having trouble keeping his own nose in the air as he tread water. He felt heavy and weak. He swirled his arms in frantic circles, trying to stay afloat, but the water was sucking him under as if his feet had turned to stone. He did not have the strength to fight the water's pull much longer. When his nostrils slipped below the surface of the water, he knew the end was near. In the distance, the elephant had turned around and was walking toward the hole in the forest from whence it came. Ellen sat on the creature's enormous tusk, her alabaster skin almost indistinguishable from the ivory tooth itself. The last thing Arnold saw before the water swallowed him completely was Ellen—his lovely, incomparable Ellen—turn her head toward him as she disappeared into the forest and mouth the words, "Save me."

* * * * * * *

"Did you *save*?! Did you *save*?!"

Arnold's eyes flew open. Ms. Driscoll, Arnold's supervisor, was shaking his shoulder and yelling at him. "The network went down again, Simkin. Before your little snooze, did you by any chance think to save your work?"

"Um, I don't know," Arnold mumbled.

"When was the last time you *saved*?" she sputtered.

"I don't remember."

Ms. Driscoll leaned her fleshy face into his and rasped, "What do you think this is, a hotel?" Arnold didn't answer; he didn't dare move. "What's the matter? Didn't get enough beauty sleep last night?" she taunted.

Arnold said nothing.

"That would explain two things: why you're sleeping on the job, and why you're so goddamn UGLY!" she spat. "Why you're so fucking STUPID remains a mystery." To the rest of the room Ms. Driscoll yelled, "Network's down. Fifteen-minute break, everyone!" Disgusted, she turned to Arnold and said, "Take a walk or get a cup of coffee or something," then waddled back to her office.

The rest of the day Arnold could not stop thinking about The Dream. It was like a log snagged perpendicular to a stream, creating a blockage that trapped the debris of his thoughts in a stagnant, bubbling backwater. Yet The Dream also had the opposite effect of narrowing his options, focusing his thoughts on what he had to do to get around the logjam in his brain. The final frame of his fateful vision, of Ellen astride the elephant's tusk calling to him, her would-be savior, haunted him. He hadn't been able to save Ellen. He couldn't even save himself. The futility of his efforts was paralyzing. Again and again he saw himself slipping below the water's surface, suffocated not so much by the water itself, but by his pathetic inability to act—to say or do anything that might make a difference—to exert his will on the events unfolding before him.

He felt the same way about his life—that he had no control over it; things just happened, and whatever happened, nothing really seemed to matter. He wondered if cavemen ever felt this way. No, he thought, it would be impossible for a caveman to be as neurotic and incompetent as Arnold Simkin—an epiphany which, Arnold felt, put a serious crimp in Darwin's theory of natural selection. Nor would it be possible for a caveman to hate his job, be dissatisfied with his life, or worry about such things as his self-esteem, lack of personal goals, muscle tone, blood sugar, supply of gum, proximity to a bathroom, the pollen count, Lyme disease, global warming, underarm odor, bad breath, social status, income potential, inability to speak a second language, Internet access speed, addiction to Twix bars, secret disdain for classic literature, or any one of the thousands of other anxieties and idiocies that occupied his mind at any given moment of the day.

No, a caveman's mind would not be cluttered with such nonsense; it would be filled with a sense of urgent purpose, focused entirely on the dual imperatives of finding food and staying warm. Nothing else would matter to a caveman. How exhilarating it must have been to plan a hunt, to apply one's intelligence to the accomplishment of a single life-or-death goal; to stalk the beast over the tundra; to sink the blade of a spear—a spear made by your own two hands!—into the flesh of a woolly mastadon; to bring the beast to its knees and deliver the death blow; to watch it fall slowly to the ground in a vanquished heap, then to cut it up and haul the bloody shanks of mastadon meat back to the fire, to the women, who would be so overwhelmed with gratitude that they would never even think about sending a guy out again for cigarettes.

Compared to his own life, a life of ceaseless tedium broken up by occasional trips to the bathroom and the snack machine, the life of John Q. Caveman looked amazingly satisfying and full. Compared to the life of a late-twentieth-century English major toiling away in the basement of a law firm for close to minimum wage, the average cavemen had it made!

Then, in an instant, Arnold knew what he had to do. He had to do it not only to save himself, but to save Ellen—to save their chance at a life together. That's what the dream was telling him. He knew that accepting a job at the zoo had been an odd choice for Ellen. It didn't fit. It didn't fit because Ellen hadn't really wanted a job at the zoo at all. What she really wanted was for Arnold to save her from the direction in which her life was headed. But in the office, as in The Dream, he had never been able to muster the courage to talk to her, to reach out to her and make their future together a reality. In life, as in The Dream, he was a weak, ineffectual fool drowning in pool of his own anxieties and shortcomings. To make it to shore, to reach his beloved Ellen and alter the course of destiny for good—to live a life guided by purpose, courage and his own free will—Arnold knew exactly what he had to do.

The next day, Arnold called in sick and drove his rusty Kia Spectra to the zoo. A dense fog hung low and wet over the parking lot. Drops of dew dripped from the trees, and a morning dove cooed from somewhere deep in the mist. Except for a Cadillac and a Jetta in the "Employees Only" section, his was the only car in the lot. He couldn't remember if Ellen had ever mentioned what kind of car she drove, but he imagined it was something sensible, like a Saturn or Subaru, or maybe a Prius. Arnold didn't feel Ellen's presence anywhere nearby, though, and since he had come to know Ellen—or know *of* her, at least, for they had never actually met or spoken to each other—his ESP (Ellen Sensory Perception, as he called it) had never failed him.

Arnold bought a ticket and nudged his hips through the turnstile. The flamingo enclosure was just inside the gate. There were about thirty birds, but they were all still asleep. The mere existence of a creature as weird as a flamingo was evidence enough for Arnold that God had a wicked sense of humor. Standing on one leg with their heads twisted around and tucked under their wings, the flamingo exhibit looked to Arnold like a recycling center for discarded, dismembered lawn ornaments, or the basement of a tropical-themed casino.

Behind him, Arnold heard a screech, then a squeal, then the laughter of children. A group of school kids was streaming through the turnstiles, and the first two boys in the pack were chasing a peacock across the plaza. For some reason the presence of children made Arnold nervous, so he hastily unfolded his zoo map and determined that the elephants were located along the path to his right.

Arnold did not stop to gawk at the iguanas, look at the leopards, or stare at the seals. He went directly to the elephant enclosure, where a large beast with giant ears—an African elephant, if Arnold's memory was correct—was busy curling its trunk around a clump of hay and shoving the grass into its gigantic mouth. Standing next to the large elephant was a much smaller elephant, who, Arnold guessed, was still quite young. In fact, according to a sign at the enclosure, the youngster was two months old and had been given the name Jocko, because he was always "clowning" around. Arnold had never heard of any clowns named Jocko, but he supposed it was as good a name as any.

Arnold watched the elephants for a long time. He was struck by how little they moved; mostly they just stood around doing nothing. Their trunks were always in motion, probing around for morsels of food, but the rest of them stood relatively still, especially the mother elephant, who looked as bored as Arnold usually felt. All of which was good, Arnold thought, because he wasn't sure how far or accurately he could throw a spear, and it would greatly increase his odds of success if his target was standing still. Arnold also noted that the elephant enclosure was extremely easy to get into, because the zoo prided itself on providing as natural a habitat as possible for all of its resident creatures. All one had to do to gain access to the elephants was hop the short fence that surrounded the enclosure and traverse a concrete moat about five feet deep and six feet wide, which, evidently, the elephants were afraid to cross.

Arnold walked around the entire enclosure, snapping pictures with a digital camera and taking mental notes on any obstacles he might encounter. There weren't many, though—just a water trough and a slim pipe that stuck up into the air about twelve feet, which, Arnold guessed, was some sort of sprinkler system or shower the elephants used to stay cool on hot days. Otherwise, there was nothing but a flat expanse of dirt and hay, mixed rather aromatically with a great deal of elephant dung, and a small building where, Arnold guessed, they kept the hay supply.

Killing an elephant was going to be easier than he thought. From the looks of it, all he had to do was climb the zoo's fence one night, work his way over to the elephant enclosure—making sure to stay in the shadows so he didn't get picked up by a security camera—then scramble across the moat, find his target and hurl the spear. The only hard part would be hitting the beast with sufficient accuracy and force to pierce a vital organ, preferably the heart. He didn't have any illusions about sticking around to watch his prey die (he would have to wait to hear about that on the news), for he had read that even a team of experienced mastodon hunters, after attacking, often had to track the creature for miles waiting for it to weaken and die from loss of blood. No, the best Arnold could hope for was one clean shot. That's all he was going to get, at any rate, so he knew he had to make it count.

Arnold heard giggles behind him. He turned around and saw that the pack of schoolchildren at the front gate had caught up to him. As the kids massed against the railing, trying to get as close as they could to the animals, their teacher—a short, girlish woman who couldn't have been more than twenty-five—was telling them how elephants keep their blood cool by flapping their ears, which have millions of capillaries in them and act as a sort of natural air conditioner. Just then, Jocko the baby elephant, curious about all the commotion, ambled over to the schoolchildren, who squealed with delight when they saw him. The teacher gave each child a peanut, which the girls held in their outstretched hands. Unfortunately, the little fellow couldn't reach across the moat to get the treats. Seeing this, most of the boys *threw* their peanuts at Jocko, who nabbed them with his nimble snout seconds after they hit the ground. Soon the mother elephant joined her baby. She had no problem reaching across the moat with her trunk to grab the peanuts of-fered by the girls. Arnold watched as, one by one, the mother elephant plucked the peanuts from the girls' tiny hands. With each peanut snatched came a shriek as the lucky girl yanked her hand away and shook it, simultaneously shocked and ecstatic from having touched, however briefly, the moist and hairy nos-tril of a creature fifty times her size.

Arnold decided it was time to go. He had seen what he came to see, so he headed for the exit. As he walked, he kept an eye out for places along the zoo's outside fence where he could ei-ther climb over it without shredding himself on barbed wire, or crawl under it. The fence was only about eight feet high, though, and didn't have any barbed wire, so it looked as though he could climb it almost anywhere.

Getting over the fence was the final piece of his plan, and now that it was in place, Arnold allowed himself a little smile. Just thinking about what he was preparing to do gave him rolling surges of confidence that he had never experienced before. He was nervous, but the nerves he was feeling were the exact opposite of the anxiety and apprehension that had plagued him practically every waking moment of his life. These nerves were the electric buzz of anticipation, the vital current of energy that comes when action is taken with a sense of mission, purpose, and vision.

Arnold had read his Hemingway, so he suspected that what he was experiencing was the thrill of the hunt. Great waves of stomach-fluttering, sphincter-twitching joy washed over him every time he imagined hurling a spear at the largest animal on Earth, felling it with his own two hands—hands that too often had been called scrawny, effeminate, or, as his Aunt Meg put it, "delicate." There was nothing delicate about what Arnold was planning. No, what Arnold had in mind was primal and true, an essential act stripped of all artifice—a natural, organic exchange of life and death, negotiated according to the laws of the jungle, not of mankind.

An ear-piercing screech came from a cage on Arnold's left. At first Arnold could not identify the creature in the cage making the noise, but after a few moments he saw a flutter of movement on a large tree branch. There, sitting lazily on the branch, a spider monkey with long, thin arms was furiously masturbating itself, baring its teeth at Arnold in a demonic, mischievous smile. Momentarily spooked, Arnold broke into a slow jog toward the exit.

Now, the astute reader has every reason to wonder why Arnold Simkin, a young man of higher-than-average intelligence who was generally averse to risk of all kinds, would concoct a plan to murder a creature as docile and friendly and huge as a zoo elephant. Anyone who knew Arnold would tell you that such a scheme was entirely out of character for him. Arnold, they would say, was a nice, harmless guy whose chief threat to those around him was his deep and relentless enthusiasm for the operas of Wagner and Verde. Someone who listens to opera *for the fun of it*—whose soul is sensitive and refined enough to appreciate the nuances of a well-sung aria—is not the sort of person who would kill an animal in cold blood *for the fun of it.* Or for any reason. That's what they would say.

Yet that is precisely what is about to happen in this story. To account for it, the narrator of this tale has attempted to give the reader some idea of what was going on in Arnold Simkin's mind at the time he committed his all-but-inconceivable crime. Certainly, love had something to do with it, though Arnold's *love* for Ellen Reese could be more accurately described as an intense infatuation. But, as anyone who as ever experienced it knows, infatuation is another of life's many paradoxes, a condition of the mind that often feels more like love than love itself.

Certainly, stress had something to do with it. Arnold's job, as we have seen, was oppressively dull. The ceaseless tedium of his workaday drudgery had obviously taken its toll. A psychologist might be tempted to conclude that Arnold's self-esteem had taken such a beating over the years that, by killing an elephant, he was attempting to reclaim his masculinity and self-respect in one brutal, premeditated act of violence. Or, that plunging a spear into the thick warm flesh of an animal was Arnold's way of sublimating his overwhelming sexual desire for Ms. Reese— a desire so explosive and primal that he instinctively recoiled from it, making it all but impossible to consummate any other way.

All of these suppositions offer a partial explanation for Arnold's peculiar behavior, but none of them is entirely correct. In the end they are all just words babbled about in a futile attempt to impose rationality on an act that is—or soon will be—fundamentally irrational. For another partial truth of the matter is that Arnold was strongly motivated by The Dream, specifically the part where the naked and vulnerable Ellen gets carried off into the woods by an enormously tusked pachyderm while he, Arnold, drowns. Arnold hated that part.

The problem with dreams is that while they may pulse with

meaning and significance while we are asleep, they are a notoriously uncertain guide for our waking lives. What the theories of Freud, Jung, Adler and others neglect to mention—or at best leave for the footnotes at the back of the book—is that maybe, just maybe, a person's dreams don't mean a damn thing at all. Maybe dreams are just the mind's way of entertaining itself while we're asleep and the television is off.

Of course, it's also possible that our dreams *are* packed with important life bulletins encoded in the elusive language of metaphor, and that human beings are incredibly inept at decoding these messages. Either way it comes out the same. Some people create great art out of their dreams and some follow their dreams into the very pit of Hell. In between, most of us spend our lives trying to decipher the secret language of our dreams, only to find that, like wisps of mist on a placid lake, they cannot be bottled for examination by the slow, inadequate meanderings of the rational mind.

Taken in this context, what Arnold Simkin decided to do is not so very strange at all. The world is full of people who do remarkably irrational things for no good reason whatsoever. Why does a poet write? A painter paint? A musician play? These are not rational activities; there is no real reason for doing them. Yet we value them just the same. Arnold's actions are just another part of that crazy human drama—no better, no worse—and it is futile to spend any more time speculating about a definitive "why" for his behavior, because there isn't one. Or perhaps there are too many. Suffice it to say that, for reasons even Arnold Simkin was incapable of fully comprehending, he had to kill a *real* elephant, not a metaphorical one, and he believed that doing so would bring him closer to the possibility of a perfect love with his dream girl, Ellen Reese. That he was spectacularly wrong in his assumptions is beside the point. This is what he believed, and this is how it happened:

Finding the proper spear was the hardest part. Buying a spear online or from a local merchant and promptly using it in a criminal act likely to get widespread media attention was not a great idea, Arnold figured, so he first tried to make his own spear.

Arnold soon discovered that making one's own spear—one that had any realistic chance of killing an elephant, at least—was no easy matter. The blade needed to be at least a foot long, and sharp enough to penetrate an elephant's thick hide. It also needed to have a long handle, so that after it was thrown and had found its mark in the animal, Arnold could follow up the throw by grabbing the spear handle and thrusting it as deep as possible in hopes of hitting a vital organ or two. Arnold had read that this is how tribesman in the African bush used to do it, before they had .50-calibre hunting rifles. The tribesmen hunted in groups, of course, and used the animal's initial shock at being attacked to their advantage by swarming it and ramming their spears home while it was still confused. Arnold was going to be alone, but he figured he could adapt this method to his needs and use the fact that he was attacking at night to his advantage. With any luck, the elephant might even be asleep, Arnold figured, and he could kill it before it even woke up.

The spear also had to be well balanced for throwing, and strong enough to withstand the possibility of the elephant trying to remove it or break it off with its trunk. Arnold soon discovered that making a spear that met all of the necessary criteria was well beyond his capabilities as a craftsman. He might as well have been trying to build a space shuttle. The closest he came to fashioning a viable spear was duct-taping a butcher knife to a broomstick, but when he tried to stick it through anything thicker than a piece of cardboard, the tape ripped and the knife fell off.

Thwarted, Arnold reluctantly turned to the Internet, where, to his amazement, there were hundreds of spears to choose from, most of which were being sold at exorbitant prices by collectors and antique dealers. To get the spear he wanted, Arnold realized that he was going to have to part with some money, but at this point he figured it would be money well spent—an investment in his future with Ellen Reese.

When it arrived in the mail, Arnold saw immediately that the tiny picture on his computer screen had not done the weapon justice. The shaft itself was seven feet long, and the blade—a long, slender teardrop of forged steal that tapered to a razor-sharp point—was sixteen inches long on top of that. The spear he had chosen was called a Zulu "Umkhonto" throwing spear, and it cost him $200. The shaft was wrapped in blades of grass, for camouflage and a better grip, and at the base of the spear was the intricately carved design of a tree. According to the booklet that came with the spear, there was once a famous Zulu warrior chief known for taking warriors who were too timid or weak in battle to this very tree and executing them by tying them to the tree and slowly inserting their own spear into their heart while the other warriors watched. The tree on the spear was a reminder that cowardice in battle was not an option.

Arnold also had to decide what to wear for the occasion—or not to wear, as the case may be. He wanted to recreate the atmosphere and feeling of a true elephant hunt insofar as possible in the city. In The Dream, he remembered, he wore nothing but a loincloth, so that seemed to be the logical fashion choice. But again, Arnold was stymied by the shortsightedness of the local clothing retailers. Prehistoric tribal wear was seemingly the *only* fashion trend that didn't come around every five years, so going over to Macy's and getting a loincloth off the rack was out of the question. Arnold knew he could order one off the Internet, but he didn't want to wait for another delivery. For the sake of expedience (and comfort, to be honest), he decided to go with an old pair of Jockey underwear that had turned gray from several hundred washings. Going barefoot didn't seem like a good idea, either. Those sharp little pebbles in the parking lot would hurt like the dickens. So he decided to wear his tennis shoes, but with no socks—something he hadn't done since second grade.

Having decided on his wardrobe and weapon, there was only one more thing Arnold had to do before he could put his plan into action. Arnold had read that in addition to being strong and versatile, an elephant's nose was also extremely adept at smelling the presence of predators, especially humans. Warriors in the bush rubbed goat and elephant dung all over themselves to mask their scent. Arnold felt that, in the name of authenticity, he should do something similar. Unfortunately, the only supply of animal feces he could get his hands on, so to speak, was from a dog—and even that proved harder to obtain than he had anticipated.

Arnold scoured his own neighborhood for two hours in search of a fresh doggy dump, but could not find a single pile of it anywhere. The week before he could have sworn the stuff was impossible to avoid; but, as with so many things in life, when he needed it the most, it was nowhere to be found. Sure, he chanced upon a few dry, crusty turds here and there, but none he could easily smear on his body. He needed the fresh stuff.

Then he got a brilliant idea: If you want fresh dog shit, he reasoned, you have to go where the dogs are. The local dog park was only half a mile away, so Arnold walked briskly toward it. A splendid meadow of freshly mowed grass, the park was a place where dogs of all kinds could be found frolicking in the sun, catching frisbees in their teeth, chasing slobber-soaked tennis balls and, Arnold hoped, defecating freely.

But even at the dog park Arnold had a difficult time finding what he was looking for. The dogs were there, and they were doing their business, as expected. The problem wasn't the dogs; it was their owners. Without exception, they were the sort of hyper-responsible people who feel obligated to pick up after their pet. There was not a single unscooped turd to be found, anywhere. Signs all over the park implored dog owners to pick up after their pet, and as far as Arnold could tell, everyone at the park was obeying the signs, displaying an unprecedented level of civic cooperation. Frustrated, Arnold approached a grey-haired woman in a blue pea coat who was walking a bushy-tailed malamute with milky devil eyes.

"Pardon me, ma'am, but may I have what's in that plastic bag you're holding?" Arnold asked.

"No, young man, you certainly may not!" she replied, recoiling at the sound of his voice.

"What are *you* going to do with it?" Arnold pressed.

The woman looked at him with the same cloudy devil eyes as her dog and hissed, "That's none of your business, sonny. Tell me, what are *you* going to do with it?"

And so it went. Arnold finally got what he needed by tricking a man with a large black Labrador retriever into giving him the dog's latest deposit. Arnold told the man he was a park employee and that personalized poop disposal was a new service the park was offering in order to encourage people to bring their pets down. The gentleman gladly gave the bag in his hand to Arnold, and seemed genuinely pleased to see tangible evidence of his tax dollars at work.

* * * * * * *

That very night, Arnold planned to put his ideas into action. There was no time to waste. With each passing hour, Arnold could feel his psychic connection to Ellen Reese fading, and the pain it was causing him had grown almost unbearable, as if she were a vital organ being slowly removed from his body one agonizing sinew at a time. If she disappeared from his life, if the sustenance she had provided him for the past year were entirely cut off, he feared he would die.

It was a cool night in late September, one that carried with it a whiff of winter. Arnold left his apartment around 2:00 A.M. A thin sliver of new moon hung like one of Ellen's earrings in the sky. If Arnold had cared to look in the opposite direction, he would have seen, too, that the belt of Orion the Hunter was creeping up over the eastern horizon. If he believed in astrology, he would have doubtless felt that the stars were favorably aligned for what he was about to do.

Arnold didn't have time to notice the stars, though. He was more concerned about the four feet of African throwing spear sticking out the window of his Kia, and, if he got stopped, how he might explain to a police officer the circumstances that led him to be driving around in the wee hours of the morning in his underwear, smeared head to toe with dog-shit.

Luckily, Arnold never had to explain himself. When he arrived at the zoo, the parking lot was completely empty. He parked in the corner of the lot, in the shadows, away from the street lamps, in such a way that his car was almost invisible. He didn't bother locking the car because he had no way of carrying the keys. Instead, he left them in the ignition, figuring they would help speed his getaway.

He slid the spear out of the crack in the passenger-side window and hefted it. The balance was good, he judged, and the weight of it felt even more formidable now that he held it in his hands, out in the open, ready to use. He had yet to throw the spear at anything, because hurling an eight-foot African hunting spear is a difficult thing to practice in the city. Even late at night the parks always seemed to be teeming with people, and during the day he didn't want to attract the attention of some busybody soccer mom who might think he was trying to skewer little Brittany for dinner. He only had to throw it once though, he reasoned, and if fate were guiding his actions—as it most certainly seemed to be—there was no doubt that he would hit his target, because the act itself was all but preordained.

Arnold crouched low and hurried to a spot where he could climb the fence without being seen. The gravel in the parking lot crunched like cereal beneath his feet, and he congratulated himself for having the foresight to wear tennis shoes. How much simpler the caveman's life would have been, he thought, if only he had had access to a Payless shoe store.

Arnold slid the head of the spear through a square in the

fence and pushed the rest through. He then jammed his toe in to get a foothold, grabbed the fence above his head and began to climb. The fence was only about eight feet high, so he didn't have to climb far—and just like that he was inside the zoo, spear in hand, ready to kill.

His pulse quickened as he surveyed the darkness for signs of a security guard or any hidden cameras. Except for the occasional snort or grunt from the nocturnal rustlings of some unseen creature, the grounds were quiet. The air was so still that Arnold's heartbeat felt like a primal drum pounding inside his chest, announcing his murderous intentions to the rest of the world. But the rest of the world didn't seem to notice or care; he was just another creature moving stealthily through the night, doing what it needed to survive.

In retrospect, however, he wished that his survival did not depend on smearing his body with dog-shit. It smelled awful to begin with, but now it was mingling with Arnold's nervous sweat, creating a noxious body slime that, Arnold felt, diminished the thrill of the hunt considerably. His senses were definitely sharpened, though, and for the first time in a long while he felt completely filled with a sense of purpose. Odd as it may sound, roaming around the zoo in the middle of the night covered in shit beat the hell out of working in a law firm. He could never go back to that way of life again, he reflected, and this thought filled him with a kind of glowing inner peace.

It didn't take long for Arnold to reach the elephant enclosure. Dark, mysterious—and quite empty—the enclosure looked much different than it had during the daytime. It was quite a bit larger than Arnold had remembered, and its flat, featureless terrain looked desolate and lonely, as if no one cared the slightest bit about the creatures imprisoned there. Elephants were among the most intelligent creatures in the world, Arnold knew. They had a complex social order, cared deeply for their young and mourned the deaths of their own with complex ceremonial rituals that lasted for days. Indeed, the evidence

Arnold had collected seemed to suggest that elephants were capable of loving each other even deeper and more profoundly than humans—which, Arnold had to concede, wasn't particularly difficult.

These thoughts did not deter Arnold from the task at hand, however. On the contrary, the knowledge that his prey was not some brainless bovine awaiting its inevitable slaughter made what he was about to do feel more legitimate. After all, it wasn't as if he were going into a field at night and bashing a cow's head in with a sledgehammer. *That* would be an act of cowardice, because there was no risk involved. Hunting down an elephant in its own habitat (or at least the only habitat available to it in the Northern hemisphere) was another matter altogether. There was plenty of risk involved—enough, anyway, to attract the attention of someone as discerning as Ellen Reese, whom he was certain would appreciate the distinction.

Arnold hopped the short fence that surrounded the elephants' enclosure and crossed the concrete moat that kept the beasts in place. The barnyard stench stung his nostrils, and he made a mental note to wear a noseplug if he ever did anything like this again. There was no sign of elephant life out in the open, so the beasts must be inside, Arnold guessed, in the concrete structure at the far end of the enclosure.

He crouched low and made his way toward the small building, which was silhouetted by the orange glow of a solitary halogen lamp located on a nearby pole. There was just enough light for Arnold to see that the sliding bolt on the metal door wasn't locked. He crept as quietly and quickly as he could to the door, taking care to stay in the shadow of the building so he wouldn't be seen. Stealthily, and without hesitation—for Arnold knew if he paused to think about what he was doing, even for a moment, he would probably panic and run—he laid his spear on the ground and slid the bolt open. He then picked up his spear, opened the steel door a crack and slipped inside.

Only one thing on Earth could generate the noxious odor

that attacked Arnold's nostrils at that moment: gallons of fermenting elephant piss. One whiff of it and Arnold's lungs began to burn. His canine cologne was relatively pleasant in comparison to this caustic assault on his senses. There didn't seem to be any oxygen left in the air, so he inhaled the offensive fumes faster than he would have otherwise, exhaling half-way through each breath when the smell became unbearable. He tried breathing through his mouth, but he could still taste the stench as if he were drinking it through a straw.

Except for a few slivers of light from the lamp outside, the building was dark. Though he couldn't see, Arnold could hear heavy breathing nearby. In front of him, to the right, he heard a brief rustle of hay. Arnold stood still for a moment to let his eyes adjust, and in that moment of blind silence he heard a slow, rhythmic thump, like a distant drum. The drum beat slowly and seemed to get closer as he listened, but the cadence of the beat remained constant. A melancholy throb, it came and went in two parts, to and fro, ebb and flow, in and out, yin and yang, yes and no, each part of the beat implying the other, as if Arnold were somehow listening to the infinite and everlasting pulse of the universe. The sound filled him with sadness. It felt like something for which he had been looking his entire life—and now that he had found it, he didn't know what to do with it, what it was, or even why he had been looking for it in the first place. Gradually the drumbeat got louder, but Arnold couldn't tell if it was coming closer to him or if he was somehow moving toward it. He was standing still, but it felt to Arnold as if his soul were being pulled toward the drumbeat, whether his body wanted to follow or not. A terrifying thought suddenly jolted Arnold back to his senses: It was the realization that the drum he was hearing wasn't a drum at all—it was the enormous beating heart of an African elephant.

Arnold couldn't see the animal, though. Everything was blackness and blobs—indistinct shapes bulging out of the darkness, as if he were looking through the frame of a severely underexposed piece of film. The one useful trick his father had taught him was, when looking at things in the dark, don't look straight at them. When he tried this, the retinal cones in his eyes could just barely detect a large round hump in front of him. The hump was about as tall as Arnold himself, and though he could see nothing else, Arnold guessed that if the elephant were sleeping on its side, this was probably its ribcage and stomach.

Arnold's own heart was beating fast now, so fast that it felt more like machine-gun fire than a heartbeat. He crouched low and slowly extended his hand until he felt something bristly and rough, like steel nubs on sandpaper. It had a slightly rounded shape, so Arnold extrapolated that it must be the elephant's leg. In his mind's eye more than his real eyes, the form of the great beast began to take shape in front of him: If the hump were indeed its rib cage and the rounded bristles its leg, Arnold deduced that its heart had to be somewhere in between.

Though it didn't move, Arnold could feel the sheer mass of the thing in front of him, as if there were some sort of gravitational pull between the animal and himself, drawing them together. He focused on the spot in the darkness where he judged the animal's heart to be. The drumbeat began thumping again, this time faster and louder than before. A jolt of energy shot through his arm, and for the first time since he had entered the building, he became aware of the deadly spear in his hand. Except that now, the spear did not seem to be so much *in* his hand as it was a *part of* his hand, an inextricable extension of himself pulsing in the dark, as if it too were alive. Arnold raised the spear to his shoulder and extended his arm back as far as it would go. His target, he realized, was the drumbeat itself—the throbbing heart of the beast that lay asleep in front of him.

As the drumbeat grew louder and louder, closer and closer, Arnold stood transfixed, with every fiber of his being locked onto the hole in the dark from which the drumbeat emanated. Then the darkness itself began to pulse and throb, and Arnold could see a pinprick of light deep inside it. The pinprick grew brighter, like a star, then exploded and came rushing at him in a rainbow of colors. The colors formed an image, and Arnold immediately recognized the image as his beloved Ellen, sitting astride an elephant's enormous tusk, waving to him—hello or goodbye, he couldn't tell. The image then vanished as quickly as it had appeared.

Another surge of energy shot through Arnold's arm. A power he had never experienced before seemed to be working through him now, dictating his actions, determining his fate. Deep in his lungs he felt a primal urge to scream, to purge himself of the emotional toxins that had poisoned his life as surely as if he had drunk them from a bottle. Arnold felt the spearhead whistle past his ear as it hurtled toward the emptiness in front of him. Into the center of the drumbeat went the spear, chasing the light that was Ellen and the evil that had spirited her away. As the spear left his hand, Arnold gave in to the fireball of despair at the core of his being and let out an ecstatic howl, an explosive cry that echoed the cries of countless warriors and hunters before him, who, in the heat of battle or at the climax of the hunt, have for centuries yelled that same mortal yell, and who now know it simply as the trumpet blast of the angels as one soul is exchanged for another. In that moment of divine fury, Arnold felt as if truth and light and happiness were within reach for the first time in his life. In that single moment, he felt more alive than he ever had before.

* * * * * * *

Ellen Reese fed Jocko the baby elephant every weekday morning at 7:30 A.M., two hours before the zoo opened its gates to the public. It was her favorite time of day because she had little Jocko to herself. The crowds had yet to gather, and the animals were at their loudest and most active right after the sun came up.

The animals; she could hear them screeching all the way

across the zoo. As she walked toward the elephant enclosure, their primal screams echoed through the bear canyon and past the big cats, mixing with the howls and yelps of a hundred other animals, forming a cacophony that Ellen found strangely energizing. The chatter of the gibbons and peacocks was especially loud that morning, she thought. But what did she know? She hadn't been there long enough to determine what was normal and what wasn't. That morning, even the lions were roaring, which was a first.

In the short time Ellen had been at the zoo, she and Jocko had already fallen into a comfortable routine. As soon as she slid the bolt and opened the door, Jocko's trunk would peek around the corner of his stall, nibbling at the air, in search of a treat. When Ellen gave the treat to him, Jocko poked his head around the corner and met her with his big brown eyes, which were already the size of a tennis ball. Then she would feed the little guy his vitamin supplements through a giant bottle with a nipple the size of a pickle.

This morning, Ellen knew something was wrong the moment she turned the corner. The door to the elephant's paddock was open, and Bobo, the big bull elephant, was already roaming the perimeter of the enclosure, sweeping the ground with his giant trunk, flinging dirt and dust everywhere. Quickly, she opened the side gate, hopped the moat, and ran to the paddock building.

Inside, Jocko's mother, Eva, was standing next to the little elephant, caressing his face with her trunk as he lay on the hay, his big eye open but empty.

"Oh no," she gasped and knelt beside Jocko, putting her hand on his cheek. But Jocko's body was already cold. What Arnold hadn't known when he entered the building was that elephants sleep standing up. The hump in the dark that he thought was an adult elephant's rib and belly was really Jocko's back. Arnold's spear had hit Jocko in the side and punctured the little fellow's lung, causing him to slowly suffocate and bleed to death.

Ellen wept at Jocko's side, lightly running her hands over his bristly body. Nature was too cruel, she thought—Jocko did not deserve to die. Then she saw the wound and the blood. She immediately thought of Bobo, with his huge ivory tusks, and assumed that the big brute had gored little Jocko sometime during the night, as sometimes happens in the wild. Realizing that she might be in danger herself if Bobo was on the warpath, Ellen quickly exited the paddock and ran for help.

Lenny Chalmers, one of the zoo's curators, was the one who found Arnold's body in the corner of the paddock, mangled and twisted and half covered with hay. Most of the bones in Arnold's body were broken, and his head had been squashed like a cantaloupe, as if he had been repeatedly slammed against the ground and stepped on by ten-thousand pounds of angry elephant—which he had. It was Lenny, too, who found Arnold's spear.

"Looks like ol' Jocko didn't just die," said Lenny. "Looks to me like he was murdered."

"Murdered!" cried Ellen in disbelief. "What kind of animal would do such a thing?!"

Lenny Chalmers did not have an answer for her.

As soon as the news stations learned that Jocko had been killed, they sent crews with cameras to document the scene. One enterprising reporter from the local paper learned from a zoo official that an unattended car had been found in the parking lot that morning, and from the unmistakable smell of it, police had determined that it was probably the killer's car. Considered part of the crime scene, the car had not been moved, which allowed the reporter to get the car's license number and, through contacts at the Dept. of Motor Vehicles, determine that the vehicle belonged to an Arnold Simkin, age 24, 5-foot 10 inches, 165 pounds, of 2502 Briar Lane in San Mateo, California—his parents' house. Arnold's parents learned of their son's death from the reporter, and were at a loss to explain how their son—whom they thought was attending law school in San Francisco—had wound up dead at the city zoo, mostly naked and covered with two or three different kinds of feces.

On Saturday, hordes of elephant lovers, well-wishers, and schoolchildren who had heard the news were streaming in from all over the city, carrying flowers, cards, candles, and gifts to commemorate little Jocko's unthinkable death. A spontaneous shrine sprouted in front of the elephant enclosure, and Ellen herself volunteered to help keep the crowd under control and answer any questions people might have about Jocko.

Around three o'clock in the afternoon, the same newspaper reporter who had talked to Arnold's parents tapped Ellen on the shoulder and asked if she had a minute to talk. He had made a few phone calls, he said, and had spoken with Ms. Driscoll, Arnold's supervisor at the law firm. Ms. Driscoll confirmed that Arnold had been employed there, though in her opinion it would be stretching things a bit to say he "worked" there. In any case, he had quit the week before. If something had happened to him at the zoo, she speculated that it must have something to do with a woman named Ellen Reese, who had also worked at the firm for a few months—and who, according to Ms. Driscoll, Mr. Simkin had a "thing" for.

When confronted with this information, Ellen looked at the reporter as if he had spat on her. "I don't know what you're talking about," she said. "I've never heard the name Arnold Simkin before, and I certainly don't—*didn't*—know him!" She confirmed that she had worked at the law firm in question for a few months, but it was only a temporary job and she didn't recall anyone by that name working there. The reporter showed her a photo of Arnold obtained from the law firm's human resources department, but she did not recognize him, she said. The reporter thanked her and left.

Ellen did not know what to think about any of it. It was all so senseless and tragic, she thought—so positively *savage*. She then leaned over and thanked a five-year-old girl for bringing a rose for Jocko, which she placed among the candles and cards left by other heartbroken zoogoers.

"He was my favorite," the little girl said.

"Mine too," Ellen said, "mine too."

. . . .

HUMANINANOTARIANISM

GOOD FRIEND RECENTLY INFORMED ME THAT he had "gone vegan." When I asked why, he said something about it being the healthiest, most ethical way to eat, and he wanted to "give it a try."

The decision had been a while in the making. He had been a "chick-a-fish-atarian" for a while, he explained, but felt hypocritical about eating some types of animals and not others. For the past couple of years he had been a vegetarian, but in recent months had been re-thinking his relationship with food, the size of his carbon footprint, and how his impact on the world affected his own personal karma. Therefore he had decided to "go vegan," a dietary decision that sounds a lot like a football cheer but isn't, because vegans, I have since discovered, do not cheer.

When I asked him what the difference between a vegan and a vegetarian was, he answered, with a puff of pride, "Vegetarians don't go far enough."

"Maybe if they ate some meat," I suggested.

No, he explained, vegetarians—while well-meaning people for the most part—are not conscious enough about their food choices. A vegetarian will still eat animal by-products such as milk, yogurt, eggs, and cheese, but vegans won't, because they are philosophically opposed to the mistreatment and exploitation of animals. Cheese, for instance, is a by-product of milk, which is sucked out of cows injected with milk-producing hor-mones by machines with long tubular tentacles that attach to the udders with cold, metallic hands. The whole thing is dia-bolical. Really dedicated vegans won't even wear leather or use feather pillows, he explained, because they used to be attached to animals. And if you go all in on veganism—which he was not yet prepared to do—you won't even take vitamins or medica-tion that comes in a gelatin capsule, because gelatin is made from horse hooves.

Having gone through the list of things one couldn't eat on a vegan diet, I asked him what he *could* eat. "Fruits, vegetables, beans, bread—anything derived from plant matter, as long as it isn't mixed in with substances derived from animals," he said. "So, for instance, I won't be putting butter on my bread or po-tatoes—I'll just be eating them plain. After a while, they say your sensitivity to natural sugars increases, so that pretty soon a potato tastes almost like candy."

That was unlikely, I thought, and in any case, who wants their potato to taste like a Jolly Rancher? It sounded like anoth-er one of those, "If it tastes good, don't eat it" diets, but I was willing to listen. I am nothing if not open-minded mind when it comes to absurd food experiments other people are trying.

"It sounds ridiculous," I said. "No butter on your bread. No cream in your coffee. Life is already cruel enough. Why pile it on?"

"It's a more enlightened way to live," he explained. "And it's not just about the food, it's about living in a way that honors the dignity of other creatures on the planet. It's about ethics and principles. And besides," he said, "on a vegan diet, your farts smell better."

"You don't say."

"It's because you're not digesting animal stuff."

"Now that's interesting," I said. "So eating vegan can make your farts smell good?"

"Not *good*, necessarily—but better."

"Hmm. How much better?" I asked.

"Noticeably."

"To yourself, or to others?" I pressed. "Because your own farts always smell better than other people's. So just because a fart smells better to you doesn't necessarily mean others in the vicinity will agree that it does in fact smell better. You'd need a true side-by-side test to be absolutely certain."

"You are absolutely right," he said, "we should set that up sometime."

Thus began an uncomfortable period in our friendship. He would come over to watch a football game, and I'd sit there with a plate of chicken wings while he noshed on carrot sticks dipped in hummus. If we ordered a pizza, he'd scrape off the cheese and only eat the sauce and crust. I'd offer him a beer, and he'd decline, saying that the sort of cheap, canned beer I prefer often contains something called "isinglass," which is made from the dried swim bladders of fish. Once, I wanted some ribs, and in an effort to appease him I went to a health-food store and bought a food product made out of tofu that was stamped by a machine to look like a small rack of ribs. Watching him eat that crap was the saddest thing in the world. He said they tasted "better than they look," but that's setting the bar pretty low, because they looked absolutely disgusting. "Better" in this case meant only mildly disgusting—but that, as far as I could tell, is as good as vegan food gets.

I didn't think he'd stick with the vegan thing for long, but his persistence surprised me. Deep down, he is one of those people who enjoys denying himself things, so the vegan diet fit his psychological profile perfectly.

Over the next couple of months, he didn't just eat differently, though—he began to change as a person. He lost fifteen pounds, grew a scruffy beard, and started biking to work. Suddenly his wardrobe consisted of nothing but plaid shirts and old jeans; gone were the Metallica t-shirts and cargo pants. In the wintertime he ditched his hoodies and bought an old wool overcoat, which, when he was riding his bike, made him look like a very poor Batman. Once, I snuck a peek at his Pandora playlist and was horrified to discover Cloud Cult and Bon Iver in heavy rotation, along with Drake, Morrissey, and . . . I can barely force myself to type it: *Coldplay*.

Something more was going on here than a mere change in diet. And I didn't like it. My best buddy was gradually turning into an insufferable boor. Whereas we used to talk about sports and girls and video games when we hung out, he had begun issuing long, boring proclamations on the "state of the world" and how everything is all fucked up—the economy, politics, the healthcare system, climate change, terrorists, drug legislation, the Miss America pageant—because capitalism is a predatory system that perpetuates inequality and rewards sociopaths for behavior that really ought to land them in jail, yada, yada yada.

His sense of humor had disappeared too—or, when it did kick in, was dark and funereal: "Did you know that in Japan, these fuckers catch sharks, cut all their fins off and dump them in the ocean to drown? Why? Because shark-fin soup is supposed to increase sexual potency in men. Killing sharks to get a boner—that's humanity for you."

We used to laugh about that kind of thing, but now he was taking it all very seriously. When I mentioned one day that he might want to think about lightening up a little, he came back at me with, "Well, I think you're a little *too* light. As far as I'm concerned, you're stuck in the world of the trivial and mundane. I've tapped into something meaningful, and you don't like it because deep down you know I'm right."

"Right about what?" I asked.

"About our responsibility the rest of the planet—about how we all need to take a good long look at how we live and, wherever possible, adopt habits and lifestyles that contribute to, rather than detract from, the greater good."

The "greater good" argument was not one I found particularly compelling. The regular good was plenty good enough for me, and even that was a challenge sometimes, because how could anyone know what the "best" good choice was in every situation?

"So, are you still biking to work?" I asked.

"Yes."

"Well, I read an article recently that said people who bike to work and back, or just exercise a lot in general, burn an average of eight hundred more calories a day than people who don't. And if you add up all the extra gasoline burned to transport those calories to the grocery store, and all the extra carbon dioxide these people exhale, it's actually worse for the environment than if they took the bus. Just saying."

"That's stupid," he said.

"No, that's science."

We argued for a while: about why it was stupid, why I was stupid for believing it, and why he was stupid for *not* believing it. But it was not a very satisfying argument. I had, after all, made the whole thing up to piss him off, so I wasn't arguing from a position of strength or heart or fact—I was arguing from the position that it was funny to watch him get all worked up over an idea held together by nothing but bullshit and spite.

But he wouldn't let it go.

"Tell you what," he said. "A woman I work with at the co-op is having a vegan dinner party this weekend. I think you should come for two reasons: to see firsthand how delicious and varied a vegan diet can be, and to meet some people who are trying to live in a conscious and principled way, in as much accordance with nature as possible, and in harmony with the essence of what it means to be a human being. In other words, people entirely unlike you."

This sounded to me like the worst of all possible parties: a bunch of self-righteous, humorless do-gooders in a room eating lentils and farting sweet vegetable gas into air already thick with patchouli and body stink. The conversation would be torture, too, because it would be my friend times ten griping about all the ways in which the world is failing to meet their inflated expectations and unrealistic ideals. What could be duller? I mean, who wants to sit in a room with a bunch of people who are frantically polishing their own halos, congratulating themselves for being so much better than everyone else?

Then again, people in my humble circumstances must always weigh the potential psychic anguish of an event against the cost savings of a free meal—even a vegan meal. Unfortunately, I had used up my last Chipotle gift card the day before and only had about three dollars in cash, so I agreed to go to the party with him, but only with the understanding that I was there to mooch a meal and nothing more. We bumped fists and parted, each wondering what was wrong with the other.

The night of the party, I found myself in a quandary over what to wear. My favorite shirt was 100% cotton, and I worried that some fanatical vegan might see it as a sign that I was one of them—someone who consciously chose plant-based clothes because of my deep concern for the planet. Also, my belt wasn't leather—it was plastic texturized to look like leather—so again, I was concerned that a close sartorial inspection might lead someone at the party to conclude that I gave a shit about that sort of thing. In the end I chose a shirt with an 80/20 cotton-polyester blend, just to be safe, and wore a bright-green windbreaker so obviously made with toxic chemicals that no one could accuse me of caring about anything.

The party was held in the apartment of a woman named Bristol, so I had my guard up right away. In my experience, girls named after cities—Madison, Sydney, Victoria, Brooklyn, Paris—were trouble, though not quite as much trouble as girls named after states—Arizona, Virginia, Dakota, Montana—and not nearly as wacky as girls named after countries—Asia, India, China, Argentina—or girls named after celestial objects: Cassiopeia, Halley, Miranda, Virgo, Aurora. At least Bristol is an English city, so my inclination was to hate it (and her) less than if she were named after some cute little city in Italy or France that was once sacked by the Gauls but is now famous for its honey and vinegar.

Whatever happened to naming your kid Susan or Mary?

My friend didn't tell me much about this Bristol girl except that she was very "present," had a great "aura," and in some circles might be considered "hot." A real-estate agent would have called her place an "artist's loft," since it was located in a warehouse on the outskirts of town, at the end of a dirt road my GPS didn't recognize, and was surrounded by other "spaces" where artists allegedly plied their craft. Bristol herself was a "designer," and by the looks of her place, she had yet to settle on a specific aesthetic. Most of the furniture was red and white plastic, except for a lumpy brown couch. The walls were covered with batik silkscreens of trippy mandelas and leaping horses, and her lamps ran the gamut from 1970s kitsch to nineteenth-century whorehouse. To get there, we rode a freight elevator up five floors, and there wasn't really a door, just a sliding slab of metal decorated with some yellow and blue graffiti.

The smell of the place was surprisingly nice; not at all what I expected: cinnamon and spice mixed with the aroma of basmati rice and curry, like a Middle-Eastern restaurant during the holidays. When we arrived, half-a-dozen people were already there, drinking wine out of paper cups and listening to music that didn't really have a beat; it just swirled and swelled and swooshed, like a baby playing in the bathtub. Later, I learned that it was the sound of the ocean played from an app designed to help people meditate. I personally found it annoying, however, because it made me need to use the bathroom, which was located two floors down at the end of a dark hallway where, I was certain, someone had recently been murdered.

Right away I could tell I did not fit in. Everyone was more or less my age—mid-twenties—but they all seemed to be going on forty. One guy even wore the kind of tweed golf cap my grandfather wears. Another dude had a beard three inches long. And one of the girls wore blue, cat-eye glasses with zirconium "diamonds" embedded in the frame, as if she were trying out for the part of the eccentric next-door neighbor in an Alfred Hitchcock movie.

Then I met Bristol.

Yes, she was attractive, but in an odd way that was more like a bird with lots of strange colors and feather combinations that inexplicably work together to make something beautiful. Her individual features weren't all that extraordinary. She had straight blondish hair that was a little thin and a roundish face with a small nose, plump lips, and teeth that were mostly straight except for one of her incisors, which stuck out just enough to be distinctive without being distracting. But her eyes—they were amazing. Sparkling green emeralds flecked with gold. Hypnotic. Enchanting. Witchy magic gypsy eyes, the kind that tell fortunes, cast spells, and raise the dead.

"Why hello, you must be Jeff's friend," she said as if she were genuinely glad to meet me, not just faking it. "I'm so glad you could come. Please, get something to drink and make yourself comfortable. Dinner will be ready in just a sec." After she said the word "sec," she held my gaze for half a beat, then spun around and disappeared into the kitchen, trailing a long gauzy skirt that made it look like she was floating across the floor rather than walking.

Jeff saw the way I was looking at her.

"Don't even think about it. That dude over there is her boyfriend," he said, pointing to a lean, well-muscled guy who had obviously eaten plenty of red meat in his life, and was so brazenly masculine that he had flames tattooed on his forearms.

"Ever hear of the band WolfSpit? He's the drummer."

I nodded in silent acknowledgement of his rock credentials.

"Oh, and he just published a vegan cookbook," Jeff added, "several recipes from which I'm guessing we're about to try."

At that moment, Bristol emerged from the kitchen holding two large, colorful bowls. Following her was a short guy carrying a crock pot and a stocky girl carrying a ceramic bowl of something that sent curlicues of steam into the air. Bristol set the bowls down on a wooden table next to the wall, as did the other two.

"Okay, folks, come and get it," Bristol said in a sing-songy voice that would have been annoying if she weren't so lovely. "We've got a nice vegetable curry over here, some lentils with tomato and dill over there, vegetarian chili in the crockpot, and a quinoa salad with tabouli and mint. Oh, and rice is in the steamer—which Evan is bringing out right now."

The guy with the flames on his arms entered the room holding a rice steamer. He set it on the table next to the curry and put his arm around Bristol, then kissed her on the cheek, pulling her toward him so hard that the vein in his bicep pulsed.

"As most of you know, all of these recipes come from Evan's new cookbook, *Thrash Vegan*, and all have been personally tested by *moi*," she said, pointing to herself. "If you like the food, please buy several copies of the book on Amazon and give it a bunch of five-star reviews," she said, laughing. "Now come, everyone—eat."

I had to admit, the food wasn't bad. Not as bad as I expected, anyway. And trust me, I wanted to hate it, because I hated Evan. I hated him for dating Bristol, for being a heavy-metal drummer *and* cookbook author (pick a lane, pal), for having awesome tattoos, for having perfect chin stubble, and for a hundred other things, most of them too petty to mention. Most of all, I hated the fact that I wasn't him, and that I was trapped in a world where I could never be him. It is cruel how life apportions talent and luck and boldness to people who don't deserve it, and withholds it from people like me, who could seriously use the extra help.

As Jeff and I were eating, though, a strange thing happened—or at least I thought it was strange, because it was so unexpected. Out of all the people in the room, including her drummer-god-author-stud boyfriend, Bristol came over and sat by me.

In fact, she ended up sitting so close it was a little uncomfortable. We were sitting on the floor, around a small coffee table. As she sat down next to me, she tucked her legs under her and a little to the side, in such a way that her right thigh was touching my leg, causing me to feel an odd mixture of terror and delight.

"So, how do you like it?" Bristol asked as I spooned some chili into my mouth. I nodded, trying to indicate that I liked it very much without having to actually say it. Then she leaned toward me and whispered, "Personally, I think the chili could use a little more cumin and salt, but that's just me."

"It's all good," I said. "Not that it couldn't be better," I added.

"Don't lie. You hate it, I can tell," Bristol said. "After this, I bet you're going to go out and get a cheeseburger."

The thought had occurred to me.

"I envy you," she said. "Sort of. Not that I'd ever want to eat a cheeseburger again—just that I can remember a time in my life when I could eat a cheeseburger and enjoy it. That's not possible anymore."

I pretended to wipe a tear from my eye, and she playfully whacked me on the shoulder. "You're friend is cheeky," she said to Jeff.

"My friend here thinks the whole vegan thing is bullshit," Jeff said. "He thinks eating meat is an American birthright, and that choosing not to eat meat is un-American, maybe even commie. He thinks everyone in this room, including you, is a pretentious poser, and that we are what's wrong with the world, not what's right with it."

Bristol raised her eyebrows and looked amused. "Is that so?"

"In my defense, let me say that I prefer to do my own wild generalizing and to insult my host directly, not through a disgruntled proxy friend who, mere months ago, could have said the same thing about himself," I said. "But yes, that about sums up my worldview."

"You're not wrong—about the people in this room," Bristol said. "But it's not about deciding whether or not to eat meat. Meat is just a symbol—a substance that happens to embody everything that's wrong with the way food is produced and processed in our culture, and the way animals are treated. Cattle farms are toxic places, full of filth and disease, so they inoculate cows against the disease with antibiotics, speed up their muscle growth with steroids and hormones, kill them in a burst of primal fear—then ship the whole mess off to be grilled and consumed by people. That stuff ends up going into our bodies, then we wonder why we have so much cancer and heart disease. The same thing is true more or less of pigs, chickens, and fish—so why eat any of them? Then there's the fact that animals are sentient creatures who have families, mourn their dead, and feel pain. Personally, I cannot look at a steak without hearing the anguished cry of the animal as it was killed. It's as if the creature is speaking to me from beyond the slaughterhouse, warning me that the meat itself is nothing but blood and pain and death."

"Well, when you put it that way, it does take some of the fun out of barbecuing," I said.

"If it were just about food, I'd be a vegetarian and call it a day," Bristol continued. "But once you start being conscious of how your choices affect the world—how we are all connected in the great web of life—every bite of food you put in your mouth becomes a political statement; a referendum on who you are, what you believe, and what truth you are living. And if you're not living the truth—or at least *a* truth, as you understand it—what's the point?"

I didn't know quite what to say. I would know *exactly* what to say if Jeff were spouting this sort of piffle at me—but when Bristol said it, she obviously meant it. And, because I desperately wanted to get to know Bristol and understand her, I listened to her, which never would have happened if Jeff were the one talking.

"Ironically, this is the last meal like this I'll ever eat," Bristol said. "After tonight, Evan and I are joining the Raw Food movement. So no more cooked food for me. Evan's already started writing a new book about it. The working title is *Eat, Raw, Play*. He's thinking of throwing some music lessons in there too, just for fun."

"That makes no sense whatsoever," I said. "A cookbook for people who eat raw food and play the drums?"

Bristol's eyes lit up in a way that made me think for a moment she agreed with me.

"I know—crazy, right?" she said. "That's what's so great about it. No one else but Evan would ever think of doing something like that."

I'd never heard of the Raw Food movement, and wondered what they did, in fact, eat. "Mostly vegetables, fruit, legumes, and nuts," Bristol explained. "Some people eat eggs and dairy in the raw movement, but we're not going to, out of consideration for the animals."

Another word about how great and principled Evan was, and how much Bristol admired him for it, was going to make me gag. In an attempt to change the subject, I pushed some food around on my plate with a fork and asked, "So what is it I'm eating here, exactly?"

"That's a quinoia and tabouli salad," Bristol explained.

"That's a lot of vowels," I said.

"Yes, it is very good for the bowels," she replied.

"That's good to know," I said, not bothering to correct her.

This girl is impossible, I thought—but something about her intrigued me, in a way no one had ever interested me before. Aside from her association with this Evan character, I kind of admired her willingness to live according to her principles and not according to her whims and desires, as so many other people our age were doing. Her idealism and self-righteousness, while occasionally suffocating, were also admirable qualities that few people in my acquaintance—other than my recently converted friend, Jeff—possessed.

It also had not escaped me that even though Evan had flaming tattoos and rippling muscles and a cool job, the thing Bristol seemed to like most about him was his dedication to the principle of conscious self-denial. What seemed to turn her on was a guy who was willing to go the extra mile to avoid eating just about everything in order to save the animals and heal the planet.

But because I am a guy, and I know how guys think, my guess was that it was all an act. At some point, I think Evan figured out what impressed his girlfriend the most, and was pursuing the whole "raw" thing because it seemed more extreme and principled than mere veganism—a tactic that was almost certainly related to the kind and amount of sex he was going to get from it. The man was simply acting in his own self-interest. Sex, to him, was more important than food—and he was evidently willing to sacrifice one for the other.

I deduced two things from this: One, that sex with Bristol must be worth it. And two, even though I couldn't match Evan in the area of muscles and body ink, and my day job as a Samsung specialist at Best Buy wasn't as sexy as a heavy-metal drummer, I *could* compete with him in the arena of principled living and self-denial. All I had to do was come up with some principles, then deny myself in such an extreme and impressive way that Bristol would look past my shortcomings and fall in love with me instead.

That was the plan, anyway.

If only it were that easy.

After three weeks of googling and several late nights smoking weed and thinking, I had the outlines of a workable plan. Not a perfect plan, mind you, but a way forward at least. When I explained it to Jeff, however, he had his doubts.

"It's a shitty plan," he said. "It'll never work. The problem is, you don't understand the first thing about ethics or principles or integrity. You're plan doesn't come from an honest place, or serve any higher purpose—it's just a Hail Mary rain of bullshit designed to discredit this Evan character and avoid eating a lot of foods you don't want to eat. She'll see right through it."

"I of course reject that characterization," I said. "This approach comes from the most honest place possible—*love*."

Jeff slapped his forehead and said, "Oh my god, are you serious? Love? You've only met the girl once."

"And I'm going to meet her again—only this time I'm going to be prepared."

"Okay, what makes you think this has a chance in hell of working?" Jeff asked.

I thought about it for a few seconds, then voiced the hunch around which my plan revolved: "I think she still likes cheeseburgers."

* * * * * * *

Owing to Jeff's lack of enthusiasm, all I asked of him from there on out was that he invite me along the next time Bristol had a party. He agreed, under protest, but made me promise in the meantime to try a bit harder to understand where Bristol was coming from and why she believed what she did. Why? Because then I would understand why my plan was doomed.

I said I would, but didn't. Then, about a week later, the invite came.

By then, I had done my research and was ready. This time, the party wasn't an occasion to celebrate anything special; rather, it was a get-together of what Jeff called "like-minded individuals" (myself excluded) for a "salon-type" discussion of various issues. Jeff warned me however that the discussion that night was going to revolve around her and Evan's recent conversion to a raw-food diet and all its corollary benefits. He didn't even want to go, because while veganism held a certain philosophical appeal for him, he wasn't ready to spend the rest of his life eating celery stalks and sunflower seeds.

The night of the "salon," as we rode up the rickety elevator to Bristol's loft, Jeff said, "One thing you should know about Bristol is that she loves to be the most politically progressive person in the room," Jeff explained. "You know, the kind of person you used to hate."

"Duly noted," I said, "and summarily dismissed."

"Fine. It's your funeral," he said as he banged three times on the metal slab that was her door. A few moments later, the door slid open and Bristol herself was standing before us, holding a glass of red wine. I thought I detected a flicker of something in her eyes when she saw me, though in retrospect it could have been a trick of the light.

"You again," she said. "I'm surprised. I thought we'd scared you away for good."

"I don't scare easy," I said in a Clint Eastwood-like rasp that came out of nowhere.

"That's good," she laughed. "Nicholas Cage, right?"

"Uh, my uncle Ed, actually," I said. "It's what he used to say right before my aunt served dinner."

Bristol motioned for us to come inside and told us to sit wherever we wanted. She was even more attractive than I remembered. This time her hair was pinned up and she wore silver hoop earrings that glinted every time she turned her head. She was dressed much more simply, in a black shift dress and those crappy Japanese slippers you can get for five bucks at Marshall's. But it all somehow worked—or at least it worked on me. I resolved then and there to do whatever it took to capture her heart—as long as it didn't take *eating* like her.

Luckily, her boyfriend Evan wasn't there. He was supposedly rehearsing with his band, but I had my doubts. Bristol didn't know it yet, but her boyfriend wasn't as committed to the raw thing—or even the vegan thing—as much as he led her to believe. I suspected from the start that those muscles of his didn't come from eating barley soup and extra-large salads. So I tailed the guy for two weeks, and lo and behold, I caught him eating at Smashburger on four different occasions, scarfing a three-egg ham-and-cheese omelet at Denny's, and more than once snacking on a foot-long Slim Jim. The kicker was the night I saw him disappear with two of his bandmates into a Timber Lodge Steakhouse. The photos from that night are a little dark, but you can tell it's him. Those arms don't lie.

I wasn't going to use the photos unless I had to. But they were in my jacket pocket, just in case.

Only about ten people were present that night. Half of them I recognized from the previous party, but most of the others were people from the co-op whom I'd never met. I didn't really want to meet them, either, but there was no way to avoid it. To begin with, Bristol asked us to go around the room and introduce ourselves. In addition, she asked us to tell the group a little bit about ourselves, and where we were along "the path"—meaning, I gathered, how much attention we were giving to what was going in our mouths. There were a couple of vegetarians, but most people identified as "vegan," or "ethical vegan." One girl said she'd been eating raw for about a week, but admitted that it was "tough," because she'd had to give up many of her favorite vegan foods—"favorite vegan foods" being, to my mind, a huge oxymoron.

Then it was my turn. I cleared my throat and said, "Hi, I'm Jeff's friend. I'm here because I'm in love with Bristol."

Everyone laughed, as if the notion of Bristol and me as a couple was so patently absurd that I must be joking.

"I'm not a vegan," I continued. "But I am here to talk about a better way to eat—a way more in tune with the rhythm of modern civilization, and far more advanced than vegan or raw—or any other diet for that matter—in terms of its overall impact on our beloved planet."

Pretty much everyone in the room gave me the "what the hell is he talking about?" face. Bristol looked confused, but tried her best to guide the discussion in the direction she had already planned.

"Well, we all look forward to hearing more about that," said Bristol. "We're all interested in more enlightened forms of consumption. Which leads me to our topic of the evening, my recent conversion to a raw-food diet. Many of you have asked me how it's been going, and I want to share with you that it's going extremely well. I won't lie to you—the transition wasn't easy. But the great thing about eating raw is that you are absorbing all the nutrients and enzymes that get destroyed in the cooking process. My body feels better now than it has in months, and I feel like my inner spirit is glowing. I feel so full of life, and so blessed to be able to share this feeling with you all."

"Perhaps you feel full of life because that's what you've been ingesting," I said.

"That's what I just said," Bristol replied. "Not cooking my food has, I believe, brought me closer to the life force of all things, the source of all that we are."

"No, it hasn't," I said matter-of-factly. "Precisely the opposite is true, in fact. The only reason you feel 'more alive' is that you are, in reality, closer to death. Because death is what you've really been ingesting, not life."

Several people in the room gasped.

"What are you talking about?" Bristol sneered in a tone that bordered on hostile.

"I call it 'humaninanotarianism,' and as far as I know, I am its only practitioner."

Everyone laughed again. "I just googled it," said a string-bean hipster dude leaning against the wall. "There's no such thing."

"Not on the Internet, maybe" I said. "But there are other types of knowledge that don't necessarily show up on your little device there. New knowledge—knowledge not yet sanctified by the executives at Google. What is that, anyway, last year's

Nexus?" I asked, pointing at his phone. "Do yourself a favor: get a real phone. Best Buy, ten to six—come in and I'll set you up."

Several people started mumbling at once, the gist of which, I gathered, was that they wanted me to shut up.

"Hear me out," I protested. "You all seem to think that eating fruits, vegetables, and other plant matter instead of meat constitutes some kind of morally superior diet. Many of you don't eat meat because you are opposed to animal cruelty, and don't want to eat anything that you can imagine was once alive. But in my view, eating vegetables—or any plant life, for that matter—is just as reprehensible as eating meat. Why? Because new research on plants confirms what we all intuitively know already: that they are alive too. It's not the same as us, but plants can hear, taste, and communicate with each other, they know up from down, and they know when their leaves or roots are going to hit an obstacle, because they will try to avoid it. Furthermore, and most important, plants feel pain. Scientists have recorded plants *screaming* when they are cut. Just because we can't hear it doesn't mean it isn't happening. The truth is, plants are living, conscious creatures, and if you are truly committed to honoring the sanctity of life on this planet—as I am—you need to stop eating anything having to do with plants. Fruits, vegetables, nuts, berries—everything."

There were several scrunched faces in the crowd, and I could tell it was going to be a tougher sell than I thought.

"Wait a minute," said a girl who was sitting on the floor. "What about, say, apples that have fallen to the ground, or walnuts that have fallen off a tree? Couldn't you eat those?"

"Well, I myself can't eat them," I said. "Because ever since I became aware that plants are living creatures too, all I can think about when I see apples on the ground is their little screams the moment they were separated from their tree, followed by that awful, sickening thud. For me, a walk down the vegetable aisle is nothing but a wailing chorus of anguish and death. All those poor plants—hacked, chopped, picked and boxed—all so that us humans can have something tasty to eat. It's the most selfish thing in the world, if you think about it. All I'm saying is that if you care about the living creatures in this fragile world of ours, and you want to be philosophically consistent, you have to give up plants in addition to meat, dairy, and all the rest. Either way, you're eating death, and ingesting all the terror and violence and cruelty that goes with it. I, for one, won't do it anymore."

Skepticism. Confusion. Anger. "What's left to eat?" someone asked. "I mean, if you can't eat animal or plant products, what else is there?"

"Well, there's water, for one thing," I said. "And if you want to, you can still eat things in the shape of an animal. But my daily diet now is split into two parts. First, I get most of my vitamins and nutrients from supplements in powder or pill form. Then, for bulk, I eat protein bars (as long as they're artificially sweetened), Oscar Meyer hot dogs, and those cheesy breads from Domino's.

"I know what you're thinking: those aren't 'good' foods. But we need to change our definition of 'good.' We've been conditioned to think otherwise, but the truth is that if you care about animals and mother Earth as much as I do, your dietary goal should be to eat the most highly processed foods modern science has to offer. Why? Because these are the foods that are farthest removed from the sick cycle of death that poisons the conventional food chain. You people have it all backwards. The truth is, the more man-made chemicals that are in your food, the better—because that means there is less animal and plant matter. And the less animal and plant matter that is in our food, the better off we'll all be, because we will finally be living in perfect, non-violent harmony with all the other blessed creatures on this planet."

Stunned silence is what I expected—and I got it, for about four seconds.

"That's the stupidest thing I've ever heard," someone said.

"I can't believe I'm hearing this," said another.

"Who is this guy?"

"What a load of bullshit.

"Are you serious?"

"Please, tell me you're joking."

And then, Bristol. Tears pooled in the twin moats of kindness that were her eyes. "I think you should leave," she said. "You obviously do not take any of this seriously. You have entered my home under false pretenses and, instead of entering into our discussion with an open mind and heart, have come to mock me, us, and everything we're trying to accomplish here. Please, go."

I expected a reaction, but not one this harsh. "On the contrary, I think it's *you* who has the closed mind and heart," I countered. "You are the one who doesn't want to listen to new ideas, especially if they don't happen to confirm what you already believe."

Two guys who were sitting on the couch suddenly stood up. "We don't like your energy, man. You should leave."

I stood up and grabbed my jacket. "History is littered with visionaries who challenged the status quo and were tossed out of meetings just like this. I count myself honored to be among them."

I didn't want to do it, but I had no choice now—I had to show Bristol the photos. I pulled the manila envelope out of my jacket pocket, opened it, and handed her a stack of four-by-six photographs. They showed Evan eating at several well-known meat-serving establishments, time-stamped and arranged in the most damning order possible. I handed them to Bristol.

"What are these?" she asked.

"Proof that your wonder boy isn't quite as wondrous as you think," I said. "The guy is a fraud. Those are photos that prove he is cheating on you. Because yes, that is a double-stack BBQ Bacon and Cheddar Smashburger he's putting in his mouth."

Bristol wheezed, trying to catch her breath, then began to

sob. "What is this? What kind of monster are you?" she cried. "Get out of my house now! And don't ever come back!"

* * * * * * *

Jeff and I didn't talk for a couple of weeks after that. All he said to me after the party was, "I warned you," then he stopped returning my calls and texts. And, in retrospect, I'll admit that I may have laid it on a little thick with the harmony and blessedness stuff, but that's the sort of thing I thought Bristol would want to hear. The weird thing is that, as I was saying it, I almost believed it myself. My argument had a certain logic to it, I thought. It wasn't a logic anyone agreed with, but I think most reasonable people would admit that it had a certain counterintuitive flair. In the end, however, I had to admit that my plan did not work, that Jeff was right, and that the whole thing was a misguided firing of Cupid's notoriously inaccurate arrow.

On the bright side, I could still eat anything I wanted.

Two months later I was looking for a birthday present for my mother. She likes this expensive organic lotion that you can only get at hippie food stores, so I ventured into the co-op where Jeff used to work. Somewhere in the back of my lizard brain I knew that Bristol used to work with Jeff too, and might still work there, but to be honest, I'd pretty much forgotten her. I'd come to the conclusion that she was too spiritually wonder-wacky for me, anyway, and that the true attraction for me was the challenge of getting her to drop her vegan-drummer-dude boyfriend for me, Best Buy Samsung guy.

When I got to the checkout counter, I saw the name badge first—"Bristol"—but I hardly recognized the person wearing it. Her hair was thin and ragged. She'd lost so much weight that her chin and cheekbones were protruding from her face, as if she had spent the last two months in a concentration camp. And her eyes—those lovely sparkly eyes—were dark, flat discs of despair.

She looked at me, blankly at first, but then her eyes flew open and she whisper-yelled. "You!"

Uh oh, I thought—still mad. I smiled weakly and said, "Hi."

"I need to talk to you," she hissed. "Now."

She immediately shut down her register and pulled me by the sleeve into the back room of the co-op. There, amid boxes of butter lettuce and avocadoes, organic carrots and rutabagas, she pulled my face close to hers and, just when I thought she was about to kiss me, said, "You have to help me."

She looked desperate. I wasn't sure I could help her out of whatever mess she'd gotten herself into, because if I had to guess, I'd say she was hitting the heroin pretty hard. She looked like a junkie, strung out and prepared to do anything—*anything*—to get her next fix.

"Look, I don't . . ."

"You're the only one who understands!" she cried. "Ever since you said that thing about the plants feeling pain and walking down the vegetable aisle hearing their screams, I can't get the image out of my head. Then it started happening to me here at work. I can't stand it anymore. I swear I can hear the bell peppers crying, and the sobs and moans that come from the potato bin—it's too much to bear! I can't sleep. I can't eat anything anymore. I'm dying. You have to help me. Show me how you got through this horror. Please, I'm begging you."

What to tell her? That it was all bullshit? That she was getting all worked up over nothing? That she shouldn't be so gullible? That she needed to chill out, smoke a joint, and order a pizza?

Then I got a better idea.

I put my hands on her shoulders and looked into her eyes, which were buried deep in sockets of pure sorrow.

"I know just what you're going through," I said. "And I know just what you need."

I led her out of the store and into my car. "Don't worry, everything will be fine," I assured her.

At the McDonald's counter, I ordered us both a McDouble Cheeseburger, diet Coke, and a McFlurry shake. We stood in silence as the server loaded our tray, then we sat down in a booth by the window.

"What is this?" Bristol said. "I can't eat this crap."

"Oh yes you can," I said. "Think about the animals, the plants, the planet."

"But this is meat. I can't eat that. And that shake is dairy. Don't you see, I can't any of this," she said as a lone tear rolled down her cheek.

"That's where you're wrong," I explained. "This isn't meat. It's a factory-created pseudo-substance that happens to look and taste sort of like meat, but in reality it's a super-processed meta-food so far removed from its animal origins that it doesn't actually qualify as meat. There's no milk in that shake, either—it's a masterfully engineered blend of potassium sorbate, sodium phosphate, magnesium hydroxide, and a dozen other chemicals that, when mixed together, magically emulsify themselves into the mouth-pleasing soft-serve concoction you see before you. And, well, the purely synthetic pedigree of diet Coke speaks for itself.

"The point, Bristol, is that you *can* eat it. Nay, you *must* eat it. I know it contradicts everything you think you know about food and nutrition. But these highly processed man-made food-stuffs—the foods everyone says are bad for you—are the only truly planet-friendly foods available to us. That's what food processing does—it puts miles of distance between you and death. Face it, the closer you are to 'nature,' the closer you are to the carnage and mayhem of modern agriculture. Harvesting is nothing but using giant machines with big sharp blades to mass-murder thousands of otherwise innocent plants. 'Fresh' just means it died yesterday. How would you like to be chopped and mulched? How much fun do you think it is to be *digested*? That's why we need to embrace these expertly engineered pseu-do-foods, not reject them. Believe me, I've been where you are.

If you really want to eat in the most ethical way possible, you need to forget everything you think you know and start fresh, so to speak. Let your old ideas die. Start your new life now."

"Are you sure?"

"It's the only way," I said. "Trust me."

With that, Bristol grasped the McDouble Cheeseburger in her shaking hands and brought it to her mouth. She then bit into it and began to chew.

"Oh my god, this is amazing!" she exclaimed as a ribbon of the dyed corn-syrup goo commonly known as ketchup dribbled down her chin.

"Yes, it is," I said, "and the best part is, your farts will smell *fantastic*."

* * * * * *

AIR DIABLO

J EREMY TAYLOR WAS LATE TO THE airport, and he wasn't happy about it. The alarm clock in his hotel room had failed to go off (for $199 a night, you'd think they could afford to stock the rooms with a goddamn clock-radio that works!), his morning wake-up call, an emergency back-up, had never come (four-star service, my ass!), he had been delayed at check-out because of an overcharge for Internet service he never used (what a fucking scam!), and he had been in too much of a rush to get any breakfast, so on top of being unhappy, he was hungry, too.

He wasn't feeling all that great, either. Until 2:00 A.M., to the best of his recollection, he had been drinking whiskey and sodas in the hotel bar and flirting with his waitress, a taut young thing with legs sculpted out of marble and blonde hair so thick and shiny it looked like a waterfall of honey flowing down her back. While he drank, he had entertained fantasies of taking this Norwegian cocktail vixen back to his room and losing himself in her firm young flesh. The more he drank, though, the clearer it had become to him that his fantasy was never going to come true. So he drank even more, in what became a pathetic and somewhat expensive effort to forget the number fifty, which happened to be his age, the number of pounds he was overweight, and the number, in thousands, that his daughter's partying career at the University of Indiana was going to cost him.

"Thirty-six dollars," the cabbie said. Jeremy gave him two twenties and demanded four dollars back in change.

It was a power thing, stiffing cabbies. When he did it, the dialogue in Jeremy's head went something like this: "Hell if I'm gonna tip some son-of-a-bitchin' Somali terrorist just so he can bring fifty of his cousins over here to take jobs away from Americans and plot a motherfuckin' coup." It was also the money, of course, because hey, four bucks is a cup of coffee and a danish. The cabbie, who was Ethiopian, and who held a Ph.D. in biochemistry from Alemaya University in Dire Dawa, tossed Taylor's luggage onto the sidewalk and sped off without saying a word.

"Fuck you, too," Jeremy muttered as he extended the handle on his bag.

It was 8:15 A.M. already, and his flight was due to leave at 9:20 A.M. If he could get checked in and the security line wasn't too long he still had a chance of making his flight, but he knew he'd be cutting it close. The second he walked through the airport's double doors, however, he realized he was screwed. The check-in line had at least fifty people in it, and the security line stretched half-way to Winnetka. This was O'Hare, the busiest airport in the world; hell, it could take him two hours to reach the gate.

Quickly, he scanned the departure times displayed on a bank of television screens that hung on the wall like the eyes of a giant insect. He had a sales call in Dallas at 2:00 P.M., an account that, if it were to come through, could make his entire month. It *needed* to come through, in fact, because if it didn't, his month was going to be shit. He needed a Hail Mary, and this was it; if it didn't happen, all hell was going to break loose.

Jeremy scanned the board—Albany, Albuquerque, Anchorage, Atlanta, Bangkok, Boston—until he found his flight, American Airlines 2775 to Dallas. His eyes tracked across the screen to the Estimated Departure Time, where he did not see the words "On Time," or the word he was hoping to see:

"Delayed." Instead, he saw the word "CANCELED" written in capital letters, in red, like a big fat "No Vacancy" sign.

Jeremy clenched his teeth and smacked his forehead with the heel of his hand. "You have got to be kidding," he said to himself. "You have got to be fucking kidding."

The line to the ticket counter was not as long as it could have been. It only took him twenty minutes to reach the front of the line, but each of those minutes felt to Jeremy like a kind of medieval torture, as if he were standing on a bed of white-hot coals in his bare feet, or being whipped until his back was a mess of raw hamburger. The minutes ticked by so slowly that he could almost feel himself aging, and every fifteen seconds or so a new dread entered his consciousness. Because if he missed his Dallas meeting at 2:00 P.M. he would not be able to re-schedule it for at least another week, by which time the momentum needed to nail the Tierney Bros. down to a one-year contract will have died. If he couldn't pull the Tierney sale off, he didn't know what he was going to do, because it wasn't like he had a ton of other prospects lined up. This deal was going to be his meal ticket for the next two months at least; with it he was a hero, without it he was goat meat. 80 percent of his income came from commissions, so if he didn't sell, he didn't eat. Not eating was the least of his worries, though. If he got caught in another slump, like the one back in '99, when every teenage dirt-bag computer geek in the country was making a million dollars every time they farted, while he, Jeremy Taylor, veteran sales guy, was making next to nothing, he was going to kill something, or some*one*.

The person whose skull he was most likely to crush was that of his wife, Tanya, who had become such a raging robo-bitch about money that he felt like cuffing her half the time anyway. Jesus, would the woman ever let up? All she ever did was shop—at the mall during the day, and on the Internet at night—and when he came home after a hard day's work, and choked down the sorry excuse for a meal she served him, all she did was bitch and moan about all the shit she wanted to buy but couldn't.

Why?

Because he didn't make enough money.

Did he realize, she would say, how embarrassing it is to have your credit card refused at the Marshall Field's jewelry counter? How such an experience scars a woman, making her feel like a second-class citizen? Like she doesn't even belong in the store? And whose fault was that? No one but his, because *he* was the one who insisted on buying the bigger, more expensive house; *he* was the one who insisted on driving the fancy Chrysler; *he* was the one who sank their nest egg into lousy stocks; *he* was the one blowing a C-note every weekend playing golf; and *he* was the one who wanted the sixty-five-inch television with the full cable sports package. All of which left her with practically nothing, she claimed, and made her look bad in the eyes of the *community*.

Well, as far as Jeremy Taylor was concerned, the community could kiss his hairy white ass—and so could everyone else—because he was doing the best he could. He already hated every minute of his life, and if that wasn't good enough for people, then fuck them. Fuck them all.

At long last, a ticket agent waved him over. She was a large woman with dark chocolate skin and a slight case of acne on her face. Her name tag read "Wanda."

"Good morning, what can I do for you today, sir?" Wanda asked.

"For starters, you can get me on a plane," Jeremy replied.

"What's your final destination today?"

"It's supposed to be Dallas, but you canceled my flight."

"American 2775?"

"That's right."

"We're sorry for the inconvenience. Let's see what we can do for you," Wanda said, typing briskly on the keyboard in front of her. "Hmmm. Looks like the earliest I can get you out is 3:30 P.M. this afternoon."

"That won't work," Jeremy informed her. "I've got a business meeting in Dallas at two o'clock this afternoon, so you're going to have to do better than that."

Wanda continued tapping on her keyboard, head down, peering at her computer screen. "I'm sorry, sir, but that's the only other flight to Dallas we have today."

"That's it?!" Jeremy exclaimed.

"Yes, but I can give you a meal voucher and a coupon for 10,000 free miles."

Jeremy leaned across the tiny counter and peered up into Wanda's face. "I don't want a fucking meal voucher," he hissed, "I want to get to Dallas."

"I'm sorry, sir, but . . ."

"If American can't get me to Dallas this morning, then book me on another airline," Jeremy said firmly.

"I'm sorry, sir, but if we can get you to your destination within ten hours, company policy doesn't allow us to . . ."

"Screw company policy!" Jeremy interjected. "I paid for a first-class ticket to get to Dallas this morning, not this afternoon. So I'm going to get to Dallas, do you understand?"

"I can appreciate your frustration, sir, but there's really nothing I can do."

"Bullshit," Jeremy said. "I know goddamn well you can book me on another airline, because you've done it before. Somebody has to be going to Dallas this morning. Find out who is, and get me on a plane."

Wanda eyed Jeremy with cold, dark disdain. It was guys like this who made her job miserable; guys who insisted on having everything their way, and who wouldn't stop until they got it. She hated being put in this position. She was supposed to be a "customer service" representative, but if she capitulated to this jerk she would get yelled at by her supervisor, and if she didn't do what the jerk wanted, the jerk himself was going to yell at her. It was a no-win situation. Nevertheless, she dutifully pecked through the schedules of airlines with whom American had certain partnership arrangements, but there were only three other flights to Dallas that morning, and all of them were already oversold.

"Delta has a flight that leaves at 2:10 P.M.," she said with a hopeful ring in her voice.

"Not good enough," Jeremy said. "Try again."

"Southwest has a flight that leaves at 11:20 A.M.," she offered.

"That might do it," Jeremy grunted.

"But it goes through Memphis, and doesn't arrive until 5:05 P.M."

"Then obviously that *won't* work," Jeremy snapped, growing ever more impatient.

Wanda tapped on her keyboard some more just to make it look like she was searching deeper into the database, but she knew it was useless—she had exhausted all of her options. *Almost* all of them, anyway.

"Sir, I've checked the schedules, and there are no seats to Dallas available until 3:30 P.M. this afternoon," Wanda informed him. "I'm sorry, but that's the best I can do."

For a few moments, it looked to Wanda as if Jeremy Taylor might back off and accept his fate, but she was wrong. Instead, Jeremy broke out in a sweat and started breathing heavily. He rolled his eyes and tossed his head back and forth like a bobble-head doll, then grabbed the sides of the counter with his meaty hands. He raised the fist of his right hand and pounded it on the counter. "What the fuck is wrong with you, goddammit!" he shouted. "I did not pay for a first-class ticket in order to get dicked around! You are an airline. You provide a simple service—to get people where they need to go. Why is that so difficult? I refuse to believe that there are no other options. And if there aren't any, I can tell you right now that I am never going to fly on this shit-bucket airline again!!!"

"Sir, there is no need to shout," Wanda admonished. "Please keep your voice down and we'll try to resolve this as best we can."

"Your best is shit!" Jeremy howled. "I want to talk to your manager, or whoever it is who supervises your sorry black ass."

That did it. Wanda could take a lot, but she could not take being condescended to, and she could not take talk about her ass—sorry, black, or otherwise. She didn't enjoy exercising her final option, but it was sometimes necessary. This jerk deserved whatever he got.

"Well, there is *one* other possibility," Wanda said.

"That's more like it," Jeremy grunted, condescension dripping from his lips like blood from a knife.

"It's an independent airline. The planes are smaller, and they don't fly as fast, but they'll get you where you need to go. The next flight starts boarding in about an hour. You can reach your final destination by noon," Wanda said with a slight twinkle in her eye that Jeremy did not notice. But even if he had, he wouldn't have known how to read it or what it meant.

"What's the name of the airline?"

Wanda looked at him with ice in her eyes. "Air Diablo," she replied.

"Book it," Jeremy ordered.

"Do you have any baggage you'd like to check?"

"Nope. Carry-on all the way."

Thirty seconds later, Wanda handed Jeremy Taylor a boarding pass. "Gate 24C, boarding at 9:20 A.M.," she said. "I hope you get where you need to go."

Jeremy did not hear her or respond. He just snatched the boarding pass from her and bolted for the security line.

Gate 24C was at the far end of Terminal Four. When he arrived, there was no one else at the gate, and there were no signs indicating that this was the boarding area for Air Diablo, or any other airline. In fact, that particular section of the airport seemed entirely deserted. There was no one waiting at any of the gates nearby, either. The only sign of life in the area was a forlorn-looking little man with big round glasses who was manning the check-in desk at gate 24C.

"J . . . J . . . Jeremy T . . . T . . . Taylor?" the little man stuttered as Jeremy approached.

"That's right," Jeremy confirmed. "How did you know my name?"

"We've been a . . . w . . . waiting your a . . . rr . . . rr . . . iv al," the little man said, blinking his eyes like an owl. "You may b . . . b . . . board any t . . . t . . . time you l . . . l . . . like."

Jeremy handed his boarding pass to the little man, who promptly ripped it up and threw it away. "T . . . t . . . take any s . . . s . . . seat you l . . . l . . . like," he said, "and thank you for f . . . f . . . flying Air D . . . D . . . Diablo."

The stewardesses were Jeremy Taylor's first indication that the Air Diablo flying experience was going to be a slight departure from the meat-moving shuttle of bodies he was accustomed to. Their name tags read Myla and Candi, and they looked like identical twins. Each of them had straight black hair, as smooth and shiny as a fresh coat of paint. They were lovelier than anything he'd ever seen in a magazine, even the magazines he bought on the road, and they smiled at him as he ambled down the walkway toward them, their even white teeth framed by plump scarlet lips, their cheeks dusted with blush. Each wore a black leather skirt cut short and tight, with fishnet nylon stockings and spiked silver heels that made their legs look long and sleek and dangerous. How they walked down the aisles in those things Jeremy could not fathom. But he did not dwell on that thought for long, because his middle-aged gaze inevitably landed on their magnificent breasts, which strained the buttons on their all-but-transparent blouses to the point where it was impossible not to imagine those buttons popping and imprisoned breasts breaking free for all the world to see. Neither woman appeared to be wearing a bra, so from the side, through the gaps in the buttons, Jeremy could see the underside of Candi's left breast, a view that made his pulse race and gave him a slight case of vertigo.

Coming in duplicate as it did, the force of Myla and Candi's beauty was stereophonic, which is to say complex and multi-dimensional. One could admire them for their surface allure, or get lost searching for the mysteries hidden in the infinite wonder of their jade and lavender eyes. Or, as in Jeremy's case, one could simply sprout a hard-on and take it as a sign that fate has smiled upon you in recompense for the aggravations of the day.

It was a small plane, with only two seats on either side of the aisle, but the aisle was wide and the seats themselves were much larger and roomier than anything Jeremy had ever seen on an aircraft before. They were leather too, black and supple, with plenty of legroom to recline and relax. Indeed, the entire cabin had a feel of luxury and exclusiveness to it that Jeremy had only experienced a few times in his life, when he had been invited for drinks or dinner at the University Club in Boston. The overhead bins were not made of gray plastic; they were crafted out of mahogany and polished to a high, golden sheen. Recessed into the armrest of every seat was a drink dispenser that served crushed ice along with a variety of soft drinks and other drink mixers, including tonic and soda. The carpet in the aisle was soft and springy, like the carpet in Jeremy's favorite room at home. Even the air onboard was nicer to breathe, as if it had been infused with cinnamon and vanilla.

Brahms played softly over the speaker system as Jeremy took his seat. As far as he could tell, there were only four or five other people on the flight. From where Jeremy sat, all he could see were the backs of their heads poking up over the headrests. Two of his fellow passengers appeared to be women—one with chestnut hair that had obviously been dyed and hennaed, the other a natural-looking blonde. The other three passengers were men, two with neatly cropped businessmen's hair and the other an older gentleman who was almost bald except for a short sprinkling of gray fuzz on either side of his shiny, freckled head.

As Jeremy was buckling his seat belt, Candi appeared beside him and asked if he'd like a complimentary cocktail. Jeremy was pleasantly surprised that in this day and age there was still an airline willing to give something away for free in exchange for a little customer satisfaction. On American, he had to pay for everything: drinks, snacks, headphones, the works. It sucked, big time.

"A Bloody Mary, thanks," Jeremy replied.

"Excellent choice. Mary's blood is especially fresh this morning," said Candi, her voice as flat and dispassionate as a plank of wood. Jeremy took her remark as an attempt at humor and smiled, but Candi gave him no indication that she was joking.

Within minutes, Jeremy had a cocktail in his hands and the plane was taxiing along the runway. This is how every airline should operate, he thought. Free drinks, plush seats, beautiful flight attendants, out of the gate and into the air on time—what was so difficult about that? Now that he thought about it, he was glad so many big airlines were going bankrupt, because their service was universally awful. They *deserved* to go out of business, in his opinion, so that other, better airlines—airlines like the one on which he was now flying—could prosper and take their place. That was the beauty of capitalism, he thought; it weeded out underachievers and made way for people who knew how to get things done.

A few moments later, his plane was in the air. It climbed at a steep angle, knifing through layer after layer of clouds on its way up through the atmosphere into the sapphire sky above. The force of the engines pushed Jeremy deep into his soft leather seat, a sensation he found rather pleasurable, as if the seat were gently hugging him. He leaned his head back and discovered that a pair of Bose noise-canceling headphones, the kind advertised in all the in-flight magazines, was embedded in the headrest. Every other airline charged three bucks for a cheapo little headset; not Diablo. These guys know what they're doing, thought Jeremy as he fitted the headphone cups around his ears. Immediately, the rush and hiss of the plane's engines hushed to a whisper and strains of the Brahms concerto that had been playing over the plane's speaker system enveloped him. He hated "that classical shit," though, and began searching for a button to change the channel.

As he searched, a deep, sonorous voice interrupted the music: "On behalf of Diablo Airlines, this is your captain speaking. Our flight time this morning is going to be two hours and eighteen minutes. Sit back and enjoy the flight. Oh, and Jeremy Taylor, I hope you're comfortable back there, because trust me, you are in for the ride of your life."

The tumbling arpeggios of Brahms' Piano Concerto No. 2 returned, but Jeremy whipped off the headphones so fast that he never heard them.

What the hell was that?, he thought.

The pilot mentioning him by name had unnerved him more than he was willing to admit. Calm down, he told himself—it was probably just another example of the airline's customer-service policies in action, some sort of strategy for personalizing the flight experience to make their customers feel special. They knew his name from the flight roster, he reasoned, and they knew where he was sitting, so of course they had all the information they needed to address him by name. He'd read about this kind of thing. They probably did it for everyone, he figured, and the more he thought about it, the cleverer it seemed. He didn't particularly like being singled out by name, and he frankly thought it was pushing the personalization thing a bit too far, but he had to admire the ingenuity and business acumen involved.

As the plane leveled off to its cruising altitude, the older gentleman who was sitting six rows in front of Jeremy unfastened his seatbelt buckle and rose to go to the bathroom. Tall and lean, the man turned toward the back of the plane and began making his way down the aisle, clasping his big, bony hands on the corner of each seat as he passed. Had Jeremy been more observant, he might have seen that the man's right hand looked distinctly different from his left. It was smooth and splotchy at the same time, with white scars that ran like tiny rivers over the back of his hand and up into the fingers. All five fingers were intact, but the hand itself looked as if it had been smashed and then reconstructed by a drunken medical intern. Chunks of flesh and bone had clearly been sewn together and fused at some point, leaving an uneven patchwork of different skin textures and scars. The fingers themselves were bent in odd places and at strange angles, making them look more like the branches of a tree than a human hand.

When the man reached Jeremy's seat, he stopped. Jeremy didn't even notice him until the man said his name.

"Jeremy? Jeremy Taylor?"

Jeremy looked up, slightly puzzled, for he did not recognize the man. Yet the man clearly seemed to recognize him.

"You probably don't remember me," the man said with a laugh.

"Have we met?"

"Oh yes," said the man. "Seventh grade. Science. Mr. Scanlon?"

Jeremy scanned his memory but all he could come up with from that part of his life was a vague recollection of some thick black desks, a few Bunsen burners and a half-dozen beakers of different sizes holding a variety of luminescent liquids.

"Scanlon. Oh, yeah, right," said Jeremy.

"What a coincidence, eh?" said Mr. Scanlon as he extended his mangled right hand toward Jeremy. "How are you?"

Jeremy reached his own hand up to shake Scanlon's, but when he saw the man's mangled appendage coming toward him, he recoiled in disgust and drew his own hand away. Scanlon held his hand in the air for a few moments before realizing that Jeremy was not going to shake it.

"I'm sorry, it's just . . ."

"No need to explain," said Scanlon. "You were never very good at explaining things, anyway."

"What's that supposed to mean?" asked Jeremy, suddenly feeling defensive.

"Just that I remember you quite well, even if you don't remember me."

"Well, it's been a long time," Jeremy said.

"Yes, you were quite a little bastard back then."

"What?"

"Shall I jog your memory?" said Scanlon. "The year: 1975. You were about thirteen, I'd guess. You used to wear a black t-shirt all the time, a ratty old thing that proclaimed your devotion to one of those wretched bands so popular with the delinquent set: Judas Priest or Black Sabbath or something. It had a demonic ring to it is all I know, because I remember thinking how appropriate it was for you, since you were one of those damnable urchins who entertains themselves by sucking all the joy and satisfaction out of the teaching profession. At the time, I remember thinking, 'No, I'm not going to let one little thug ruin twenty years of dedication,' but you—you were determined to push me to my limit. Just so you know, I was aware of everything you did: I know that you purposely spilled ink on Mark Bryson's stool just before he sat on it that one day. I know you burned Emily Kwan's notebook and threw it into the sink, pretending to be the "hero" who put it out. I know you put sulfur in Mary Fletch's chem kit so that she would inadvertently stink up the room during Project 14—all so you could get a few laughs by accusing her of farting."

At the mention of this episode, Jeremy had to laugh. He did remember doing that, and thirty-something years later he still thought it was funny.

"Of course, I also remember a few things you may not find so amusing. You pressuring Linda Clemens to have sex with you behind the bleachers at the spring dance, for instance—and, despite her objections, you penetrating her in what I believe would now be referred to as 'date rape.' You jerking off in Mrs. Driscoll's desk drawer. You blowing people's lockers up with firecrackers. You pulling fire alarms, calling in bomb threats, faking your father's signature on absence slips, smoking pot and drinking Boone's Farm in the parking lot, stealing car parts and selling them for dope money. Yes, I remember it all."

At the mention of these youthful transgressions, Jeremy squirmed in his seat and a thin film of sweat formed on his forehead. "So what? I was just a kid," he said, feeling ever more defensive.

"No, you weren't just a kid. You were a punk, a cretin, a thoughtless little scab."

"Whatever, old man," Jeremy sneered, waving Scanlon away. "Don't you have to go empty your colostomy bag or something?"

"Of course, there's one other thing I remember," Scanlon said. He leaned his head down toward Jeremy and spoke in a menacing whisper. "I remember the day I caught you cheating on an experiment. When I pointed out the fact that you were copying a stolen assignment, you denied it. When I reached for the papers themselves—the irrefutable evidence—you poured alcohol on my hand and lit it on fire."

Scanlon stuck his mangled right hand out, six inches in front of Jeremy's face. "When I didn't scream or shake my hand like a madman—because I know that rubbing alcohol burns rather coolly, and if one doesn't make sudden movements, will simply burn off without harming the skin—this didn't seem to satisfy your taste for drama or revenge. While I held my hand steady in the air for all the class to see—because, teacher that I am, I saw an opportunity to instruct your fellow students about certain interesting properties of heat dispersion in burning liquids—you decided to compound your crime, and your ig-norance, by pouring hydrochloric acid on my hand. You said at the time that it was a desperate attempt to put out the fire you had started, but I know better. I know that deep down in your ugly heart you wanted to inflict pain on me, to disfigure me. You wanted to exert the only pathetic form of power available to you at the time—the power to hurt people. And you did. Congratulations."

"Fuck you," Jeremy sputtered. "I don't need to listen to this shit. Go away."

"No, listening to this shit is precisely what you need," hissed Scanlon. And, with a swiftness that belied his age, the old man strode toward the back of the plane and disappeared.

A few minutes later, one of the flight attendants, Myla, asked Jeremy if he might like a bite to eat. Breakfast had eluded him that morning, so the mention of food suddenly made him feel ravenous. A bag of pretzels wasn't going to do the job, though.

"Do you have any *real* food onboard?" Jeremy asked, hopefully. "I haven't eaten yet today—I'm starving."

"How about eggs, sausage, pancakes, some orange juice and a cup of coffee?" Myla cooed.

"You're kidding, right?"

"Not at all," Myla replied. "Or, if you prefer, I could get you some cereal or an early lunch."

Jeremy shook his head in disbelief. "No," he chuckled, "the eggs and all will be fine."

"Eggs over easy, with half the yolk cooked solid, the other half runny?"

Jeremy peered up into Myla's emerald eyes with a mixture of astonishment and longing, for that was precisely how he liked his eggs, and no one—not even, or perhaps especially, his wife—ever seemed to get them right.

"Yes, that'll be perfect," Jeremy confirmed, silently wondering how it was possible for this little airline to turn a profit given that the plane was almost empty and the services so extraordinarily generous.

Five minutes later Myla returned with a steaming-hot breakfast served on what appeared to be fine china. He had learned not to expect much from in-flight meals, but this was not the microwaved glop he was accustomed to—it was a real breakfast, worthy of any Denny's or Waffle House. From the looks of it, they had cooked his eggs perfectly, too, with half the yolk congealed into a solid ring around a pool of liquid yellow, just the way his mother—the only person in the world who ever got his eggs right—used to serve them.

He severed a sausage link in half with his fork, then stabbed the half closest to him and guided it into his mouth.

The moment he began to chew, he realized something was wrong. The consistency wasn't right; not enough resistance against his teeth and too fine a texture for sausage, or any other meat product for that matter. He chewed a few times in that state of alarm that hits people when they suspect that they may have just eaten something rotten. When the actual taste of the sausage hit his tongue, Jeremy wretched involuntarily and spat the offending link back onto his plate like an infant rejecting his first taste of broccoli. He reached for the orange juice to rinse his mouth of the foulness that had enveloped his tongue and was now working its way down his throat like a river of fetid sludge. The moment the orange juice hit the back of his throat, he lurched forward and spewed the juice all over the seat back in front of him. His stomach heaved a few times, and when it stopped, a thin stream of bile hung from his lower lip like a spider web.

Jeremy jabbed frantically at the attendant "call" button above him and wiped the bile from his lips with a napkin. When Myla arrived at his side, her perfect white teeth on display like a necklace of fine pearls, Jeremy coughed a couple of times into his fist and barked, "What the hell is this? This tastes like shit!"

"Perhaps that's because it *is* shit," Myla said, smiling like a beauty contestant. "Your cat Tabby's, to be precise."

Jeremy felt his stomach churn and gagged once more into his napkin.

"And the orange juice is, of course, pee-pee," she said with perky delight. "Hers," Myla said, pointing to the blond-haired woman a few rows away who was just now getting out of her seat. Jeremy looked up and recognized the woman instantly.

"Sis?" he said. "What are *you* doing on this flight?"

Jeremy's sister, Kate, was not one to mince words. "I couldn't pass up the opportunity to give you some shit," she said matter-of-factly. "Not that anything I do from now until the end of time could ever undo all the crap I took from you while we were growing up. Though I have to admit that watching you choke on my urine did have its cathartic side. Oh, and by the way, I have genital herpes and I'm in the middle of a flare-up this week, so watch out."

"I don't deserve this!" sputtered Jeremy. "What did I ever do to you?"

"What didn't you do!?" Kate shot back. "I can't possibly recap an entire childhood of humiliation and abuse, so let's just say that growing up with you as my younger brother was like lying naked in a tub full of broken glass while some little alien fucker in skateboard shoes pokes you with a stun gun to see how much you twitch."

"Oh, come on—don't you think you're exaggerating a little," Jeremy objected.

"It would be impossible to exaggerate the full magnitude of your awfulness toward me," said Kate, folding her arms like a pretzel.

"All right then, so what about it?" Jeremy protested. "You were my sister. Bugging sisters is what little brothers *do*—it's practically the *job description* for little brothers. It's what we're *supposed* to do."

"No, little brothers are *supposed* to sneak peeks at their sister's diary, not make copies of it and give it to all her friends. Little brothers are *supposed* to spy on their sister while she's getting dressed, not set up a video camera and sell the footage to his friends. Little brothers are *supposed* to try to get their sisters to chew pepper gum and smell their socks, not lace their food with Drano or light smoke bombs in their room while they're sleeping. Little brothers are supposed to be juvenile, annoying brats, not terrorists in training!"

Jeremy lifted the plate of food in front of him and handed it to Myla. "Get this stuff away from me," he said. "And while you're at it, see what you can do about getting rid of her."

"You know, Jer-bear, you can't just keep pretending this stuff never happened," said Kate firmly. "It's going to come back to haunt you somehow, some way. You could get arthritis, fibromyalgia, shingles, mono, ulcers, or any number of other ailments. Your immune system could fail. An aneurism could explode inside your brain. You could get cancer. Whether you want to believe it or not, physical illness originates from sickness in your soul. And as much as I think you deserve to have all of those things happen to you, I wouldn't want to actually *see* them happen to you."

"Not much chance of that, since we never see each other anyway," countered Jeremy.

"That's not the point," said Kate. "We never see each other because we can't stand each other. Remember?"

"So? Hating each other doesn't stop other families from getting together."

"Let's not make this a referendum on our family," said Kate, exasperated. "This is about you, and only you."

"Oh is it? Well, I'm sitting here thinking it's about the fact that you just tried to fucking poison me for a bunch of shit I may or may not have done to you as a kid, and that you're fifty-three years old and still whining about how I screwed up your life and turned you into a pussy-lapping lesbo."

"That's not it, and you know it."

"Do I?"

"Yes, and if you don't know it yet, you'll know it soon," said Kate with a hint of mischief in her voice.

"Thanks, sis, nice of you to drop by and brighten my day," said Jeremy, dismissing her with a wave of his hand. "What the hell are you doing on this plane, anyway?" asked Jeremy. "Since when do you fly anywhere, for any reason?"

Jeremy's sister did not answer him; by the time he asked

the question, Kate was already half-way down the aisle to the lavatory at the back of the plane. Myla, who had been standing patiently nearby with Jeremy's breakfast plate in her hand, just smiled at him and headed for the front cabin, her hips rolling to and fro as she made her way up the aisle.

"Bitch," muttered Jeremy under his breath. Then, after a pause, he added: "*Bitches.*"

Jesus, Jeremy thought, can't I get a moment of peace and quiet? He'd been in the air less than half an hour and already he'd been accosted by two of his least favorite people in the world. What were the odds of that happening—on an all but empty flight aboard an airline no one had ever heard of, no less?

From the drink dispenser in the armrest, Jeremy squirted some soda water into a cup to rinse his mouth of the lingering aftertaste from his fecal breakfast. He didn't dare ask for anything else to eat for fear that it too might be tainted. He checked his watch. 10:32 A.M. There was still an hour and a half of flight time before touchdown, so Jeremy decided he might as well get some work done. He'd given the same presentation a thousand times, but the Tierney Brothers account in Dallas was a special one, so he figured he ought to personalize his message a little—stick their logo on his PowerPoint maybe, or make up some kind of tear-jerking story that would have them eating out of his hand.

He flipped open his laptop computer and began poking away at the keys. He had never learned to type properly. Instead, he used the index and middle fingers on each hand to hunt and peck his way through the alphabet, a method that made him look a bit like a Tyrannosaurus Rex, albeit one with bad posture and a lousy haircut.

A few extra PowerPoint slides demonstrating his knowledge of the Tierney Brothers' business wouldn't hurt, he figured, so he opened up his presentation, created a new slide and began typing in some bullet points.

"Twenty-three percent market penetration," he typed, but

when he looked up, those weren't the characters that appeared on the screen. What appeared on the screen, in capital letters next to the first bullet point on the slide, was, "I WANT TO FUCK CANDI."

Startled, he tried to backspace over the words to delete them, but the cursor just glided over the words as if they were made of glass, making them brighter as it slid across the screen. He tried typing over the words, but nothing happened. On the next line, beside the bullet point, he typed, "Fifty percent market penetration possible," but the words that appeared on the screen, in capital letters and bright yellow type, were, "I WANT TO FUCK CANDI NOW!"

Just then, Jeremy heard a voice over his left shoulder.

"Can I get you anything?"

Jeremy glanced up and saw Candi leaning over his shoulder. She must have sneaked up behind me, he thought. Her face was only about a foot away from his now as she leaned over and her magnificent bosom grazed his shoulder. From that position, Candi could easily read what was on Jeremy's computer screen, and Jeremy knew it. He snapped the lid of his laptop closed. "No thanks, I'm fine," he said.

"Are you sure?" Candi cooed.

"No. I mean yes, I'm sure," said Jeremy, flustered.

"All you have to do is ask," Candi said.

"I'll keep that in mind," said Jeremy.

Candi leaned even closer, until her lips were only a few inches away from Jeremy's left ear. "You know—if you keep it all in your mind, your head could *explode*," she whispered, emphasizing the "p" in a way that blew a ticklish puff of warm breath into his ear and sent a melting shiver half-way down his spine.

"Is that work?" Candi inquired, pointing at Jeremy's laptop, "or pleasure?"

"W . . . w . . . work," Jeremy stuttered.

A mischievous light danced in Candi's eyes. "It looked like

fun to me," she said, twirling a few strands of her silken hair with her finger.

Like most middle-aged men with thinning hair and an expanding waistline, Jeremy fantasized constantly about what it would be like to caress the flawless skin of a centerfold, to engage in unspeakable intimacies with a woman half his age, scarcely older than his own daughter—to rub his belly blubber against the firm, athletic flesh of a nameless nymph torn from the smooth, slick pages of a magazine. When confronted with someone who fit that description in real life, however—one who radiated erotic availability like heat from an open oven— he didn't know quite what to do. He was content to follow her lead.

"Why don't you come with me," she suggested, laying an exquisitely manicured hand on his shoulder.

The thought that jumped immediately to Jeremy's mind at that moment was that the services apparently being offered to him were going to cost extra. He couldn't help it; that's the way his mind worked. Whether he was buying a house or purchasing a pack of chewing gum, he automatically weighed the assets, liabilities, opportunity costs, and tangible benefits of any given transaction—then, inevitably, went ahead and purchased whatever it was that had caught his fancy. At the moment, he fancied Candi—and in a sense, he was right, for Candi's services were almost certainly going to cost him more than he was willing to pay.

Jeremy unfastened his seat-belt buckle and rose, as if in a trance, from his seat. Candi locked her sparkling eyes on Jeremy and curled her index finger, beckoning him to follow her. Like a fish tracking a worm, Jeremy moved down the aisle toward the back of the plane, admiring Candi's firm, round bottom as he went. To him, Candi's hips and legs were a kind of poetry in motion, a symphony of symmetry that promised the music and rhythm of pure, carnal release. Not that he'd ever heard such music himself, for his sex life was largely dutiful and perfunctory, no more satisfying on average than a glass of water or a good, long belch. Coupling with his wife had become a joyless chore for the most part, one he avoided if at all possible. Actual sex—the heaving, sweating, grunting kind—was for actors in movies and people from Europe. Truth be known, he was no closer to experiencing it at fifty than he was at fifteen. He had read about it, though, and had seen it on screens both large and small, and so, naturally, he was mesmerized by the imagined transcendence that such frenetic flesh-melding seemed to offer. Once, before he died, he wanted to experience it himself, firsthand, since the powers of gratification in his own hands were somewhat limited.

It did not occur to Jeremy to ask why a woman of Candi's obvious charms would want to lure him to the back of an airplane for an impetuous, furtive grope—only that she had done so, that she was evidently sincere, and that he deserved this little bit of luck, because until then his day—not to mention his life for the past twenty years—had been a complete wreck.

Ahead of him, Candi passed the lavatory and ducked around the corner into the flight attendants' galley. Jeremy followed, his head reeling, unable to fully appreciate or comprehend the strange reality that was unfolding before him. As soon as Jeremy turned the corner, a hand reached out and grabbed his shirt sleeve, pulling him to the side. Candi had wedged herself into a corner out of direct view from the passengers going in and out of the lavatory. No one else was in the attendant's galley; Candi and Jeremy were alone. The hiss of the engines was loud enough to muffle any noise they might make, so a number of previously unthinkable things (at least for Jeremy) were suddenly, alarmingly, possible. Candi had made her intentions clear by opening the top button of her blouse and moistening her ruby lips with a layer of glistening saliva. She pulled Jeremy toward her with such force that he almost tripped and fell. His face mere inches from hers, she grazed his cheek with her lips and her hot breath tickled his ear.

"Quick, we haven't got much time," she whispered.

Jeremy buried his face in Candi's chest and ran his hand up the back of her thigh. Her flesh was not soft and squishy, like his wife's, it was firm and unforgiving, like a football or the head of a drum. Jeremy kissed Candi's neck while his hands searched for some sort of gap in her clothes or clasp he could undo, but he couldn't find one; the armor of her undergarments seemed impenetrable.

"Hurry," urged Candi.

Jeremy didn't know how to go much faster than he already was, but he nonetheless began sliding his hands around frantically, groping and squeezing, looking for a way to get her stockings off while simultaneously bouncing his lips against her neck like a woodpecker in search of a worm. The logistics of removing Candi's stockings while undoing his own belt and zipper and maintaining a sufficient erection to consummate the adventure were formidable. Jeremy was not making progress on any of these crucial fronts, and his frustration soon turned to despair, then to panic as he felt the moment slipping away.

He needed to regroup.

He tried breathing into Candi's ear. He tried fondling her breasts through her sheer, starched blouse. Then he tried to kiss her on the lips.

As soon as his thin, chapped lips touched her plump, red ones, she spat and pushed him away.

"You sick bastard! You'd do it, wouldn't you?!" Candi sputtered.

Dumfounded, Jeremy took a step back and searched his muddled mind for something appropriate to say. Instead, he just stood there, his belt buckle undone, his shirt half pulled out of his trousers, looking at her as if she were a creature from another planet.

"You've got a wife and daughter, for God's sake," Candi scolded. "What in the hell do you think you're doing!?"

At that moment, an elderly woman stuck her head around

the corner. She had brownish-red hair, dyed to keep the gray out, and wore an innocuous skirt-and-blouse combo that fashion writers would kindly call sensible. The woman saw Candi in the corner and said, "Miss, I wonder if I could get some . . ." but cut herself short as soon as she saw Jeremy.

"Jeremy P. Taylor, what in God's name are you doing back here?!" the woman said sternly. "Have you no dignity? No self-respect? Tuck your shirt in, young man, and don't give me that look."

If there was a look on Jeremy's face, it was one of confusion and disbelief. "Mom?" he said, as meekly as a six-year-old. Then, more forcefully, "Mom, what are you doing here? This is ridiculous!"

"Not half as ridiculous as finding you here."

The woman turned and peered back up through the fuselage of the plane.

"George. George! Get back here this instant!" she yelled. "I want to show you something!"

A few moments later, an older man with milky blue eyes and the posture of a camel made his way into the aft cabin where Jeremy, his mother and Candi were standing. The man looked at Jeremy but did not appear to recognize him. He then saw Candi standing in the corner and stared at her two beats longer than Mrs. Taylor apparently felt was necessary. She slapped him on the arm and pointed at Jeremy.

"Look what has become of your son," she said.

The man leaned closer to Jeremy and squinted. "My god, is that you, J.J.? You look terrible." Mrs. Taylor folded her arms and pursed her lips, evidently pleased that her assessment of the situation had been confirmed.

"Your son tried to have his way with me," Candi interjected.

Jeremy's father looked at her and blinked a couple of times. "What went wrong?" he asked.

Mrs. Taylor slapped him on the arm again and said, "What

he means is, we're sorry for any impropriety on our son's part, and hope you can find it in your heart to forgive him."

"I can't do that," said Candi.

"I see," said Mrs. Taylor. She then turned to Jeremy. "Don't you have something you want to say?"

"No, not really," Jeremy replied.

"An apology, perhaps?"

"I have nothing to apologize for," said Jeremy. "She . . ."

"She would disagree with you, I think. Your wife would too, I believe."

"Don't bring Tanya into this."

"Why not? She's the only one who isn't here to speak her mind."

"This is a setup, isn't it?" accused Jeremy.

"A what?"

"You know, a trap—an ambush."

"It most certainly is not!"

"Then what do you call it? A coincidence?"

"I don't know what you mean. To suggest that I—we— somehow had a hand in all of this," his mother said, waving her hand theatrically. Well, it's insulting. It hurts my feelings, if you want to know the truth."

"Mom, your feelings get hurt when the mail doesn't come on time."

"You are as insolent and mean-spirited a boy as ever," said Jeremy's mother. "To think that I gave birth to you, that I raised you, that I nursed you on my bosom."

"Mom, please."

"Only to have you turn out like this."

"Stop it, mom."

"It's more than a mother can bear."

Jeremy's mother then turned and faced the cabin door. On the door, next to a large red handle, an "emergency exit" decal showed a cartoon woman dressed in the same demur fashion as Jeremy's mother, grasping the handle and pulling upward to disengage the door. Seconds later, Jeremy's mother assumed precisely the same pose as the woman in the decal, then jerked the handle up and pushed the door out, as the instructions indicated. There was a loud sucking sound as the seal on the door was broken, then the door immediately disengaged from the fuselage of the plane and fell away like a piece of tissue paper tossed out of a speeding car.

"Mom! What the hell?!"

"I didn't want it to end like this. But . . . goodbye," said Jeremy's mother. She took two steps forward and hurled herself out of the plane, above a vast expanse of nowhere, into the baby-blue emptiness beyond.

"Jesus!" Jeremy cried.

Jeremy's father poked his head out of the open portal and said matter-of-factly, "Guess I'd better go see where she's gotten to." He sighed, then stepped out of the plane as if he were on his way to pick up the morning paper.

And just like that, Jeremy Taylor's parents were gone.

"Now it's your turn," said Candi as she shoved Jeremy from behind. Jeremy tried to prevent himself from being sucked out the same door his mother and father had just exited, but his weight had already been moving forward when Candi pushed him, and there was nothing in the cabin to grab onto. He windmilled his arms as he lurched forward and clawed at the empty air, snapping his fingers open and shut in an instinctive attempt to grasp something that might break his fall. As his body was sucked out into the slipstream of the jet, Jeremy shot his arms out and grabbed the edge of the fuselage where the door had been. A violent wind peeled back the skin on his face and tore at his clothes. He knew he couldn't hold on for long, and at least some part of him realized that he was not going to be able to pull himself back inside the plane, but there was nothing else he could do except hang on for dear life. His eyes stung from the jet's furious slipstream, and his arms felt like they were being ripped out of their sockets. Had he been capable of thinking rationally under such circumstances, Jeremy would doubtless have concluded that letting go was his only reasonable option. But that decision was never his to make. The last thing he saw before his world went white was an exquisitely manicured hand peeling his fingers away from the fuselage one by one like postage stamps until, at last, he had no more choices left.

A numbness came over Jeremy as the world fell away and the emptiness below enveloped him. But the shock of falling was soon replaced by an eerie calm, which then turned to a comforting silence, as if he were suddenly surrounded by a sky full of pillows and snow. In an instant, the terror of falling yielded to the exhilaration of flying. He suddenly felt like he was being held aloft by unseen puffs and currents of air, as if the sky were as dense as water and he was merely swimming through it, happy as a dolphin, free as a bird.

This sensation did not last long, though, for the trees, water, roads, cars and buildings below that had before seemed so distant and toy-like were now growing in size and accelerating toward him at a frightening speed. Jeremy's fleeting sensation of flight was quickly replaced by an acute sense of falling and the encroaching terror of certain death.

Jeremy awoke with a jolt, and before he could catch his breath, another jolt hit him with such force that it felt like someone was pounding his chest with a couple of sledgehammers. He opened his eyes and saw a number of faces peering down at him. There was a tremendous commotion and various people in uniforms, people he didn't recognize, kept coming in and out of his peripheral vision. He tried to say something, but the connection between his brain and his lips seemed to be missing, for he could not move his mouth or tongue. A voice drifted through the chatter and he found himself trying to focus in on it by mentally filtering out all the other noises around him.

"It's his birthday today," the voice said. "According to his driver's license, he just turned fifty."

Two men in blue uniforms slid some kind of board under Jeremy, then there was a lot of jostling and the ceiling began to move. Jeremy was rolled outside and hoisted into what he judged was the back of an ambulance. The doors slammed shut and someone shouted, "Let's get this man where he needs to go!"

A dark-skinned woman with a slight case of acne leaned over Jeremy and put her hand on his forehead. She looked into Jeremy's eyes and half smiled at him in a way that could have been friendly, or not. Jeremy couldn't tell.

"Happy Birthday, huh?" she said, somehow aware that Jeremy could not respond. "I just hope we're not too late," she added, patting him gently on the arm.

She reached to grab a stethoscope off a shelf behind her, and when she did Jeremy's eyes grew wide with fright.

Her name tag read: "Wanda."

* * * * * * *

THE GREAT SPARROW WAR

THE GREAT SPARROW WAR OF 2010 started like so many other wars, with a small incident that touched off sensitivities about a larger issue that raised questions about territorial and political sovereignty, which led to sanctions and a food shortage that sparked a rebellion and ended up in an all-out flurry of total insanity, followed by the emergence of a victor—and finally peace, of a sort.

At least that's how I remember it. Then again, I won the war, so my recollection is not the least bit objective.

It started on a sunny spring day in May. The cardinals were whistling, the robins were singing, and a bunch of other birds were making the noises they do, chattering over each other like a bunch of teenage girls hopped up on Red Bull and Justin Bieber. I was sitting on my back deck, enjoying a morning martini, when my neighbor, Stan, walked out of his house carrying a bucket full of birdseed. I tipped my drink in his direction and he responded with a slight head bob. There was no need for words. We'd been neighbors for fifteen years, and the secret to our neighborliness was avoiding polite chit-chat. He ignored me, I ignored him, and that's the way we both preferred it.

Besides, I hated Stan. He was one of those fastidious little fuckers who putters around in his garden all summer long, weeding and pruning and fussing over what everyone agreed was an absolutely fabulous garden. In fact, I'd heard that exact phrase—"absolutely fabulous"—waft over the fence hundreds of times over the years, because Stan was also one of those socially active little bastards who hosts parties for the singular purpose of showing off his fabulous garden to his fabulous friends—most of whom, I had to admit, were rather handsome.

In addition to his garden, Stan had an impressive collection of birdfeeders: several colorful tubes in various sizes, two huge trays full of fruit and seeds, a special feeder for finches that forces them to eat upside down, and one that looked like a little log cabin. Every other day or so, he hauled several buckets of birdseed outside and proceeded to fill his feeders, using a different kind of seed for each one. Sunflower seeds in this one, a "songbird" mix in that one, safflower and corn over here, red milo over there, and little black niger seeds for the upside-down finches. Then he cut up a few oranges and an apple and put the pieces on a tray, and topped off the hummingbird feeder with sugar water, which he colored red even though the feeder itself was made of red plastic, so the liquid inside looked red no matter what. Stupid Stan.

The whole ritual took at least twenty minutes, and looked tedious as hell—but I will say this, it brought in the birds. Cardinals, juncos, nuthatches, chickadees, waxwings, titmouses, towhees, grosbeaks, robins, finches woodpeckers, warblers—they all congregated at Stan's house and put on what I came to think of as a natural fashion show. Vibrant colors, weird hairdos, bizarre feather combinations—honestly, it was like living next to Yves St. Laurent, if Yves St. Laurent designed clothes for actual birds rather than skinny women who look and eat like them.

Reluctantly, I must admit that I enjoyed the birds. I'm not the sort of person who goes on about how much I love birds and nature and shit. In fact, nature-loving environmentalist dickheads drive me crazy. When these sandal-footed save-the-world types start talking about how amazing nature is and how we all ought to drive less awesome cars and recycle our gin bottles and go hump a tree for good luck because the planet is half-a-degree warmer now than it was fifty years ago, well, it makes me want to start a multi-national corporation and go mow down a rainforest, just to piss them off. I won't, of course—I'll do what I do best: sit on my deck, pour myself another martini, and fart.

So no, I wasn't demonstrative about my affection for Stan's birds. But I did spend a great deal of time sitting on my deck looking out over Stan's backyard pretending not to give a shit about them. Apparently, he noticed—because on the aforementioned day in May he did something he never did: He put his seed buckets down, walked toward me, leaned over the fence and, much to my horror, opened his mouth and started talking.

"Ray," he said, "I just wanted to let you know that I'm moving in a couple of weeks."

Stunned, I did not rise to the bait and express my dismay with words. Instead, I let my eyebrows do the talking.

"My mother is ill, so I'm selling this place and moving to Florida to help her out," he said.

I raised my eyebrows another notch.

"I wanted to ask you a favor," he said.

At that news, arched eyebrows were not enough to convey my surprise. I had to open my eyeballs wide too, as wide as they could possibly go. In fifteen years, Stan had never asked for a favor, and our unspoken agreement was that he never would. And vice-versa. He was breaking that pact now, so whatever it was, it had to be important. Or really super gay.

Turned out, it was both.

"I notice you enjoy watching the birds in my yard, and I was wondering if you might be willing to take my feeders and put them in *your* backyard?" he said. "The new owners don't want them, and the thought of abandoning my birds makes me positively sick to my stomach. These birds depend on me. But if you would agree to feed them, I could rest easy knowing they were in your capable care."

Glad-handing bastard. I scrunched my eyebrows low and

squinted at the little fucker to see if he was trying to pull a fast one. Me, take care of his birds? Me, spend twenty minutes every other day scooping birdseed into plastic tubes? Me, take responsibility for a flock of creatures I don't care about? Me, do him a favor? Please.

He could see that I was conflicted.

"Think about it?" he said. "Because if *you* don't do it, nobody will."

I spent several days weighing the pros and cons of the situation. No matter how many cons I stacked up, though, the fact remained that if I did not agree to take over the feeding of Stan's birds, there would be no birds to watch. And, much as I hated to admit it, I liked those goddamn birds. If all those birds didn't come to Stan's feeders, I'd have to strap a pair of binoculars around my neck and start looking for the damned things up in the trees. I've tried that before, and it's hard work. Quite often it means you have to get out of your chair. Plus, the little bastards are impossible to find, your arms get tired holding the binos up, and you have to set your drink down every time you want to look at a bird. It's ridiculous. Life is much easier when all the birds come to you. So, though I was loathe to admit it, in this particular case the path of least resistance—the path I usually prefer—was to agree to Stan's proposition and start feeding the birds myself.

Giddy with gratitude, Stan spent half a day setting up the feeders in my backyard and explaining in excruciating detail which kind of seeds went into which type of feeder—all of which I promptly forgot. It didn't seem to matter, though, because in those first few weeks after Stan left, my backyard was a damn Audubon society convention. In fact, it looked to me as if the birds were glad they didn't have to worry about messing up Stan's prissy little garden. And for a while I took some degree of pleasure in feeling as if I had provided a refuge for these feathered freeloaders. The theme of my garden is "every weed for itself," and the birds didn't seem to mind the least bit that my juniper bushes weren't planted, or that my chrysanthemums didn't exist, or that my gorgeous hydrangeas were a figment of my imagination.

They loved their new home, or seemed to—until I ran out of food.

Stan had given me a generous supply of birdseed, but after a month or so it was gone. I'm a cheap, lazy bastard, so I didn't get around to buying any more bird food for a couple of weeks. And in that time, the birds disappeared.

Birds, evidently, have no sense of loyalty. They're like every other liberal social parasite; they're just looking for a handout, and when the freebies stop coming, they have no more use for you.

To be fair, Stan had warned me that this could happen if I didn't keep the feeders full. But I wasn't about to spend the kind of money he did on eight different kinds of birdseed. So I went down to Walmart and bought the cheapest fifty-pound bag of bird food I could find. I filled all the feeders to the brim, as instructed, and waited for the birds to return.

But they didn't. That afternoon, the feeders sat there, full and untouched.

When I checked them the next morning, however, all the feeders were completely empty. I'm a late sleeper, so I didn't get outside until about 11:00 A.M., but by that time the damage had been done.

When bird feeders get emptied that quickly, your first thought is squirrels. But Stan had thoroughly squirrel-proofed my whole operation with all kinds of domes and baffles, so if it was squirrels, it had to have been some sort of special-ops team trained specifically for a mission in my backyard. It takes months to train squirrels for that type of operation, though, so I doubted they were the culprits.

Of course, there was always the possibility that the

neighborhood was full of hungry birds because I had neglected to feed them for a couple of weeks. So I filled the feeders up again, and waited.

It didn't take long for a few birds to arrive. But they weren't the interesting, colorful birds I was used to—they were brown and bland and small. They were sparrows, the lowliest, most boring birds on the planet—and pretty soon there were about fifty of them swarming my feeders, flitting and fluttering around, beaks pecking away at every opening, flinging birdseed all over the place like a bunch of winged savages. I tried to shoo them away, but they were back in a matter of minutes, and had emptied the newly filled feeders in less than an hour. When they were done, they perched themselves in a line along the fence, spaced with military precision an inch apart, and proceeded to fluff themselves with an arrogance I found outrageous, given their size and stature in the bird kingdom.

To be fair again, Stan had warned me that this could happen. If I didn't spring for the premium bird food sold at the hoity-toity wild-bird store, he'd said, the good birds wouldn't like it and would go dine somewhere else. Apparently, Stan had for fifteen years been using the finest possible bird seed—the caviar of cracked corn; the fois gras of sunflower seeds; the filet mignon of millet—spoiling the birds in our neighborhood so thoroughly that they had developed a reflexive disdain for regular old bird-food-in-a-bag.

When I told the lady with the gray ponytail at the gourmet bird-food palace what had happened, she clucked her tongue like a chicken and said, "Sounds like you've got a sparrow invasion on your hands. Sparrows are the bikers of the bird world," she explained. "They travel in packs and guard their territory very aggressively. Once they've established themselves, it's hard to get rid of them."

Keeping your feeders full of insanely expensive bird food was important, she explained, because regular old bird food in a bag is mostly "filler" and "junk seed," which is why it's so cheap, and why it disappears so quickly. "Songbirds just won't eat it," she claimed. "Sparrows will pick through the filler to get to something they can digest," she said, "but to other birds, that's like digging through a dumpster in the back of McDonald's to get your dinner. They just won't do it."

Elitist little fuckers. No wonder Stan liked them so much.

So I melted some plastic and purchased a boutique buffet of exquisite seed in order to recreate the culinary experience to which my birds had apparently grown accustomed. Black-oil sunflower seeds from Madagascar; de-shelled safflower seeds from India; cracked corn from fields in the heart of Iowa—I got it all, and served it up to my flock with not nearly as much resentment as I should have had under the circumstances.

But the good birds did not come back. And the sparrows did not go away. Instead, the sparrows raided the feeders full of the crazy-expensive food I had provided, and drained them just as efficiently as they had with the cheap-ass food. As it turns out, sparrows do not gag and puke on premium bird seed; they love it, and eat it in staggering quantities, with no regard whatsoever for its cost, and no visible appreciation of its quality.

To be fair, the lady at the bird-food store warned me this could happen.

"Once you've got sparrows, it's like having a house full of mice," she told me. "Mean mice that the other mice don't want to deal with. In this analogy, of course, the 'other' mice are the birds you want," she clarified. "You know, the colorful, pretty ones."

Sparrows are not pretty; they're ugly. Have you ever seen a common house sparrow up close? I have, through binoculars, and I can tell you that they are not the sweet little tweetie birds their name suggests. They're nasty-looking little devils, with black pinhole eyes and craggy little feet and chipped beaks. The females have markings that look like little flame tattoos, and the males have these little helmet heads that make them look like Wermacht infrantry-men. Sparrows don't smile like other birds, either. Up close, you can see them snickering as they ravage the food supply and fight each other for a spot at the dinner trough. They don't eat like birds, they eat like pigs—brown, beaked pigs with wings. The whole spectacle is disgusting, not to mention expensive and depressing.

All my attempts to dissuade the little bastards proved useless. As I watched these vagrant thugs set up camp in my yard, I found myself developing a grudging respect for Stan. How had he performed his bird magic all those years? What had he done that I hadn't, other than keep the buffet coming? Was it really possible to ruin fifteen years worth of communal bird gathering by interrupting their food supply for a couple of weeks? Apparently so. But I had not given up. Oh no. The sparrows had declared war on me, so I, in turn, was declaring war on them.

All wars are won because one side has knowledge the other side doesn't—whether it's tactics, weapons, strategy, or skill. What the sparrows didn't know about me is that killing them all would not cause me to lose a wink of sleep, and might even provide me with some measure of satisfaction, since it had been a while since I killed anything larger than a mosquito. Biggest thing I ever killed was a deer, and after that disaster—tracking the thing, gutting and dressing it in the field, hauling it out in pieces—I vowed never to kill anything again that I couldn't carry in one hand. A sparrow was just about right—and, though it is sad in retrospect to admit, I looked forward to the battle to come.

In the meantime, my new neighbors had moved in, and I was not pleased with what the new-neighbor lottery had sent me. Any time new neighbors move in is cause for alarm, because you never know what you're going to get. You hope it will be some hot housewife who likes to sunbathe in the nude, or someone who has a nice bass boat. What you don't want is a young couple with kids, or some neo-hippie do-gooders who want to grow their own vegetables and put a giant smelly compost heap on the other side of the fence, five feet from your grilling station. But that's what I got—Trent, a freelance journalist, his wife Jasmine, who sold jewelry on the Internet, and their two noisy kids, Jonah, 6, and Caitlin, 4—both of whom were supposedly "gifted," but whose special talents, as far as I could tell, were screaming very loudly and working their little schnauzer into a barking frenzy.

I hated these people from the moment I met them. In the first two weeks, they had ripped out half of Stan's garden, planted said vegetables and several "indigenous" plants, as they explained to me—because, according to the ineffably idiotic Jasmine, "the monarchs don't have enough milkweed to eat on their migration to Mexico, because of all the farmland and such, so it's our responsibility as a species to help them on their sacred journey."

They installed "rain barrels" to catch the water spewing out of their gutters, put solar panels on the roof—and, in the space where Stan's birdfeeders used to stand, they erected a huge cabana that blocked the view from my deck of just about everything to the south and west. Cabana is just a fancy word for a permanent tent, of course, and it was a big one—12 x 12 feet, with a canvas roof raised in the center to the height of a basketball hoop.

Every evening around six o'clock, Trent and Jasmine got together under the cabana to drink fizzy water and concoct ever more outrageous plans for their new property. All of them involved things designed to destroy my life: a kiddie pool in summer; a hockey rink in the winter; sparkle lights on the trees during the holidays; motion-detector lights at every door; outdoor speakers for their "music"; a batting cage for Jonah; an open fire pit for roasting marshmallows; a koi pond; a meditation garden; a badminton court. You name it, they thought of it—and the stupider the idea was, the more likely they were to do it.

By far the worst idea they had—which I overheard one evening while I was grilling a steak on my side of the fence—was to clear the space along the side of their house, the space between my house and theirs, and use it to raise chickens. I repeat: chickens. Ten feet away from my bedroom window. Which, apparently, they were legally allowed to do, owing to some recent change in the city ordinance that now allows people to do stupid, time-wasting shit in their backyard that our forebears had the wisdom to dispense with by building grocery stores and creating various types of cellophane and Styrofoam packaging. I mean, eggs cost a buck-fifty a dozen, and chicken is like five bucks a pound. How much money can you possibly save by raising the damn things yourself? I don't get it. Never will.

My fury over the new neighbors and their whole insipid outlook on life had been on a slow boil for a while, but it spilled over one day when, as I was enjoying a Stoli martini on my deck, Trent leaned over the fence and asked me for a "favor." As I mentioned before, Stan and I had an arrangement—no favors—and it was clear I was going to have to educate young Trent about the rules of the neighborhood. But, to be kind, I decided to hear him out.

"I've noticed that you have a lot of birds in your backyard," he began. "But I've also noticed that after they eat, as they fly out of your yard, they deposit a not insignificant amount of poop on the roof of our lovely cabana," he said, pointing to the structure. "As you can see, it appears to be a favorite target of theirs, so I was wondering if you might be willing to move your feeders to another spot in your yard, so that our cabana is no longer in their flight path?"

I gave him both the eyebrows and eyeballs.

"How about it? It's a neighborly gesture that would be much appreciated," he added.

I stared at him for a long while, and eventually spoke to him in words both thoughtful and measured. "Young man," I said. "Who in this day and age uses the word 'poop' in a sentence?"

"Well, we have little children, you see, and we don't like to expose them to coarse language," Trent explained.

"But you're talking to me," I said. "I'm a grown man and your kids aren't around, and yet you still use the word 'poop.'"

"Force of habit, I guess," he said, straining to smile.

"Tell you what," I said. "I'll move the bird feeders if you abandon your chicken project."

He crunched his face up into a ball. "Uh, I can't do that. Caitlin, my daughter, really wants those chickens. I can't disappoint her—you understand."

"I do not," I said. "Disappointing children is what parents do."

He broke eye contact with me and looked at the ground, shaking his head from side to side. "Look, I'll help you move the bird feeders, if that's the problem. It's no big deal."

"It's a big deal to me," I said. "I hate chickens. That's the problem."

Ol' Trent apparently wasn't in a mood to negotiate, and he didn't seem to know what to do with an ornery old man who wouldn't listen to "reason." The look on his face was somewhere between disappointment and pain. "We can talk later," he said, then turned around and went back inside his house.

After a few minutes, his mush-brain wife Jasmine came out. "Excuse me," she said. "I know my husband just talked to you, but if I might add something to the discussion. I know you like feeding the birds, but the truth is that providing easy food for them like that just makes the birds dependent on you—and that's not fair to them. It sounds counterintuitive, I know, but truly the best thing you can do for your birds, and the environmentally correct thing to do, I might add, is *not* to feed them. The beauty of it is that if you didn't feed the birds, you'd be solving our little problem here," she said, pointing at the cabana—"*and* you'd be doing the right thing!"

The eyebrows/eyeballs combo spooked her, I think, because she didn't say anything else; she just turned around and went back inside the house.

As I said before, most wars are won because one side does

something the other doesn't expect. Sometimes, the surprise comes in the form of a new alliance, a partnership borne from the logic of the proverb, "The enemy of my enemy is my friend." At least until the common enemy is vanquished, after which things can return to normal.

What Trent and Jasmine didn't know was that I had already started thinking about it, and I was beginning to see my sparrows in a new light—as a secret weapon. From where I sat, his cabana hardly had any birdshit on it at all. But I knew it could have much, much more—and I knew how to provide it. So I beelined it down to Walmart and bought five bags of the cheapest, worst bird food I could find. Then I went to Walgreens and got a couple of jars of powdered laxative. Then I got a big plastic tub and mixed it all together into a nice concoction that I named "Birdshit Bombardier," and filled those feeders full.

In a matter of days, Trent's cabana was half-covered in bird shit. My birds had shat so many shats on it that it was starting to develop a hard, crusty shell. It was really starting to smell, too, especially on those hot midsummer days when the sun is relentless and you just want to sit outside under your cabana and sip cold fizzy water and forget about the fact that your neighbor is an asshole who won't do you a simple favor. But you can't, because the stench is really something to behold, and your delicate flower of a wife simply won't go out there anymore. Neither will your kids. Even your dog doesn't like the smell.

Trent had the police out once, but they never talked to me, so my guess was they told him there was nothing they could, or would, do. By this time, the folks next door and I weren't on speaking terms anymore, which is just the way I wanted it. My birds were free to fly wherever they wanted, they stayed in their house, and all was right with the world.

After a while, however, even I got tired of looking at the mountain of birdshit accumulating on Trent's cabana roof. Birdshit is ugly. It's an icky white mess, and the more of it there is, the uglier it is. The thing is, I was the one who had to look at it all the time, not Trent or his family—so, ironically, I was the one who was annoying myself.

Then I got an even more brilliant idea. What would happen, I thought, if I mixed different-colored dyes into my bird-food concoction to brighten up the scenery?

The results were spectacular! In only a few days, Trent's cabana was covered with psychedelic splatters of red, blue, yellow, and green—a whole palette of colors spreading and streaking in such artful combinations that they put Jackson Pollock's later work to shame. Except that *I* was the artist here—the savant of sparrow shit—and Trent's cabana was my masterpiece. Other people could have the colorful birds, I thought—the so-called 'good' birds—because my bad birds could shit an entire rainbow! Who else could say that?

In order to complete my artistic vision, however, I needed more sparrows. So I bought a birdhouse tower with twenty houses in it, along with half-a-dozen bird baths. I bought a pallet full of bird seed, and refilled those feeders three or four times a day. Pretty soon I had hundreds of sparrows living in my backyard, sunning themselves by the pools I had provided, and generally living large and happy. They didn't mind eating colored, laxative-laced Walmart food—and in exchange for their digestive largesse, I got to watch my masterpiece evolve and grow into a beautifully crap-tastic slab of chromacolor sparrow shit, with ever-more-exciting layers and hues piled on top of each other according to the rhythm and chance of nature, aided somewhat by some carefully applied pharmaceuticals.

Trent tried to voice his objections to me every now and then, but I could see that the fight had largely gone out of him. Every time he walked into his backyard and threw his hands up in exasperation, I just tipped the rim of my glass in his direction and took a sip. Each day, I grew prouder of what I had accomplished. Every afternoon, I took photos to chronicle the evolution of my work, which grew more glorious by the day. Enchanted by the continuous cascade of colors, I sat for hours on my deck, watching the birds fly back and forth, bombarding Trent's cabana with their chromacolor excrement. It was a beautiful spectacle, and I couldn't have been happier.

Then, one day, a huge thunderstorm blew through. Torrential rains poured from the heavens. As the rain came down, it softened the crusty shell of colored bird shit that had accumulated on Trent's cabana roof. As the rain continued to come down, pieces of my masterpiece began to loosen, then ooze and slide down the roof onto the bricks around the cabana. Whole slabs of it slid off and hit the ground with a heavy wet splash, and the colors swirled around on the bricks, with nowhere to go, because that idiot Trent knows absolutely nothing about proper drainage.

The next morning, after the storm, I looked over at Trent's cabana and saw that the roof was washed clean. For a moment I was disappointed, because I had worked so hard to mess it up. But then it came to me: this was a whole new canvas, just waiting for the sparrow-shit artist to impose his genius on it once again. Suddenly, I realized, I had found my purpose in life—my reason for being. In that moment I knew, with a clarity that usually escaped me, that I was a true artist, one who had finally found both his medium and his method.

I began doing research on the Internet to find out if any other artists in the world were doing anything similar. (They weren't.) There were people who made sculptures out of roadkill bones, and people who glued seeds to paper and called it art. There were people who used feathers to make clothes, and people who sewed squirrel pelts together to make blankets. But no one was doing what I was doing: allowing birds to do the work for them. From the looks of it, I had discovered an entirely new art form, a means of expression no one on earth had ever attempted.

Monetizing the idea was the next obvious step. Art collectors will buy anything if it's weird enough, I reasoned. In India, elephants smear paint on pieces of paper and tourists buy them by the thousands, so why wouldn't people pay for an organic birdshit collage? And once the idea caught on, what was to stop me from developing my own line of dyed birdseed? My own brand of outdoor cabana roofs and other types of canvases? Start my own art gallery?

Nothing, that's what. Because this is America, the greatest nation on Earth. In a matter of days, I worked up a business plan and began researching potential investors. My life suddenly had a clarity and direction it had been lacking for some time. Without realizing it, or even bothering to look for it, I had found my true purpose in life, my calling—my *destiny*.

Life is strange that way. I never would have found my calling without Stan, a man I hated for fifteen years. Or without those damned sparrows, whom I now consider my paintbrushes. Or if I hadn't met my insufferable neighbors Trent and Jasmine, who forced me to stand up for the bedrock principle of freedom in my own backyard. They pushed me to the brink of human tolerance, where all good men discover the stuff of which they are truly made—and for that, I must reluctantly thank them.

Like all wars, this one is not entirely over, of course; it has simply moved to a different front. It's about the chickens now— those damned, infernal chickens, which are now installed on the side of the neighbors' house and, judging by the noise, seem to be multiplying in number every other week. But mark my words, I will win this battle too. All I need is another stroke of genius borne of necessity and cunning, which has always been the victor's secret weapon in the timeless art of war.

* * * * * * *

WALK OF FIRE

AM NOT A BIG FAN OF fear. Some people love it, I know—idiots who spend their free time jumping off bridges with rubber bands tied to their ankles, hurtling themselves out of airplanes, navigating treacherous river rapids, climbing vertical rock faces by their fingernails, or otherwise cheating death for their own personal amusement. I am not one of those people, it's safe to say. I figure the odds of life are stacked enough in death's favor as it is; cheating only makes it worse.

When I was a kid, my mother had a pet phrase she invoked to admonish anyone foolish enough to engage in unnecessarily risky activities, such as using a bar stool to reach the peanut butter jar. "Don't tempt fate," she would say, her voice low and raspy from years of doing exactly that with a pack of Lucky Strikes a day. When she really meant it, she left long pauses full of portent between each word—"Don't . . . tempt . . . fate"—so each one had time to sink in.

The curious thing about my mom's pet phrase was that the moment she said it, the very thing she was warning me about inevitably happened. It was as if fate could actually hear her, and if I didn't pay immediate attention it would spring into action just to show me who was boss. That day with the peanut butter jar is a perfect example.

I was eight years old and short for my age. Using the bar stool, an admittedly unstable ladder with four long, metal legs connected to a six-inch disc of plastic on top, I had raided our pantry hundreds of times without incident. That day, however—the day my mother warned me specifically not to tempt the cruel and tempestuous demons who guard the snack shelf—was the day my foot slipped, the stool went skidding across the kitchen floor, and I, eight-year-old Calvin Flynn, knocked my two front teeth out on the edge of the counter and had to be rushed to the emergency room for reconstructive dental surgery. To this day my front teeth are slightly grayer than the rest, as if the shadow of fate has discolored them forever. Every time I look in the mirror I am reminded of that day; it's one of the reasons I don't like to smile.

Given my history and admittedly risk-averse nature, you are perhaps wondering why I am about to walk barefoot across a scarlet ribbon of flaming-hot coals?

It wasn't my idea, believe me. Brian Tilcher is to blame. He is the suck-up in our office who, when asked by our regional sales manager for ideas about team-building exercises, suggested that we all attend a Terry Glaser seminar and do the infamous "Walk of Fire." My suggestion—a trip to Disneyland—evidently wasn't sadistic enough for our manager (who shall remain nameless because calling him by name would imply a level of humanity he does not possess). Until the Walk of Fire suggestion came up, it looked as though we were going to go play another spirited game of SplatBall at the Northdale Mall. But having a marble-size ball of paint explode on the side of your head isn't as painful or potentially humiliating as the Walk of Fire. No one can actually get hurt in SplatBall. But the Walk of Fire—well, it apparently had the right blend of sadism and stupidity to get management's approval.

So here we are.

The coals are burning at a temperature of 1,100 degrees, Terry Glaser is telling us. Or, as Tilcher is whispering in my ear, "Hot enough to fry the bacon off a pig." He, Tilcher, isn't quite as enthusiastic about the Walk of Fire as he was a month ago, when he suggested it. But Tilcher is one of those jock types who prides himself on his willingness to do any jackass stunt imaginable, as long as there is free beer involved.

Terry Glaser is much taller than I expected: at least six-foot-five, with perfectly sculpted hair, and teeth so big and white and straight that it looks like he's wearing dentures. We're at his "sanctuary" in the hills somewhere between Los Angeles and Santa Barbara, having driven up from L.A. this morning. The place is a castle—literally. Part of it is, anyway. Back in the 1920s, William Randolph Hearst supposedly had an entire castle shipped from Scotland, then decided not to use it and his family auctioned it off piece by piece over the years. The parapet ended up here somehow, so what you really have is a standard-issue adobe-and-red-tile California estate with a chunk of medieval castle plastered on to the end. It looks kind of silly, to tell you the truth—like Walt Disney visited for a day and left in a huff.

The bed of burning coals is laid out on the back lawn, five feet wide, thirty feet long, the orange flames having settled into a scorching simmer that looks about as hot as the surface of Mercury. Judging from the bags stacked up on the side of the house, Glaser uses a combination of standard Kingsford briquettes and hardwood charcoal. If this were a barbecue, my dad would at this moment be laying out a few T-bones on the grill, and the hiss of raw meat on hot metal would mean dinner was about ten minutes away, so I better start setting the table, or else.

Unfortunately, it's not a barbecue, or at least it's not supposed to be. The fire can't hurt us, Glaser claims, if we just "believe in ourselves," in the power of our minds to "overcome life's obstacles, no matter how daunting or impossible they may seem." To emphasize his point, Glaser is explaining why there are no ambulances on the premises in case something goes wrong. It's because ambulances are "agents of fear," he says. If an ambulance were present, it would imply that things could go wrong, that we were "allowing the possibility of danger to exist," thereby inviting it to "invade our reality." This was about "confronting our fears, not giving in to them"—and if we don't give in to our fears, there is no need for an ambulance.

The scary thing about Glaser is that if you spend a day with him, as I have just done, this line of reasoning almost starts to make sense. The guy has a way of stringing sentences together that seem to flow logically but always end up in some bizarre place where the rules of law, society, and general existence as you know them do not apply. But before you can backtrack to figure out where he zigged on the trail of reason, where the logical sleight of hand might have occurred, the whole argument disintegrates like your breath on a cold winter morning. In the end all you're left with is a trail of verbal vapor accompanied by a vague sense that he may have said something profound, though you're never quite sure.

"Fear is energy, like everything else, and that energy can be channeled and used in any way you choose," Glaser told us this morning. "In fact, fear is nothing but love in disguise. Take away the mask, expose fear for the impostor it is, and it miraculously becomes your friend, your ally, your lover—that which you love, and which loves you back, rewarding you for having the courage to seek, find, and accept the truth."

See what I mean.

The Truth is one of Glaser's favorite themes. According to him, the world is divided into three different kinds of people: those who "get it," and run their lives accordingly; those who don't get it and never will; and those who will do anything to avoid not getting it, including cough up a thousand dollars for the privilege of walking barefoot across a bed of flaming charcoal. Of course, this breaks down neatly into three basic subgroups: People who have taken a Terry Glaser seminar, people who haven't, and people whose checks to him have already cleared.

I'm being cynical, of course, but I don't know what else to

be, since I don't seem wired to accept everything Glaser says at face value, unlike my colleagues Janice, Lorraine, Kimmy, Dirk, Leon, Brian (whom I've already told you about), and he who shall remain nameless, my pathetic and lame-brained boss.

It started this morning. We all met at the office, where the boss picked us up in a rented mini-van. Kimmy showed up with a box of Krispy Kreme donuts, but wouldn't let anybody have one until we were on the road. Leon protested, claiming Krispy Kremes had to be eaten hot in order to appreciate the full profundity of their cosmic deliciousness. Tilcher, whose gift for innuendo is apparently limitless, remarked that Kimmy could always be counted upon to tease you with something hot and sweet, then leave you cold and hungry. This of course riled Janice and Lorraine, our resident lesbian feminists, who told Tilcher he was a pig and a loser and that he ought to jerk off more often, if that was possible. By the time Kimmy relinquished the Krispy Kremes, they had been downgraded from spiritual sacrament to "okay, but not great" (Dirk's opinion), to "pretty good, but not as good as I expected" (Kimmy and Brian's assessment) to "kinda gross," (from Janice and Lorraine, whose workout regimens put saturated fat in roughly the same food category as hemlock and cyanide). I didn't even try one. When you grow up in Fresno, as I did, you already know there isn't a donut on the planet that can compare with the legendary Dream Fluff cinnamon swirl; it's just an indisputable fact of life.

Now, you would think a group of people who had the independence of mind not to gush mindlessly about the glory of Krispy Kremes would know when they are being conned by a two-bit hustler, but nothing could be further from the truth. Glaser had them in the palm of his hand before the first coffee break, during which no coffee was available, incidentally, only herbal tea and water. The reason for this, according to Glaser, was that we needed to "purify our systems" before the Walk of Fire. I found this ridiculous for a number of reasons, not the least of which was that, during breaks, Glaser always went outside for a smoke. Secondly, aside from Glaser's seminars, I have never heard of a spiritual tradition that doesn't require participants to spend months, if not years, preparing themselves—through rigorous self-discipline, fasting, and meditation—for such mind-over-body rituals as fire-walking. One look at Tilcher will tell you that it would take a hell of a lot more than a few glasses of water to purify *his* system.

However, none of these apparent absurdities deterred my workmates from swallowing Glaser's message whole, like a jello shot at Hooters. Even Janice, who normally has a pretty good bullshit detector, began to tear up when Glaser started hammering us with one of his favorite catch-phrases: "*See* it, then *be* it." He didn't just say this once, mind you. Throughout the day he repeated it over and over, sometimes five or six times in a row, stressing different syllables each time: "SEE it, then BE it. See it, THEN be it. See it, then BE IT!" The way Glaser phrased it, I couldn't help but hear the echo of my mother's ominous words about fate, which could explain why his spiel didn't have the desired effect on me.

By lunchtime, my cohorts were enraptured by the idea that all they had to do to double their numbers was *imagine* selling twice as many copiers a day. Me—I was just hungry. When I leaned over and whispered to Dirk, "That's not imagination, it's fantasy," the guy looked genuinely hurt, like I'd attacked his heritage or insulted his girlfriend or something. Actually, it turns out I'd done something far worse: at that moment Dirk was evidently on the verge of believing in something for the first time in his life, and I had made him feel like an idiot. Making Dirk feel that way isn't too difficult, because he *is* an idiot, but I felt bad about it anyway.

Pretty much the whole day has gone that way for me. Glaser telling us that the secret to success in selling is "faith in the power of YES," me thinking what a load of crap he's shoveling, then looking around to see the faces of Leon, Kimmie, Dirk and everyone else, even the boss, all wide-eyed and attentive, as if they really had drunk coffee at the break and were now sipping from the golden chalice of Wisdom and Truth. Glaser saying something inane like, "To light the fire of desire, go higher!," and me feeling like I'm trapped in a Dr. Seuss book. Glaser telling us what an extraordinary salesman Jesus was; me thinking that it's been more than two thousand years and the man *still* hasn't closed the sale. Glaser telling us to shut our eyes and imagine that the bed of coals we are about to walk on is a soft carpet of cool, freshly cut grass; me wondering why I have to *imagine* walking on grass when there are about five acres of the stuff all around me.

Our boss was the first to walk the coals, for which I have to give him credit, even if he is a Neanderthal shithead. The Germans have a great word, *schadenfreude,* for those times in life when you enjoy other people's pain. I thought I was going to experience a whole ecstatic wave of *schaden*-joy about half an hour ago, but it didn't happen. In fact, nothing today has happened the way I thought it would.

Right before the Walk of Fire, Glaser had us all join hands in a circle and focus our thoughts on coolness and light so that we might stride painlessly through the ordeal "on a cushion of spiritual comfort" and emerge on the other side with our "whole, true selves," having vanquished the twin demons of "fear and negativity." While Glaser spoke, I looked around and saw that I was the only one who didn't have his head tucked down into his chest, eyes closed, like a child praying to keep monsters away. It was almost dusk, and in the darkening sky above I saw a large bird with black wings and a white head circling above us. When I realized it was a bald eagle my heart jumped, but I couldn't tell anyone about it because they still had their heads down and their eyes closed. By the time Glaser finished, the bird was gone.

The mood prior to the Walk of Fire was jovial but tense. At Glaser's request, the boss took his shoes off, then peeled one of his brown acrylic socks off and waved it in Kimmie's face.

She rewarded him with a krinkled nose and a sincere "eeew-wwwww," and, out of nervousness, everyone laughed a little harder than they should have. It broke the tension, though, and Tilcher cracked a pretty good one about how the boss had an unfair advantage because his feet were so big and smelly. The boss got him back by saying something about how by the end of the day Tilcher was going to find out why they called it being "fired." Everyone laughed extra hard at that one because we all secretly wished the boss wasn't kidding.

Most of the time the boss isn't so good-humored. In fact, most of the time he is a complete asshole. If you're the sort of person who believes in karma or cosmic justice of the "what goes around comes around" variety, my boss is the kind of person who ought to wake up with scorpions in his bed, or get syphilis from his wife, or have his toenails fall off from some disgusting fungus. But nothing bad ever happens to the guy. He just goes around yelling at everyone, calling us "maggots" and "worms" (he never uses our real names), making us all miserable, especially me. He seems to enjoy the fact that I hate my job, and acts as if he has a managerial mandate to make me hate it worse. The only thing that keeps me going is that the money is pretty good, and when I'm selling I don't have to spend much time at the office listening to his bullshit. It also irks him that I sell a respectable number of copiers, and I enjoy irking him—which is a little sick, I know. But hey, I'm Irish.

So, because my boss is such an eighteen-karat son-of-a-bitch, I was thinking about half an hour ago that if I were master of the universe, now—during the Walk of Fire, in front of all his little maggots—would be a good time for some karmic payback. The boss was standing at the edge of the coals wiggling his toes while Leon and Tilcher razzed him.

"I wonder what barbecued boss-man tastes like?"

"Like chicken, only fouler. Get it? *Fowl*-er?"

Glaser admonished us all to keep quiet and start concentrating. I was standing about ten feet away, and could feel the heat of the coals on my face and hands. Warm, heavy blasts of air mixed with the cool ocean breeze made it feel as if I were jumping in and out of water, like a dolphin or a duck. Glaser stood on the other side of the coals from me. Heat waves rising from the coals made him appear to wiggle and dance as he spoke. He looked liquid and insubstantial, like a mirage in the desert, and his voice coming through the heat got alternately louder and softer, as if someone were playing with his volume dial.

The trick, according to Glaser, was not to *allow* the fire to burn you—to use the power of your mind to will yourself across the coals on a "cushion of consciousness." But I knew with absolute certainty what happened to people who were foolish enough to tempt fate like this, and I knew that fate was about to teach the boss a lesson. He was going to take two steps and start howling in primordial pain; the bottoms of his feet were going to blister, pop, and melt; the sweet-sick smell of burning flesh was going to waft up from the coals and fill our nostrils; he was going to dance and hoot like a city dweller navigating hot sand at the beach—hot!, hot!, hot!, hot!—and, best of all, the boss was going to be humiliated in front of me, in front of everyone, exposing him for the sham of a person he is, weakening his reign of idiocy and abuse, making a farce out of his whole marine-sergeant façade. The man didn't have a conscience, much less a consciousness, so it had to unfold that way. Fate had no choice but to intervene.

But it didn't happen that way. Not at all. The boss took a few tentative steps, clenching his jaw as he went and breathing loudly through his nose like a winded horse. Glaser encouraged him from the sidelines—"it's just cool, soft grass; think cool, soft grass"—as the boss continued forward, wobbling a little here and there, but maintaining his balance and composure the whole time. He never cried out in pain, never let us see the agony he was enduring. About half way through, he picked up his pace and walked off the coals like it was nothing.

Everyone except me cheered and clapped, and the boss

looked as surprised as we did that he had made it across. "Well, whaddya know?" was all he said. He inspected the bottoms of his feet; not only were they unscathed, they weren't even dirty.

Then Leon tried, and he too made it across. While he was getting cheered, Leon did a little swagger dance thing with his hips and shrugged. "Piece o' cake!" he shouted.

After that, everyone—Kimmie, Dirk, Janice, Lorraine, even Tilcher—Tilcher!—made it through the Walk of Fire without any burns or yelps or other embarrassments. Janice, arguably the most spiritually advanced one of us by virtue of the fact that she does yoga three days a week, even said it felt "kinda nice." Tilcher just went, and as soon as he was done, he stood on the other side of the coals, pointed his fingers at me and started taunting me as if he just made the winning touchdown in the Super Bowl.

Now it's my turn.

I had a couple of reasons for waiting to go last, but now they don't seem so much like reasons as excuses. First, I read somewhere that the real trick to fire-walking is to let the coals burn down to the point where when you step on them, a layer of ash forms between your feet and the flames. As long as you don't keep your feet in one place for too long, you were supposedly okay. Second, I wanted to see what happened to everyone else, because if anyone ahead of me got hurt, my plan was to quit my job on the spot and file a lawsuit against the company for unnecessary employee endangerment. Or something along those lines.

Now, with everyone else having completed the Walk of Fire—even that bonehead Tilcher—I have no choice but to go through with it. But if he can do it, I can too, I figure. So here goes.

I'm now standing about a foot away from the edge of the coals. The wind just shifted, blowing a hot furnace blast into my face, and I can feel a warm, itchy tingle on the tips of my toes. On the other side of the coals, through a shimmering curtain of heat, I can see Tilcher with his arm around Kim-mie. Everyone is laughing and no one is paying attention to me; they're all too proud of themselves, giddy with a fresh sense of accomplishment—a feeling I'm sure is all too rare for most of them. "All right now, Calvin, just focus and walk," Glaser is saying. "Remember, it's just a carpet of cool grass—cool, soft, green grass—just like the grass at home when you were a kid."

I don't know why he had to say that. I'm aiming my left foot for the darkest spot in the simmering coals, figuring that's the coolest place, the place where others have traveled safely before me. Surprisingly, I don't feel a thing, which is a relief because I was sure that . . . now I'm swinging my right foot around and putting it down. My ankles can feel the heat but not my . . . wait a second . . . oh no . . . now I can feel it . . . white-hot spikes poking up through my heel . . . jagged razors slicing through the skin between my toes . . . I'm trying to move my feet but can't . . . can hear Glaser's voice . . . "keep moving" . . . but it's too late . . . I recognize this pain . . . this remorseless force . . . I felt it on the way to the hospital the day my front teeth got knocked out . . . I felt it the day my mother was killed . . . the day my father went to prison . . . that night, three years ago, when I wanted to kill myself but couldn't . . . and I'm feeling it now, growing stronger, it's fury traveling up my legs and into my hips, paralyzing me . . . white-hot . . . inevitable . . . ines-capable . . . because . . . we didn't have a lawn when I was a kid . . . we lived in a goddamn trailer park!

* * * * * *

I'm lying in a bed with stiff sheets, in a room with too much light. It feels like morning. I'm hungry. My feet are all wrapped up in bandages, like a couple of giant Q-tips, and my mouth is dry—dryer than I can ever remember. A middle-aged, moth-erly sort in a blue uniform just walked in. She's calling me "sugar" and sticking a thermometer in my ear. Her name tag says "Maureen."

"Guess we can at least say one thing about you—you didn't get cold feet!" she says, laughing at her own joke.

"How bad is it?" I ask.

"Not too bad. You've got a few blisters on the bottoms of your feet," she says. "You'll have to stay put for a day or so, then you can go home. You're lucky."

"How so?" I ask.

"You're the seventh one this year. Most of the others got it worse than you, though."

"The others?"

"They always end up here," says Maureen. "What I don't understand is why anyone would do such a thing? I mean, it's just so . . . stupid. And dangerous."

"I couldn't agree more," I say.

"Then why did *you* do it?" she asks me, point blank.

"I don't know," I say. "Got caught up in the moment, I guess."

"Well, you get some rest," she says, patting me on the arm. "I'll bring you something to eat in a little while." She leaves, humming a tune I recognize but can't quite place.

I'm looking around the room, but there aren't any flowers—nothing to indicate that anyone in the outside world knows where I am, or cares. There is an envelope with my name on it sitting on the tray next to my bed. Inside is a note from the boss. "Call me on my cell," is all it says. There's a phone on the wall within arm's reach. I grab it and dial. It rings four times, then he picks up.

"It's Calvin," I say. "Calvin *Flynn*."

"Flynn, yeah, hey," he says through a hiss of static, "You okay?" It's the first time I've ever heard him say my name.

"Never been better," I reply.

"A shame what happened yesterday, a damned shame," he says. "Listen, I'm not big on small talk, as you know, so I'm just going to lay it on the line. I have to let you go. I like you and everything, and I wish it could have worked out, but, well, what can I say? It's got nothing to do with yesterday—it's just that, how can I put this? It's just that I'm a hammer, so I need nails, and you're not a nail. See what I'm saying?"

"You're saying I'm not a nail," I say, "and you're a hammer."

"Exactly!"

"Which is odd," I say, "because I see you more as a screw-driver, since you're not so much pounding me as screwing me," I say.

"Now, don't take it like that," he says. "Admit it: you hate this job, you hate me, and secretly you're relieved. We all know you don't fit in here, so what's the point of dragging it out?"

He's right, and I know it, but I'll be damned if I'm going to admit it.

"The point is . . ." but the second half of my sentence won't come. I don't have a point. So I do the next most satisfying thing I can think of and hang up.

There's a knock on my door and a large head with finely sculpted hair pokes into my room. I recognize the face but can't quite—wait a minute—it's *him*: Terry Glaser. He smiles and his teeth seem to stretch half way across the room.

"Hope I'm not disturbing you," he says.

"No, as long as you don't set my feet on fire," I say. He walks over and stands beside me. From this angle, looking up at him, the guy looks about twelve feet tall. His hands are huge, his nails perfectly polished ovals, pink and smooth. I hadn't noticed before, but his skin looks too tight for his face; every time he smiles it looks like his cheeks are going to rip open. Strangely, the skin under his chin is a slightly different color from the rest of his face. Could it be? Yes, the guy is wearing makeup. What a freak.

"Terribly sorry about that," he says. "I felt sure you were ready. I had every confidence you would make it."

"You were wrong," I say.

"Yes, it appears so," he says, a sheepish grin stretching across his taut, tan face. "It's never happened before."

How about that? Internationally acclaimed multi-millionaire and Today-show-approved motivational guru Terry Glaser, whose seminars purport to lead people to The Truth, and whose life is supposedly dedicated to the principle and pursuit of Truth, is staring me directly in the eye and lying through his white-capped teeth! I can't believe it. Actually, I can believe the lying part—I just can't believe he's lying to me, and that I know he's lying. It's like playing poker with someone after you've gotten a peek at their cards; it's kind of funny.

"Tell you what I'm going to do," he says. "Since you were such a cooperative participant, and since you got so close to achieving your goal the first time around, I'm going to let you take my seminar again—free of charge. How does that sound?"

I'm laughing out loud now, but I can't help it. If he thinks I'm going back up there to inflict more pain on myself, he is sadly mistaken. I'm not even thinking of the fire-walking part, I'm talking about the prospect of sitting through another day of see-it-and-be-it stupidity, of watching Glaser coat the room with his sugary platitudes, and even worse, watching other people gobble it up like candy. I couldn't stand going through that again.

"You've got to be kidding," I finally say, trying to catch my breath.

"Not at all," he says, "Absolutely free. No charge whatsoever."

I am doubled over now, clutching a pillow to my chest and guffawing into it.

"Truly, it would be my pleasure," I can hear him saying, and every word that comes out of his mouth makes me want to laugh even harder.

"You're serious?" I manage to say.

"Totally. It's not something I would normally consider," he says, "but in your case I feel compelled to make an exception."

"Well, you can forget about it," I say. "There is no way

I'm going to go back and barbecue my feet again. I was stupid enough to do it once; I'm not stupid enough to do it again."

I have to say, the look of puzzled disbelief on his face is almost sincere. If I didn't know he was a lying huckster, I'd say he was genuinely hurt by my response to his offer.

"But you must try," he says.

"Why?" I counter. "What possible good could come of it?"

Rubbing his hands together kind of nervously, like he's washing them in the bathroom sink, Glaser takes a deep breath and says, "You could get your life back, for starters," he says, serious as can be. "You can regain control of your *fate*."

There's that word—my mother's word—the word that has haunted me my entire life. I was feeling fairly sure of myself until he said it, until he used that specific word. I feel a little off balance now, like I'm a bobblehead doll whose head just got jiggled. But I can't let Glaser know that.

"Just the same, I think I'll pass," I say.

Glaser is looking down at his hands, half smiling and half frowning. "You don't know what you're saying," he says in this soft, tender way that seems totally out of character for him.

"Forget it," I say, a little more emphatically than I intended. "I am not going back up to your house and burning the shit out of my feet again."

Glaser looks disappointed, almost like he's going to cry.

"You don't understand. You have to do it. You have no choice in the matter," he says in a way that almost makes *me* want to cry. "Well, that's not entirely true," he backpedals, "you do have a choice; it's just that *not* doing it is such a bad choice that I feel obligated to do everything in my power to dissuade you from making that mistake."

"Don't worry about me, I'll be fine, as soon as I get these bandages off my feet and get out of here!" I say, pointing toward the hospital door.

There's that look again, the look that says I don't know what I'm talking about and that I'm about to do something really stupid—a look disconcertingly similar to the look my mother used to give me the moment she was about to utter that damn phrase of hers: Don't Tempt Fate. Glaser isn't using those words exactly, but that's what he's trying to say, I'm pretty sure.

"Look, it's not good for either of us if you don't complete the Walk of Fire," he says sort of ominously. "It's not good for you because your life will unfold in ways you won't like and may not be able to accept—and it's not good for me to have you going around telling everyone that I caused your misery and suffering. It'd be . . . uh . . . bad for business."

A realization just popped into my head: Glaser is afraid—of me! He doesn't want me blabbing to all my friends that his seminars are bullshit. The guy is basically a businessman, he's afraid of bad publicity, and he came all the way down off his mountaintop not out of concern for my well-being or to offer me a second chance at completing the Walk of Fire. He's here doing damage control!

"Your business isn't my problem," I say, just to be nasty—and to let him know that I know why he's really here.

He's doing that bowed head thing again, looking down at his hands, dejected, like I've just turned down a marriage proposal or something.

"Okay, have it your way," he says. "But just to make sure there are no hard feelings between us, I'm prepared to give you $25,000 in return for your silence on the matter."

Whoa—I wasn't expecting that one. Up until now I just thought we were going to go our separate ways, and my most ambitious hope was that he would leave sooner rather than later. But now he's throwing cash on top of the deal, which makes me think he's got something to hide; maybe more than the other seven unfortunates the nurse mentioned, the ones he lied about before.

The sales negotiator in me suddenly takes over and I blurt, "Make it $50,000 and you've got a deal."

"$50,000 it is," he says a little too quickly—so quickly that

I immediately realize I could have gotten more out of him. He grabs my hand and gives it three quick pumps.

"Let's do this," he says, reaching into his back pocket for his wallet. "I'll give you $1,000 now to tide you over for the next few days," he says, pulling a thick ream of cash out of his bill-fold. Then he peels off ten crisp, new $100 bills and hands them to me. "In a few days, when you're back on your feet, why don't you come on up to the house and I'll give you the rest. I'll send a driver down to get you. You'll be my guest."

I fan the bills to make sure they are real and not some hallucination induced by the antibiotics and painkillers dripping into my arm. When I look up, Glaser is already half-way out the door.

"Get some rest," he says, "you'll need it," and disappears around the corner.

A minute later Maureen, my nurse, walks in. She discreetly picks up my half-filled urine bucket and dumps it in the toilet.

"Did he offer you money?" she asks as she checks my chart at the foot of the bed.

"Yes," I say, "How'd you know?"

"That wad of hundreds in your hand was my first clue. Of course, it's none of my business how much he gave you," she adds, "but whatever it was, it's not enough. If I were you, I'd sue him."

"I thought of that," I say.

"Everyone does," she says. "But he makes everyone sign a waiver—you too, I'm sure—and he's got enough lawyers and money to make it stick."

I remember signing something back at the office when the whole event was being planned, and I have a sinking feeling it was the waiver she's talking about.

"Oh well, it'll be enough to keep me going until I figure out what to do," I say.

"And what *do* you want to do?" Maureen asks innocently.

"I . . . I don't know," I reply.

She looks at me with kind, motherly eyes. "Well, you're young yet," she says, patting my leg. "You've got plenty of time to figure it out."

A week later I find myself crawling into the back of a black Mercedes Benz sedan. As soon as the door closes, I get this weird feeling in the pit of my stomach, like something momentous just happened—or is about to happen. I've never had a premonition before, but if I had, this is what I imagine it would feel like—like I just closed the door on one part of my life and opened the door to another. If this is a premonition, though, it'd be nice if I could tell whether it is good or bad, whether I end up happy and fulfilled at the end of it—or dead. Honestly, I'm getting the feeling it could go either way.

The good part, at the moment, is that I'm cruising up the California coast on my way to collect $49,000—which, the way I live, could hold me for a couple of years. With that kind of money in the bank, I could do almost anything I want: sleep late every day, go to concerts, travel, read, play tennis in the afternoon, go on long bike rides, keep up my tan, eat out once or twice a week. The works.

The thing that's got me rattled at the moment (and I know this is ridiculous) is that, in movies, the bad guys always drive a black Mercedes. Whenever a black Benz shows up, evil is never far behind. They're like those crows in "The Omen," telling you it's time to crunch down in your seat and brace yourself, because someone is about to die.

Not that I believe in omens and "signs" and stuff like that. That's the sort of mystical mumbo-jumbo my mother was always yammering about. She believed that events in this world happened according to a certain logic, in a certain order, and that most of it was pre-determined—but not all of it—and most of the time you couldn't see the pattern until it was all over. In her view, there was some wiggle room in the gray territory between good and evil, and this space existed for human beings to assert their free will—to nudge the universe a tiny bit in one direction or the other. I'm kind of putting words in her mouth here, but I think she believed that if you paid close enough attention to things, you could see certain patterns emerging and anticipate what was likely to happen next—or at least get a pretty good idea. The trick was in reading the patterns correctly, which, to be kind about it, she did not do especially well.

The thought that's bugging me right now struck me last night, while I was watching "The Sopranos." To put it bluntly, I'm afraid Glaser might try to kill me. I know that's not a rational thought, because in real life people don't go around offing everyone who upsets them. But we're talking about $49,000 here. I keep telling myself that it's not a lot of money to Glaser. The guy's a multi-millionaire; he can afford it. But to me it's a lot of money, and when I bargained him up from $25,000 I wasn't even thinking, I just reacted.

What you also have to understand is that I've spent the past week trying to find out as much as I can about the other seven people Maureen the nurse mentioned—the ones who got toasted before me. All I could find was one extremely short and sketchy newspaper blurb in the *L.A. Times*, and the two people mentioned in the article—a Mr. Ted McNulty and a Ms. Laura Blaine—evidently aren't the sort of people who end up in Internet databases. Aside from the article, which only reported that there had been two incidents in one week at "The Castle House" that had landed people in the hospital, I could find no mention of these folks anywhere on the Web. I tried to pump Maureen the nurse for more information as well, but hospital records are confidential and she's the sort of person who plays by the rules. All she told me was "be careful," and I assured her I would be.

At the moment, however, that seems like a hollow promise. Gliding up the coast in a new Mercedes driven by a guy who looks like he's never laughed in his life, I can't shake the feeling that I'm asking for trouble—that I'm tempting fate in a way my mother would not approve of. I just keep telling myself that he's got more to lose than I do, so stay cool, stay focused, and don't let your guard down.

We are pulling up in front of an iron gate with the head of a lion shaped into the grillwork. I don't remember the gate from the last time I was here, but it's possible I wasn't paying attention. The driver reaches his arm out the window and slips a card into a slot. The gates swing inward and on up the driveway we go.

I'm guessing it's about a quarter of a mile from the front gate to the house along a freshly paved road that winds up through a cluster of oak trees perched on smooth, low hills of golden grass. Dapples of sun hit my cheeks as we drive, and I can't help but think how nice it must be to retreat from the world along this road, to call this land home.

We emerge from the trees into a large circular driveway with a fountain at the center. The statue in the middle of the fountain is another lion, sitting regally on its hind legs, spitting three streams of water out of its mouth. I step out of the car and the glare of the sun off the house's white stucco is momentarily blinding. An old guy wearing an orange Hawaiian shirt with blue flowers on it greets me, and motions for me to follow him inside.

"Mr. Glaser is waiting for you on the veranda, Mr. Flynn," the old guy says. I follow him up a flight of stairs covered in plush white carpet—the softest, fluffiest carpet I've ever felt in my life. It's like walking on the back of a rabbit.

At the top of the stairs, the old guy motions for me to walk past him. I do, and find myself standing in a huge room with a ridiculously beautiful view of the ocean. In the center of the room is the biggest couch I've ever seen, a black, leather, V-shaped number with eight sections, four on each side. In the middle of the V is a bluish glass sculpture shaped like a drop of water, sitting atop an elegant wrought-iron platform. Each corner of the room has a little palm tree planted in a blue ceramic pot, with fronds swaying in the ocean breeze like kites. The reason the breeze can reach the plants is that the entire wall is open to the elements, providing a spectacular view of the Pacific Ocean, its shimmering blue surface stretching into eternity.

Outside, on the deck, Terry Glaser is sitting in the sun, reading the Wall Street Journal. He is wearing Topsiders with no socks, a pair of khaki shorts and a green polo shirt. He looks relaxed, at ease, not at all like someone who might have murder on his mind. The old guy in the Hawaiian shirt walks over to Glaser and whispers something to him. Glaser folds up the paper, slaps it on the table and stands up. He greets me with a big, broad smile, his teeth shining like a beauty contestant.

"Calvin, my friend, how was the ride up?" he says, pumping my hand a time or two more than necessary.

I don't want to talk too much. I want to keep my eye on the old guy and make sure no one sneaks up behind me. "Fine," I say.

"Beautiful, isn't it?" he says, waving his arm theatrically. "Perfect weather. Perfect setting. Everything perfect, just the way it should be, don't you agree?"

I don't like the way Glaser tags on a question at the end of every sentence. Makes it seem as though if you don't agree with him, you're in for an argument.

"Picture perfect," I agree.

"Speaking of which," he says, reaching into the pocket of his shorts, "I've got a good one you might like." From his shorts pocket he pulls a tiny digital camera and flicks it on. "It's of you standing in front of Aslan," he says, showing me the little LCD screen, which he shades from the sun with his massive right hand. Sure enough, it's me standing in front of the lion, just as I got out of the car a few minutes ago. That the guy would take such a picture I find creepy. How many other cameras does he have around, I wonder?

"Aslan?" I say.

"Yes. You know, the lion from the Narnia Chronicles?"

I remember reading the books as a kid, and that I liked

them—I think—but I don't remember a thing about them. "Sure," I say.

"I had him specially made by a sculptor in Florence. Took two months to ship him here, but there he is. I like him because in the books, Aslan is the one who makes everything possible. If you remember, he opened his mouth but didn't roar—he sang a song, the most beautiful song ever heard, and Narnia was born. The three streams of water coming out of his mouth symbolize Beauty, Truth, and Honor, because those are the principles I believe in. I believe that each human being is the creator of their own destiny—their own world, if you will—just as Aslan was the creator of his world. Don't you agree?"

No, I don't. If you ask me, the one who made Narnia possible was C.S. Lewis, the guy who sat down in front of his typewriter and thought it all up. Aslan wouldn't have been able to create a toadstool without him. But I don't feel like getting into a philosophical argument with Terry Glaser. I've heard enough of his drivel to know what a slippery slope that is.

"You could see it that way, I suppose," I say.

"You see it differently, then?" he says with a hint of combativeness in his voice.

"No, I just meant there are different ways of looking at things," I say, "and that's one of them."

"What's another one? How do you see it, for instance? I'm curious," he says. I can see that he is enjoying watching me squirm.

"I don't know," I say, fumbling for words. "I mean, it's just a story, so I guess you can take it as far as you want to."

"Just a story?" he says. "Like the Bible is a bunch of stories?"

"Yeah, like that, sort of, I guess," I say, sounding like an idiot even to myself. "It's open to interpretation."

"Is it?" Glaser says with a strange look on his face, like he knows something I don't.

The old guy arrives with a pitcher of iced tea and pours me

a glass. "Are you hungry? Would you like something to eat?" Glaser asks. I shake my head no.

"Want to get right down to business, do you? No small talk. Just hand over the money and run, is that it?"

"Preferably, yeah," I say, trying to sound like I'm not losing my nerve. The old guy has disappeared. For all I know he's got a gun pointed at my head this very moment.

Glaser leans back in his chair and folds his hands behind his head. "Well, you're going to have to put up with me for a little while longer, because it would be irresponsible of me not to at least try to get you to change your mind."

"You can talk all you want, but I'm still walking out of here with $49,000," I say firmly. "That was the deal."

"Indeed it was," he says. "And I have no intention of depriving you of your money if, after we're done, that's what you decide you want."

"No games, either," I say, trying to sound tough, like I mean business.

"Of course not," says Glaser. "This is most definitely not a game. Which is why I am still prepared to offer you another opportunity to complete the Walk of Fire."

I can't help but laugh. "You've got to be kidding," I say.

"Not at all," he says, suddenly looking very serious. "Trust me, the last thing you want to do is go through the rest of your life having only partially completed the Walk of Fire."

"Why's that?" I ask, but I'm not really interested in the answer.

"Because not completing the Walk of Fire is—how should I put it?—extraordinarily bad luck," says Glaser. "Bad things tend to happen to people who don't see it through completely. I don't know precisely why; I just know that it happens. *Things* happen. Unfortunate things. Sometimes truly awful things."

"What sorts of *things*?" I press.

Glaser takes a deep breath and says, "Who knows? Car accidents. Heart attacks. Weird, incurable diseases. Strokes.

Power-tool mishaps. Drug addiction. Lost jobs. Insomnia. Could be anything really, and that anything could feel like nothing, until it's something, and then it's usually too late. Do you follow?"

No, I don't. To me, this sounds like a threat. I swivel my head around to see if anyone is sneaking up behind me, but there's no one there—just a vast expanse of clean blue tile. Out of the corner of my eye I can see the edge of the castle parapet poking up over the roof line, and I make a mental note that it would be a good place for someone with a rifle to hide.

"You look a little jumpy, Calvin," says Glaser. "Is everything okay?"

If he's planning to kill me, I figure my best chance at surviving is to call his bluff right now.

"If you're thinking of killing me so that you can keep your money, think again," I say in the most authoritative voice I can muster. "I've told at least six people exactly where I am today, including my uncle, who is a lawyer," I lie. "If I'm not back in the city by sundown, they've been instructed to call the cops, so there's no way you could get away with it."

Glaser looks genuinely stunned—a little hurt, even.

"Is that what you think? That I'm going to kill you?" Glaser says, then busts out laughing, like I've just told him the world's funniest joke. Finally, he says, "Calvin, I like you. You're an up-front, honest kind of guy who says what's on his mind, and I admire that. So I'm going to be just as up-front and honest with you as I can be. The fact is, if you don't complete the Walk of Fire, I won't need to kill you."

I don't like the sound of that.

"You're just trying to scare me," I say.

"I wish it were that simple," says Glaser. "But you are correct, I am trying to scare you. I'm trying to scare some *sense* into you."

I don't like where this is going, so I say, "What makes sense to me is for you to give me my money so that we can go our separate ways."

Glaser is staring through me with his ice-blue eyes, as if they are some kind of deadly freeze ray he has heretofore refrained from using.

"How about this?" he says. "How about I pay you another $50,000 if you agree to try the Walk of Fire again?"

The soles of my feet are suddenly aching, and my hands are cold and sweaty. I quickly calculate the pain-to-profit ratio of this offer and decide to go with the safe bet: $49,000 and a short goodbye. "No way," I say.

Glaser looks more desperate now—more *urgent*. "You're not making this easy," he says, rubbing the back of his neck with his big, smooth hands.

"I don't see how it could be any easier," I say. "Just give me the money and I'll be on my way."

"It's got nothing to do with the money," Glaser says, his face a little contorted now, as if he has some stomach gas that's causing him pain. "It's about your soul—or what might happen to your soul if you don't complete The Walk."

Here we go, I'm thinking—he's going to go off on some pseudo-mystical rant full of ethereal pronouncements denouncing the heathen who don't believe in The Truth According to Terry Glaser. I am about to be showered with aphorisms, buried in jargon, drowned in a vat of sentimental sap. Gassy nothing-words are going to start gushing from his mouth like water from a broken faucet; ideas for my self-improvement are going to start filling the air like a cloud of toxic gas, slowly suffocating me with their relentless idiocy.

But again, what I expect doesn't happen. Instead, Glaser leans toward me and says, "Look, Calvin, here's the deal: this Walk of Fire thing isn't some game you can choose to play or not—it's real. And by 'real' I mean it represents a force that, believe me, you do not want to reckon with."

He's saying this with a straight face, so I assume he's serious.

"To tell you the truth," he continues, "I myself don't know entirely how it works. I learned the technique from a gypsy friend of my grandfather's. The old man died before he had a chance to teach me everything, so all I know is what he showed me. That's just enough to do what I do, but not much more. And for most people, that's enough. I get them in a room, pump them up, get them feeling good about themselves, throw in a little light hypnosis and bam, they're ready to walk the coals.

"And you know what? It works. I can't believe it myself sometimes. All kinds of people come up here, unremarkable people stuck in dead-end jobs they hate, suffering through lives that lack form and momentum, much less meaning and purpose. Then they walk the coals, and I'll be damned if it doesn't change them. None of them believe they can do it when they arrive, but when they finally do it—when they survive an experience they thought was impossible only hours before—it *transforms* them. It literally turns them into different people—people with the courage to confront the impossible and overcome it; people who realize that fear isn't something that needs to overwhelm and paralyze them; it's not something immutable—it's something they have power over, something they can change. Once they realize that, fear is like silly-putty in their hands. When they leave here, they believe they can do anything—at least for a while. For most of them, getting through the Walk of Fire is the most profound experience of their lives—the closest they will ever come to experiencing an actual miracle."

Glaser lets the word "miracle" hang in the air like a party balloon. He's glaring at me with those icy blue eyes of his, waiting for me to say something, to respond to this shamelessly self-serving testimonial. But to me, trusting Glaser to tell the truth about his seminars is like trusting Ronald McDonald on the nutritional value of a Big Mac.

"Well it didn't work for me," I say. "Go figure."

"That's exactly what we have to do," says Glaser, smiling. "We have to figure out why it didn't work for you."

"It didn't work for me because the whole thing is bullshit!" I suddenly find myself shouting. "You fill these people full of crap all day long. You tell them how powerful and special they are, how they can guide their own destiny, how everything in their lives has led up to this one special moment—how it was no accident they broke their leg when they were ten or cracked up their parents' car when they were a teenager, or had to work at that shitty sales job for fifteen years to feed three bratty kids and pay alimony to the shrew who divorced them, or got hepatitis from some oyster they ate at a Red Lobster one night—because destiny has led them to your doorstep, where they earn the special privilege of paying you a grotesque amount of money to risk serious personal injury. The sick thing is, they *do* believe you! Just like they believe that if they sell a few more widgets every week they'll succeed; if they marry and have kids they'll be happy; if they buy an Acura instead of a Kia they'll be cooler; if they drink Coke instead of Pepsi they'll be more real; if they eat Wheaties instead of Fruit Loops they'll run faster; if they drink Bud Light some chick with 38 double-D boobs will give them a blow job! The reason it didn't work for me is that I'm not stupid! You can't sit me in a room and spoon-feed me that shit. I'm not that gullible."

Glaser takes a sip of iced tea and then holds the glass up to the sun and studies it for a few seconds.

"Strange, isn't it, that a beam of light can travel millions of miles through space only to end up bouncing off an object and into our eyes, then it's gone? Yet isn't it also strange, just like you said, that two people can be looking at the same thing, illuminated by identical beams of light that have traveled parallel to each other until now, and see totally different things? To you, these ice cubes in my glass may be nothing but frozen chunks of water, with certain properties of coolness that one comes to expect from drinking thousands of glasses of cold beverages.

To me, they may signify something else entirely—I might see faces in the curvature of the cubes, or detect hidden subliminal messages, see things that other people might maintain aren't really there.

"Or," he says, suddenly pouring his iced tea all over the table, "these ice cubes may just be ordinary pieces of . . ."—he picks one up and holds it up to my nose—"plastic," he says, tossing the ice cube in my lap.

I pick it up and, yep, it's plastic.

"The fact is, I don't like cold drinks because they make my teeth hurt," Glaser says. "But I do like the way ice cubes look in a glass. I like the way the sun shines through them and creates little rainbows. So, plastic ice cubes are my compromise."

The guy is even more of a freak than I thought. But the look on my face must have told him that I am completely and utterly confused, not to mention tired of listening to him. I just want to get my money and go home.

"You have no idea what I'm talking about, do you?" Glaser asks, pointedly.

"None," I say. "So you prefer plastic ice cubes to real ones. So what?"

"So, we're trying to figure out why you burned your feet so badly that you had to go to the hospital, when all your friends—whom I assume you consider less intelligent and more gullible than you—all made it through the Walk of Fire, no problem."

"Tell you what," I say. "If you give me my money, we can forget it ever happened, with no hard feelings. How about it?"

"The puzzling thing is," Glaser continues, ignoring my proposal altogether, "and let me add that I also find it fascinating and somewhat problematic—is how you could burn your feet when there was no fire?"

Now he has me stumped, and a little alarmed.

"What do you mean?" I ask.

"I mean," says Glaser, "that it's impossible for anyone to burn their feet during the Walk of Fire, because there *is* no fire.

It's a trick, if you must know. The only thing that touches any-one's feet is a warm piece of Plexiglas covered with ash. Beneath the ground there are eight high-powered digital projectors that use mirrors to project an image of burning coals onto the Plexi-glas, which acts as a kind of screen. We pump hot air through vents located around the perimeter of the walkway to make it seem as if the coals are giving off heat. As you've seen, the ef-fect is quite convincing. All of which explains why most people complete the Walk of Fire without incident. But the question remains: How did you burn your feet? Or, perhaps the better question is, why?"

I suddenly feel sick to my stomach. He's bluffing, I try to convince myself, but I truly don't know what to believe. The ground feels like it is shifting under me, as if an earthquake has just occurred, making me feel off balance and vulnerable.

"Look, Calvin, the fact is, I'm a businessman," says Glaser. "I can't afford to get sued by every scumbag who thinks his hotshot personal-injury attorney can squeeze a few-hundred grand out of me. More to the point, I can't have people like you around trying to shake me down every week. It's bad for business. My shareholders don't look favorably on that sort of thing."

It's now early afternoon and the sun feels twice as hot as it did just a few minutes ago. In my mind I race through every-thing I know or think I now about Glaser, searching for a foot-hold on the truth, trying to remember some crucial but elusive detail that might prove Glaser is lying.

"What about the charcoal bags on the side of the house?" I blurt.

"For show, mostly," says Glaser. "To make people think the coals are real. And believe it or not, I do like to barbecue every now and then."

Still, I am not willing to accept Glaser's explanation. When I walked the coals, I did it just like everyone else—apprehensive but determined, doubtful that I could do it yet unwilling to accept the possibility that I couldn't. Why, that day, was I the only one whose feet got scorched?

"What do you think happened that day?" I ask. "Do you think I faked getting burned somehow?"

"No, I don't think you faked it," Glaser says. "I think that, far from being the cynical skeptic you pretend to be, you wanted to believe in my message so badly that your mind burned your feet for you. When you attempted the Walk, your belief was so complete that your mind couldn't accept another reality—or, to put it another way, your imagination momentarily created a reality that wasn't there."

"You're saying I hallucinated the whole thing?"

"No, your burns were definitely real," says Glaser. "What I'm saying is that for some reason you may have wanted—or needed—to burn your feet, so much so that your mind would not allow any other outcome."

"That's crazy!"

"Is it?" says Glaser. "Let's see: Ever since you got out of college you've been working for someone you hate, doing a job that bores you, trying to figure out what your next move will be, but you have no idea what you ought to be doing with your life and no idea how to figure it out. You show up here for a seminar that you figure is going to be a waste of time, but your subconscious mind recognizes an opportunity even if your conscious mind does not. Your subconscious knows that if you keep going in the direction you're going, you're likely to fry yourself in a much hotter fire, so it seizes the opportunity to singe you a little in order to get the larger message across. And let's face it, up until about five minutes ago, you thought you were going to walk out of here with $49,000 in your pocket and a reprieve from having to make that hard decision about what to do with your life. So you see, it almost worked."

A wave of anxiety just crashed in my stomach, which is now a roiling, peptic volcano.

"So, you're not going to give me the money, is that it?" I say.

"Actually, I'm going to do better than that," Glaser says, smiling. "My offer to give you the $49,000, plus another $50,000 if you're willing to do the Walk of Fire again, still stands."

"Let's do it," I say without hesitation. "Fire up the projectors."

"The catch is, this time you have to do it for real," says Glaser.

"What do you mean, 'for real'?" I ask.

"I mean with real coals," says Glaser, his voice low and cool. "Now that you know it's a trick, it obviously won't work—there's nothing to be afraid of anymore. If you want the psychological benefits of the exercise, you have to be willing to walk through your Wall of Fear. Walking the coals—real or not—is relatively easy. Overcoming your fear is the hard part."

I must look as pale and frightened as I feel, because Glaser is suddenly looking at me with an expression of pity that's almost paternal.

"Now, don't start to panic on me," Glaser says. "I probably shouldn't tell you this, but walking real coals isn't all that different from walking illusory ones. In fact, I used to use real coals. Remember, I learned this technique from an old gypsy, and believe me he used real wood—usually a combination of oak, ash, and birch. Later, when I learned that it didn't matter whether the coals were real or not—because the outcome was the same—I adapted my own technique, with a little help from modern technology. And even then I did it primarily to lower my insurance premiums. It was a logical business move."

I must not look very convinced, because Glaser is leaning toward me now, folding his hands together, with his elbows on his knees. For a moment he had what looked like a mischievous twinkle in his eye, but that's gone and has been replaced by a look of genuine concern.

"Calvin, I know this is nerve-wracking. But the fact of the matter is, you don't have much of a choice," Glaser is saying. "I'm going to share some more information with you, because I think it's in your best interests to know the truth. The truth is, I lied to you when you were in the hospital the other day. You aren't the only one I've offered this deal to; there have been others. I will also tell you that none of the ones before you accepted my offer. They were all smart, independent-minded people—like you—who thought they could ignore the challenge posed by the Walk of Fire and return to their normal lives, as if nothing had happened. Unfortunately, they're all dead now—all victims of untimely accidents and illnesses that can only be attributed to the cruel hand of fate. I don't know exactly why they had to die. I only know that they did, and if you ask me, it's because they chose to ignore their fear rather than confront it. You don't want to make that same mistake, do you, Calvin?"

Something about the situation suddenly strikes me as funny and I start to laugh. "Those are my choices?" I say, no longer trying to hide my dismay. "Almost certain tragic death or the Walk of Fire?"

"The Walk of Fire and $99,000," Glaser corrects me. "But perhaps that's not enough to persuade you," Glaser adds. "Tell you what. I'm a very rich man, and I don't have any children, so the amount of money doesn't really matter to me. What do you say I kick the offer up to a million dollars? Does that make your decision any easier?"

A million, did he say? That much money is almost beyond my comprehension. I can hardly imagine it without the help of one of those *USA Today* perspective charts—you know, the ones that show how high a million Oreo cookies would reach if you stacked them next to the Empire State Building. After thinking about it for a minute or two, though, it occurs to me that a million dollars isn't all that much money—especially to someone like Glaser, whose personal worth is, if I recollect accurately, somewhere around $780 million. I also remember reading that this isn't Glaser's only house—he's got five more: three in the U.S., one in Europe, and one somewhere in the Caribbean. I'm sure many people would say take the money and run, but a million is only, what, five- or six-hundred thousand after taxes? I don't know why, but I suddenly want—no, I *need*—more.

"Throw in this house and you've got a deal," I say—and as I'm saying it, I realize that, yes, that's what I really want: his money, his life—*and* his goddamn house. I want it all, because my parents were trailer trash, my prospects at the moment are iffy at best, and this may be the only chance I get in this lifetime to play for stakes this high.

"My *house*?" Glaser repeats, and suddenly he too is laughing. It's hard to tell what he's thinking now. His smile hides his eyes, and he's all teeth at the moment, white, shiny, and straight. He's shaking his head as if he can't believe I would have the guts to throw his house into the deal. A swirly feeling goes through my stomach as I realize that he might just decide to renege on the whole offer and send me on my way, releasing me to my doom—a doom I suspect he would have some hand in engineering. If he wanted to kill me, though, I figure he wouldn't waste this much time negotiating with me. Either he genuinely means what he says, which I'm starting to believe may actually be possible, or he's got some secret that he's willing to pay handsomely to protect or hide.

"Calvin, I like your style," he says at last. "You don't have a pot to piss in, or even a clue what to do with your pathetic excuse for a life, and you're up here throwing chips on the table like a wild man, hoping I'll get scared and fold. I have to admire that. You're ambitious, and you're trying to make the most of the opportunity before you, even though you have no cards and no idea what game you're playing, or even with whom you're playing it."

One thing I learned selling copiers is that when the final offer is on the table and you're trying to close the deal, for God's sake don't open your mouth and blow it. Shut up and let him talk himself into the deal, I tell myself. Then Glaser stands up and stretches his arms. I can't tell if this is a good sign or a bad one.

"Walk with me," he says.

Together, we stroll along a brick path to the base of the castle portion of the house. Up close, this part of the house is much larger than I thought. Glaser opens a giant, creaky oak door and motions for me to step inside. It takes a few seconds for my eyes to adjust, but when they do I see an exquisitely furnished room with fat red leather chairs, a variety of medieval weaponry on the walls, and a bar stocked with hundreds of bottles of every conceivable kind of liquor. Behind the bar, above the liquor bottles, is a stained-glass window with the head of a lion outlined in purple, green, and red.

"What do you think?" Glaser asks me.

"Pretty cool," is all I can think of to say, but what I'm really thinking is that the place is magnificent, like one of my weirdest fantasies come true. Glaser repeats the whole Hearst-didn't-want-it-so-it-ended-up-here spiel almost word for word the way he tells people in his seminars. Then he tells me how he had it converted into his guest quarters, and rattles off a bunch of names of people who have stayed here: Burt Reynolds, Arnold Schwarzenegger, Billy Joel *and* Christie Brinkley, Tiger Woods, Wolfgang Puck, Ted Koppel, Katy Couric, Jay Leno, Tom Cruise, former president Jimmy Carter and Bill Gates, to name a few—all of whom, according to Glaser, had completed the Walk of Fire, and whose lives were supposedly transformed by the experience—for the better, he assures me. Then he realizes he's babbling and cuts himself short.

"What I really brought you here to tell you is this," he says: "You're an interesting fellow, Calvin—you won't walk the coals, but you're not afraid to ask for what you want, and I admire that. I could use someone with your abilities—your drive—on my team. I'm not prepared to give you my entire house—that's ridiculous, as I'm sure you know. But what would you say if, after this is all over, I were to offer you a job?"

This I did not expect.

"You could live in the castle here," he says, waving his arms around, "and you could have the run of the place when I'm not here, which is about forty weeks out of the year. Don't worry, I'll still give you the million—but if you work for me, you would then be in a position to invest your million dollars rather than blow it on drugs and girls and whatever else you kids do to kill time these days. You'd be set for life, in other words, and you'd have a job, an investment portfolio, and a fairly decent place to live. How does that sound to you?"

All of a sudden, Glaser doesn't seem like such a bad guy anymore. I mean, what would you do if someone offered you a million dollars, a star-studded seduction palace and gainful employment, all in one breath?

"What would this job entail?" I ask.

"Think of it as an apprenticeship," he says. "First, you'd have to learn the business, then you could help out with planning and scheduling—and if all that works out, you could help develop new business opportunities for the company. My seminars and speaking engagements are only part of the business. I've also got books, tapes, videos, online catalogues, a clothing line, a chain of health spas, and a few other ventures I'm not at liberty to discuss at the moment. But you can learn about all that in due time. What do you say?"

How the ball suddenly got in my court, I don't know. It all sounds too good to be true, and if there's one thing my mother drilled into my head as a child, whenever anything seems too good to be true, it usually is. But what I'm starting to think is: screw my mother and her useless, woe-is-me, you-better-be-careful bullshit. Screw her attitude that anything good in this life has to come with an equal dose of bad. Fuck the idea that the other shoe always has to drop, that whatever goes up must come down, that fate will always kick your ass in the end. No wonder her life didn't amount to shit; she wouldn't let it. She spent her whole sad excuse for a life looking for the next bad thing to come around the corner. And you know what? It eventually did, in the form of my father, with a baseball bat in one hand and a bottle in the other, on a night when he wasn't in the mood to be reminded by her what a loser he is.

"Can I think about it?" I ask.

"I'm afraid not, Calvin. This is a one-time offer, take it or leave it," says Glaser.

I'm thinking how much fun it would be to invite Kimmy up here—how there's no way she could resist me if she knew I had a million dollars in the bank and lived in a place like this. As soon as that thought flits through my head, though, I find myself thinking that Kimmy is strictly minor league, not worth the effort. If I lived here, there isn't a beach babe in California who wouldn't succumb to my charms. I'd be invincible, a veritable superhero of seduction who would use his power to rescue beautiful women from the evil clutches of Frat Boy, Geek Guy, and Surfer Dude.

"I'll take it," I say, and I mean it. I want this to happen. I want to put an end to my life as it was before, a life that was becoming a tedious march into meaningless oblivion.

"Fantastic," says Glaser. "Now all you have to do is complete the Walk of Fire—for real this time."

I'd forgotten about that part.

"Is that really necessary?" I ask. "I mean, I'd work just as hard either way, I promise, so what's the big deal?"

Glaser smiles a little and says, "The big deal is, you'd be working for me. Surely you can see that it would be hypocritical of me to encourage folks to cross the Walk of Fire if I can't even get my staff to do it? No, everyone who works for Glaser Enterprises must complete the Walk of Fire—it's a non-negotiable requirement of the job."

"Everyone?" I repeat, just to clarify.

"Everyone," he says.

I'm feeling cornered, maneuvered into a situation where I have no choice. I have to believe it's illegal to require job candidates to prove their worth by making them walk across a bed of flaming-hot charcoal. But this is no ordinary job offer, so I guess I shouldn't expect an ordinary interview. I need time to think.

"Fine then, what do you say we do it, oh, two weeks from today, after my feet are fully healed?" I say, trying to buy some time. When I was in Boy Scouts, they sold this goop at sporting goods stores to toughen up the callouses on your feet before a hike. I figured two weeks would give me time to do that or think of a better way to protect myself. Because, tempting as it is, and despite the fact that I want what Glaser is offering now more than ever, my feet were still tender from my last attempt—over Plexiglas!—and I really, really don't want to go back to the hospital. Maureen the nurse would never forgive me. There also is the small issue of pain, blinding and merciless, ripping through my body like a thunderbolt. I'd prefer to avoid that, too.

"I think it would be better for both of us if I we just got it out of the way, don't you?" Glaser says.

"No, I don't!" the look on my face must be screaming.

"Let me put it another way," says Glaser. "It's now or never."

God I hate ultimatums, especially the way they have of limiting your options.

"Trust me on this, Calvin, the Walk of Fire is not that big a deal," Glaser adds. "The biggest obstacle is not the coals, it's your mind. Control it, and you control the outcome."

I nod as if I know what he means, and Glaser takes it as an acknowledgement that I am ready. I'm not, but my mind feels paralyzed, unable to form a coherent thought or resist Glaser's entreaty to follow him. Glaser leads me out of the giant oak door and around a path to the back of the house. It's a warm day, but the breeze off the ocean feels refreshingly cool. We turn a corner and I see the old guy standing in front of what looks like a giant bonfire, orange and glowing, sparks and cinders shooting high into the air.

"Edward has prepared the coals for you," Glaser says matter-of-factly.

Suddenly I can feel my heart beating in my ears. So, I think, he was expecting this! He knew this was going to happen—that I would be unable to resist his offer. I can't help but feel manipulated, but by the same token I know that I am the one who let it happen. I am the one who came to the negotiating table with one set of terms and decided mid-stream to go for a better deal. I could just as easily walk away from it all right now, I tell myself: take my money and go. But somehow I already understand that it would never be that easy, that other obstacles would present themselves if I went that route—other unforeseeable circumstances that, in their own way, would be just as perilous and foreboding.

The old man—Edward, was it?—is using a garden rake to spread the coals out into a fat ribbon of fire. Glaser and I watch in silence for a few minutes as Edward rakes the coals, taking care to space them evenly. Instinctively, I begin looking for signs that this too may be a trick—convinced as I am that if Glaser can fool people one way, he can surely fool them in other ways. Unfortunately, the coals feel all too hot and real.

"Don't you have to do some sort of hypnosis on me for this to work?" I ask.

"I've been preparing you all along," says Glaser matter-of-factly. "The technique is simple. I'd be happy to teach it to you someday, when you're ready."

"I don't know if I'll ever be ready for this," I say, to let him know that I still have my doubts.

"It's all about focus and faith," Glaser says. "Are you focused?"

"I don't know," I say.

"Is your full attention on the coals; the task at hand?"

"The coals have captured my attention, yes" I say, "but . . ."

"Do you have faith in yourself?"

"Yes, but . . ."

"Do you have faith in me? Faith in the profundity of the opportunity that awaits you on the other side of these coals?"

Now he is doing something unexpected: He is leaning over and removing his shoes from his feet.

"To show you that I am not a charlatan or a hypocrite, I am going to walk the coals myself first," he says. "I want you to know that I would never ask or expect you to do anything I wouldn't do. Your trust in me is very important."

Glaser closes his eyes for a few moments then looks upward. I follow the path of his eyes and see a speck moving high in the sky. It looks like an eagle—possibly the same one I saw before, when I and my workmates were holding hands before the last Walk of Fire—but it is too far away to tell. Glaser lifts his right foot and takes a step onto the coals. He closes his eyes and pauses for moment, then continues. His first few steps are slow and tentative, but he picks up the pace seven or eight feet in and then walks the rest of the way as casually as if he were taking a stroll on the beach.

At the end, he steps off the coals onto the grass and says, "There, you see, it's not so difficult." He then inspects the bottoms of his feet to show me that he has no burns or blisters.

"Now it's your turn," says Glaser.

I step up to the edge of the coals, and can feel the heat on the tips of my toes. Once again, I find myself looking at Glaser through a prism of fire. His body and face are distorted by the shimmering veil of heat. The only thing I can see clearly are his teeth, gleaming white like a bone bleached by the sun.

I don't entirely understand the mechanisms at work, but for one reason or another, fate has led me back to the edge of these coals. And I know—or suspect quite strongly, for one can never really know—that were I to flee now, to turn my back on the challenge before me, fate would somehow conspire to bring me back yet again, and again, and again, ad infinitum, until I've met the challenge and overcome it. Some sort of cosmic intelligence that I can't quite comprehend—the will of God, perhaps? The hand of fate? The pull of destiny?—seems to be guiding me here, urging me to do precisely that which I dread the most.

Why it has to be this way, I do not know. Why the forces of destiny can't just pull me toward a Dream Fluff donut and let it go at that, I don't understand. What I do understand is that if I don't at least try this again, I will regret it the rest of my life. When I'm fifty, if I'm still selling office machines and my wife's a bitch and my kid's a crack addict and I'm driving a twelve-year-old Chevy, I'll wonder if I didn't squander the greatest opportunity of my life. In the end, I am more afraid of that than I am of any physical pain I might endure. The worst that can happen is I end up seeing Maureen the nurse again, I tell myself. She wouldn't be too impressed with me, but at least I could say I tried, that when I had the chance to have it all—the money, the house, the job, the swimsuit-model girlfriend—I didn't back away or flinch; I dug my heels in, gritted my teeth and went for it.

* * * * * * *

My mother always warned me I would fry in hell, but she was wrong: I got barbecued instead, and, believe it or not, hell wouldn't have me. That's what they're telling me anyway—that I'm lucky, and should be grateful that fate decided to smile on me at the very last second.

I'm not so sure.

Near as I can tell, they used a chili-sage spice rub on me, and from where I'm sitting now, it looks as though Glaser and the old man are washing me down with a moderately priced Merlot, though I suspect I would taste better with a good Napa Pinot Noir or Cabernet—something with a bit more character. They are complaining that my thighs are a little stringy, and I find this hilarious. If Glaser wants tenderer, juicier thighs, I'm thinking, he should try roasting a fifteen-year-old girl next time, not a skinny Irish kid like me.

"I thought we almost had ourselves a new associate," Glaser is saying to Edward.

"Me too," says the old man. "It's a pity."

"We followed the rules, though, didn't we?" Glaser says.

"That we did," says Edmund.

"Shades of truth, but no outright lies."

"Yes, sir."

"A bit of persuasion, some temptation, a nudge here and there, but nothing too overt."

"You did the best you could," says Edward. "They have to come of their own free will."

"Another step or two and he would have been mine," says Glaser, shaking his head.

"Maybe we'll have better luck this weekend," says Edward.

"Who's coming up?" Glaser asks casually, picking a piece of gristle out of his mouth and putting it on the side of his plate.

"Some finance executives from Ernst & Whinney," says Edward. "Half a dozen, maybe."

"A bunch of money men," Glaser sighs, taking a sip of wine. "Sounds promising."

"I agree," says Edward.

"We're due, wouldn't you say?"

"That we are," says Edward.

Glaser raises his glass and proposes a toast. "Here's to humanity," he says. "May it always need me to make things interesting."

"Amen to that," Edward says.

"Amen," echoes Glaser, and they both chuckle, as if sharing a private joke they've told each other many times before.

* * * * * * *